"I'm just another ranch hand at the Bucking Bull."

Emily took a long breath. She was replaceable. "In fact, our one other ranch hand, Zeke, is returning tomorrow. When he's around, I'll have less to do."

"You feel less essential," Jonah murmured.

"Yes."

"And you don't have a cowboy or a ranch of your own to make you feel indispensable."

"No."

And none of that was on the horizon. Just the hard Sawtooth Mountains. So much open space. So many possibilities. If she could find one she liked.

Emily risked a glance at Jonah, just a glance because the road was steep and the curves dangerous. But that one glance told her what she hadn't wanted to believe. She should have been listening to her head, not her heart.

No single kiss was going to turn Jonah into the man of her dreams. He was from another world and he most definitely didn't have room for one insignificant cowgirl in his plans.

Dear Reader,

I'm fascinated with history and it was with great joy that I first brought the legend of Merciless Mike Moody to the page in *Rescued by the Perfect Cowboy*. Now Jonah Monroe wants to write a script about the stagecoach bandit, but to do so he needs to research the myth a little deeper as well as get a feel for the trails Mike Moody used around Second Chance, Idaho.

Enter cowgirl and unexpected tour guide Emily Clark, a woman with a biological clock and her heart set on winning the love of a cowboy. She has little patience for city slicker Jonah, while he's been smitten by the former rodeo queen from the moment they first met. Do opposites attract? I think so!

I had so much fun writing Emily's sass and Jonah's snark. I didn't want their story to end! I hope you come to love The Mountain Monroes as much as I do. Each book is connected but also stands alone. Happy reading!

Melinda

HEARTWARMING

Enchanted by the Rodeo Queen

USA TODAY Bestselling Author

Melinda Curtis

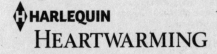

HARLEQUIN
HEARTWARMING

⊕ HARLEQUIN®
HEARTWARMING™

ISBN-13: 978-1-335-88965-2

Enchanted by the Rodeo Queen

Harlequin Enterprises ULC
22 Adelaide St. West, 40th Floor
Toronto, Ontario M5H 4E3, Canada
www.Harlequin.com

Printed in U.S.A.

Recycling programs
for this product may
not exist in your area.

Prior to writing romance, award-winning *USA TODAY* bestselling author **Melinda Curtis** was a junior manager for a Fortune 500 company, which meant when she flew on the private jet she was relegated to the jump seat—otherwise known as the potty (seriously, the commode had a seat belt). After grabbing her pen (and a parachute) she made the jump to full-time writer. Melinda's Harlequin Heartwarming book *Dandelion Wishes* will soon be a TV movie!

Brenda Novak says *Season of Change* "found a place on my keeper shelf."

Jayne Ann Krentz says *Fool For Love* is "wonderfully entertaining."

Sheila Roberts says *Can't Hurry Love* is "a page turner filled with wit and charm."

Books by Melinda Curtis

Harlequin Heartwarming

The Mountain Monroes

Kissed by the Country Doc
Snowed in with the Single Dad
Rescued by the Perfect Cowboy
Lassoed by the Would-Be Rancher

Return of the Blackwell Brothers

The Rancher's Redemption

Visit the Author Profile page
at Harlequin.com for more titles.

THE MOUNTAIN MONROES FAMILY TREE

Harlan Monroe
(deceased)

Darrell Monroe
(Oil/Finance)

- Holden Monroe
- Bo Monroe
- Kendall Monroe

Carlisle Monroe
(Hotels/Entertainment)

- Shane Monroe (twin)
- Sophie Monroe (twin)
- Camden Monroe

Ian Monroe
(Yacht Building)

- Bryce Monroe (twin, deceased)
- Bentley Monroe (twin)
- Olivia Monroe

Lincoln Monroe
(Filmmaking)

- Jonah Monroe
- Laurel Monroe (twin)
- Ashley Monroe (twin)

PROLOGUE

ADAM CLARK WAS only five, but he knew one
thing better than his ABCs and his 1-2-3s—
the legend of Merciless Mike Moody.

"He had a gun and a horse and a hideout
on top of our mountain," Adam told the new
boys in town. They sat on the curb in front
of the general store in Second Chance, eating Popsicles.

"Your mouth is red," one of the boys said.
He and his brother were mirror images of
each other and not yet in kindergarten.

With only a month left in the school year,
Adam was jazzed about being a first grader
this fall. Kindergarten was baby stuff.

He wiped his mouth on his shirtsleeve.
"Merc'less Mike robbed a stage." Adam
wasn't entirely certain what a stage was but
he didn't let anything but a lick of his Popsicle slow his story down. "And he rode off
on a big black horse." Bigger than Dad's big
black horse Deadly.

Adam paused, trying to remember his

dad's face. He'd died when Adam was three, practically a baby. His mom was getting re-married now to Shane Monroe, the uncle of his Popsicle-eating friends.

"Drip," one of the younger boys said, point-ing to the red Popsicle juice on the ground be-tween Adam's brown cowboy boots.

Adam sucked on his melting Popsicle before going on with his story. "Merc'less Mike's horse threw a shoe, so he stopped right there." Adam pointed to the old smithy a few doors down. "And he yelled at my great-great-great-great-great-great-grandad to shoe his horse." He counted all those greats—six of them—on the fingers of his free hand just like his Aunty Em had taught him.

Popsicle juice dripped on his fingers hold-ing the stick. It took Adam a bit to lick them clean, although they were now stained red. Not that Adam worried about being messy when Aunty Em picked him up from school, like she'd done today. She was the one who'd bought them Popsicles and was now inside picking up their groceries.

Aunty Em was the best aunt ever. She was one of the toughest cowboys in Second Chance. A glance inside proved it. Someone from the Flying R was asking her advice, prob'ly about bulls. Bulls were the family business and important stuff.

"Look." One of the little boys grinned at his brother, mouth rimmed with red. "My brother's a mess."

"Yup. We're all a mess." Adam got on with his story. "Merc'less Mike stabbed my great-great… Ah, you get the idea. He stabbed Old Jeb and raced up that hill." Adam pointed across the road with what was left of his Popsicle.

Splat.

The last bit of red ice fell off the stick and to the ground.

"Darn it." Adam stood, wiping his fingers on his jeans and his mouth on the neck of his T-shirt.

"The man on the horse got away?" One of the boys squinted at the mountain across the road. "He didn't die?"

"He died, but not before he hid his gold." Adam threw his Popsicle stick in the trash can. "And do you know how I know?"

Wide-eyed, the younger boys shook their heads.

Adam's chest swelled with pride. "Because me and my mom and my new dad found it."

CHAPTER ONE

OLD.

That's what thirty and unmarried was.

Old.

Emily Clark rested Deadly's hoof on top of her knees and picked out pebbles. They fell onto the barn's breezeway floor at the Bucking Bull Ranch and lay there waiting to be stepped on or swept away.

Like me. Waiting for Prince Charming.

Prince Charming didn't reside at the Bucking Bull or in Second Chance, Idaho. In fact, Emily had no idea where to find her forever someone.

Meanwhile, she'd turned thirty. Her eggs were aging out as surely as a swayback horse put out to pasture.

"Happy birthday to you," Adam, her youngest nephew, crooned as he ran into the barn. He skipped through the rest of the song at high speed. At nearly six and about to finish kindergarten, Adam thought he was hot stuff. He stopped next to her and kicked aside a pebble she'd removed from Deadly's hoof. "Happy birth-day to-oooooooo…you!" He gave her the angelic smile that got him out of trouble ninety-nine percent of the time, one rimmed with red from the Popsicle she'd bought him in town earlier. "Can you take me riding?"

"No."

"Can you take me on Merc'less Mike Moody's trail?" Meaning the dirt access road that bordered their property and led to the former bandit's small cave and hideout.

"No."

Why on earth had the desperado robbed several stagecoaches only to live in a cave at the top of a mountain?

Why on earth was Emily working on a ranch that was miles from a decent pool of eligible cowboys?

Emily lowered Deadly's hoof and straightened the kink in her back. Her brother's horse had a habit of leaning on her. Emily supposed she shouldn't complain. Kyle used to lean on her, too. Working his horse made her feel closer to him.

Behind Emily, the big black gelding's equally big and black brother, Danger, nickered.

"Mom's horse is talking to you." Adam

spun around, arms out. "Can you take me into town for a milkshake?"

"No."

"Can you reach the candy shelf and sneak me a chocolate?" Adam was nothing if not persistent.

"No."

"No?" Her nephew wound down and fell spread-eagle to the ground. "What can you do for me?"

"Well, now..." Emily tipped up her straw cowboy hat and bent over to look him in the eye. "I can *not* tickle you."

Adam made a noise like a leaky balloon, mouth twitching.

"Or I can *not* command you to muck out your pony's stall." Which she'd done for him before she'd saddled up because she was the kind of aunt who covered for angelic nephews.

Adam giggled.

"Or I can *not* let you have all the frosting on my birthday cake." Because heaven forbid Prince Charming happened along and she had extra padding on her hips from cake frosting or Granny Gertie's chocolate chip cookies.

Not that she'd ever been skinny.

Not that she aspired to be, either.

"Okay. Okay." Adam rolled to his feet and

ran toward the farmhouse. "Happy birthday, Aunty Em!"

"Happy birthday," she mumbled, leading Deadly to his stall.

The gelding was too proud to let a little thing like a jagged scar across his chest put a crimp in his stride. He always had his head up. He never plodded. Although, admittedly, he might plot to take control of the reins. He was a handful to ride and Kyle had been riding him when the pair had been ambushed by a feral bull two years ago. Only Deadly had made it back to the barn safely that day.

Inwardly, Emily flinched.

No morbid thoughts allowed on my birthday.

"You think too much, Em," Kyle had once told her. "You gotta move forward. And sometimes you gotta set aside what makes sense, take a risk, reach for what you want and hang on tight."

And sometimes you have to be careful and prepare for worst-case scenarios.

Deadly turned around in his stall and nudged her in the chest, solid nose to her breastbone.

She grunted and closed the stall door. "Thanks for the love pat, fella."

A truck pulled into the yard. Emily went out to see who it was.

A tall man with wavy red hair and a red goatee climbed down from the driver's seat one leg at a time. He was so citified he didn't realize you had to hop out of a truck and land with both feet firmly planted. Jonah Monroe's gaze lit upon Emily. "Hey."

"Not today," Emily muttered to herself. "Are you looking for Shane?" His cousin. "He's inside." Shane was engaged to Kyle's widow, Franny.

"I never go looking for Shane." Jonah's grin widened. "You're the person I wanted to see."

"Happy birthday to me," Emily said under her breath.

You could hardly throw a rock in Second Chance anymore without hitting a Monroe.

Why couldn't a different Monroe have been looking for her?

Jonah and Shane Monroe were the cousins of Bo Monroe, a gorgeous, burly Texan who had more nicknames among the women in town than a mockingbird had songs to sing—Brawny Bo, Whoa Bo, Mr. Bodacious. Emily wanted nothing more than to be the apple of Bo's eye. Instead, she was invisible.

But not to Jonah. The quick-quipping scriptwriter from the Hollywood branch of the wealthy Monroe family seemed to see everything, including Emily's infatuation with Bo. And it wasn't like he let his observations slide. He called her out on it. Constantly.

Emily, Bo doesn't like to be mooned after.
Emily, Bo likes intelligent conversation.
Emily.
Emily.
Emily.

Emily swallowed back a growl of frustration. "What can I do for you, Jonah? Are you here to buy eggs?"

Jonah opened his mouth to speak.

"Oh, I'm sorry. We're out." Emily cut him off and pulled the barn doors closed behind her. It was bug season and if they didn't close the barn doors between chores birds swooped through and left a trail of droppings in their wake. She had just enough manners not to shut herself in the barn and Jonah out, but only just.

Jonah stared at her.

Oh.

Jonah's one redeeming quality was the startling blue color of his eyes.

Emily didn't care that he wore a slim-fitting gray T-shirt or cigar jeans, or that he looked like he'd climbed carefully out of his fancy truck on Hollywood Boulevard. She didn't care that he had some bicep definition—proof that he didn't sit at a keyboard all day. She didn't care that he had ginger coloring like a certain handsome prince of England.

Jonah Monroe is not my Prince Charming.

She tipped her hat back and forced herself to look into his eyes.

Although he's not bad to look at.

Those were her eggs talking.

Desperate, those eggs. They sometimes wanted to override Emily's decision that Jonah wasn't husband material. They didn't understand that he was too sarcastic, too bitter, too likely to be a vegetarian since there wasn't an ounce of fat on the man. She lived on a cattle ranch, ate red meat and had never met a carb she didn't like.

Jonah blinked.

Oh.

It was like being caught in a car's high beams. Since she'd known him there had been moments like these when he wasn't talking that she tended to agree with her eggs.

"Let's start again." Jonah's smile was slow-building. "I'm looking for you, Emily Clark. Don't you want to know why?"

Yes.

"No." Her hair was in a messy ponytail and she smelled like leather and horse sweat.

Okay, possibly lady sweat, too. It was May and a hot day.

Jonah's grin widened. "I was looking for you because I'm thinking of hiring an aide."

"A what?" Franny planted her cowboy boots and crossed her arms.

"An aide. An assistant."

"A secretary?" Emily looked down at her grubby cowgirl self. Could he not see with those incredible eyes of his? She wasn't secretary material. "Do you even have an office?"

Jonah was writing the screenplay of Mike Moody's adventures. As far as Em knew, his office consisted of the couch in the common room at the Lodgepole Inn.

"I've decided to move out of the inn and into my own space." Jonah's shoulders squared and his chin lifted, like a teenager announcing he was moving into a campus dorm room.

"Bully for you," Emily said with a goodly dose of sarcasm. "If you're looking for a secretary, you might try Lisa Esperanza. She lives down the highway and does medical transcription." Em pretended to type, moving her fingers over imaginary keys. "She can help you with dictation or whatever."

"I'm moving into your bunkhouse," Jonah

said when she took a breath, preparing to give him more suggestions.

"Wh-what?" She choked on air. "The bunkhouse? Who gave you permission?"

"I did." Granny Gertie came out on the front porch. She'd suffered a stroke five months back and was just progressing to moving about with a cane instead of a walker. "Jonah, come in and we can talk specifics. We're going to have birthday cake for Emily."

"It's your birthday." Jonah didn't ask *if* it was Emily's birthday. He moved quicker than a snake disturbed from a nap, wrapped his arms around Emily and gave her a squeeze. "Happy, happy day."

Oh.

That was no casual hug. That was a show of arm strength. The eggs were impressed.

By the wrong Monroe!

Panicked, Emily disentangled herself from her least favorite Monroe and marched toward the house.

"Cake," Jonah said, hot on her heels. "Isn't cake normally reserved for after dinner? It's what? Four thirty?"

"You can do anything on your birthday." Gertie grinned at Jonah the way she used to grin at Shane when he was paying Franny attention. Her widowed sister-in-law and Shane had ended up engaged, although not because of Granny's grin.

"Barking up the wrong tree, Granny," Em mumbled as she hurried past her and inside, hanging up her hat and pulling off her boots. She needed to wash up and change before cake.

"I'm thankful I've got trees to bark at," Granny teased. "Jonah, dearie, I thought you weren't moving in for another day or so. What brings you by?"

"Cake," Jonah said, as big as brass.

Emily gritted her teeth as she traipsed to her room.

"CARROT CAKE." Jonah Monroe sat at the dining room table at the Bucking Bull Ranch soaking up the chaos created by three rambunctious boys, Jonah's cousin Shane and the Clark women. "My favorite."

Shane gave Jonah a sharp, disbelieving look.

"It's my favorite," Jonah said again. He just didn't eat it anymore.

"How many candles, Mom?" Davey was the oldest of Emily's nephews, at nine. He rummaged through a kitchen drawer, holding up his finds in one hand. A birth defect had left him without the other, not that the kid let that slow him down. "We have two boxes."

"I don't need thirty candles on my cake." Emily opened a cupboard and brought out a mismatched stack of dessert plates. Although she'd checked her straw cowboy hat and brown boots at the door, she was country through and through, from her blue checked shirt with pearly snaps, to her blue jeans, faded in intriguing places. Her honey-brown hair tumbled to her shoulders, and her mouth was full of sass. "Three will do."

"But we have enough." Grinning, Charlie swiped the candles, possibly unaware that one box said it was trick candles that didn't blow out, possibly very much aware there was a joke afoot. Although he was only seven, he was a mischief-maker with brown hair as wild as his nature.

This is going to be good.

If Jonah had to extend his stay in quiet Second Chance, he had a right to find life's little pleasures. These three young cowboys were going into a script someday. He could see it now.

EXTERIOR. MOUNTAIN RANCH. Three boys run through a field chasing a gleeful Labrador with a slobbery baseball in his mouth.

Jonah caught the family Labrador's eye as the black dog squished a slobbery tennis ball. He snapped his fingers to call him over.

"You can light a signal fire with thirty candles, Aunty Em." Adam hopped in place as if he was on a pogo stick. "And then send out smoke signals. *I. Am. Thirty. I. Am. Thirty.*"

Emily's smile became strained and she looked everywhere but at Jonah.

"Go for thirty, Aunty Em." Jonah had to get in on the fun even if it made Emily's brown eyes narrow when she finally looked at him. "I enjoy a good bonfire."

"Why you'd want to witness a bonfire is beyond me." Emily's grumble was more like a junkyard dog's first growl at an intruder. "Since someone might decide to roast you instead of marshmallows."

"Everybody loves s'mores," Jonah said with barely contained glee.

Their repartee inspired more hops, chortles and shoulder shoving from Emily's nephews.

This woman.

He wanted her.

He fell back in his chair.

As my assistant. Only as my assistant.

He wanted to be inspired by her snappy dialogue. He wanted to be invigorated by their back-and-forth rivalry. Being with her was worth more than the former rodeo queen could know.

"What's all that racket?" Gertie asked from her easy chair, which was a safe distance away from all the hopping and mischief-making. She closed a small music box.

"Quiet down," Shane shouted over his soon-to-be stepsons' excitement.

"Boys." That was Franny, Shane's fiancée, and the mother of those three budding cowboys.

When the three boys were nearly calm, Jonah couldn't resist sighing and saying the trigger word once more, "S'mores."

It had the desired effect—chaos.

"Cake and s'mores. Cake and s'mores," Adam chanted and bounced.

"I'm so hungry I can eat three of everything," Charlie boasted, hands on hips like a triumphant superhero.

"And gack all over the back porch after." Davey gave his younger brother a look that challenged superheroes to prove their superness. "Just like you did when you ate all your Easter candy at once." He made a gagging noise. Repeatedly.

Jonah was in heaven. Being with the Clarks reminded him of the trips he and his eleven siblings and cousins used to take with Grandpa Harlan.

"You're evil, Jonah." Emily did a not-so-good job of *not* smiling. "Burn-at-the-stake evil, even for a Monroe."

Shane shot Jonah with another look of disbelief. "You don't even like s'mores."

Could his cousin butt out? Just this once?

Emily's grin disappeared. "And I bet Jonah doesn't eat cake, either. Just look at him. Skinny enough to slither through a dog door."

"Touché." How could Jonah take offense at such a brilliant line? Or at his crafty cousin—the main reason he was in sleepy Second Chance—for feeding Emily the opportunity that had inspired her?

Dog door? Jonah chuckled.

Turned out Second Chance had redeeming qualities.

He'd seen it the day Shane had guilted him and Bo into visiting, telling them they had to contribute to the town's well-being before year's end when they were scheduled to decide what to do with Second Chance—keep or sell. He'd walked up the long set of steps to his cousin Sophie's curiosity shop and seen Emily on the porch. She'd been slack-jawed at the sight of Cousin Bo—couldn't fault her for that since Bo had that effect on most women.

Since Emily had been running Sophie's store while Sophie was on her honeymoon, Jonah had gone in as a courtesy. She'd been tossing lines at him ever since.

"Good boy, Bolt." Jonah patted the Labrador's head, keeping him near.

Another redeeming quality? Merciless Mike Moody, the century-old legend about a stagecoach-robbing desperado. Talk about a reason to stay a while. The myth had everything a screenwriter wanted—action, violence, greed. Unlike fool's gold in the Old West, Mike Moody had turned out to be worth something.

There was gold in them thar hills.

And last month Jonah had been there when Shane and the Clarks had found Mike Moody's stolen gold. Here was Jonah's chance to break out of the box and break into mainstream film. Gritty Westerns were all the rage.

"We're not having cake *and* s'mores," Franny said with a heavy sigh.

"Can we not argue on my birthday?" Emily had swung Adam onto her hip. She was very sturdy, which was good considering she worked with horses and bulls.

Charlie and Davey were each armed with a

box of candles. They loaded the cake, seemingly without counting.

Shane handed Jonah a glass of water, retaining a bottle of beer for himself. "How's that script coming?"

Killjoy.

Jonah's mood deflated. "It's coming." As a writer, he was good at the bluff. "You know, first drafts are always difficult."

That was the same thing he'd told his agent this morning, to which Maury had replied, "Get me a treatment." Meaning a story overview. "Too big a gap between projects to promote and people will think of you as a has-been, especially since your dad sacked you in January. I don't represent writers with the stink of failure."

Sensitive guy, his agent.

Jonah should've had a rough draft of the script done by now or at the very least a decent treatment. He'd listened to Gertie recount the Mike Moody myth several times. He'd been there when they'd discovered the gold. But the characters were flat on the page. The dialogue uninspired. His gut was in constant turmoil because his future was riding on the success of his interpretation of the story. And what had he done? In a moment of weakness, he'd sent a treatment to his father for feedback.

His father. The head of Monroe Studios. The man who'd fired him.

The man who hadn't replied yet and might not ever.

"Don't waste your time developing new ideas, Jonah. You're a script jobber. You write what I tell you." His father's words had been like bumpers on the bowling lane of Jonah's life.

Write me a teen ensemble series, Jonah, one with three spunky leads who are also high school nerds.

Write me a teenage witch movie, Jonah, one with a lead whose warlock boyfriend has died.

Write me...

Jonah could write anything given tight parameters, but what he wanted right now was to read something—a reply from his father that confirmed he was on to bigger and better things.

Speaking of replies, Shane was waiting to hear more about the script about Mike Moody's adventure. Nonwriters asked questions like this all the time. They wanted a snippet of story, an example scene, a bit of dinner conversation.

Jonah deflected. "How's that search for a town doctor coming, Shane?" No doctor wanted to work and live at a small crossroads town in the middle of the Idaho mountains.

"Yeah, Shane." Franny, the concerned mother of scrape-prone boys, perked up. "How's it going?"

In the kitchen, Emily spun one way and then another, back and forth, Adam still on her hip.

"I'm dizzy." Adam giggled.

"If I was a bull, that'd be my goal." Emily swung the little boy off her hip and to the ground, making a buzzer sound. The Clarks sold bucking bulls to rodeos. Big, mean fellas. "Sorry, cowboy. You didn't last eight seconds."

Jonah grinned. He never felt uninspired around Emily. She had an energy about her. And when she was near, sparks flew.

Not romantic sparks, thank Hollywood.

Unlike his sister Laurel or his cousins Shane and Sophie, Jonah wasn't interested in setting down roots in Second Chance with a significant other. His life was in Hollywood. Besides, he was still smarting from his last venture in dating, which hadn't ended well.

Well… He'd written a script about the experience, but that was more catharsis than career move. It was a romance and possibly a harder sell than a gritty Western. At least, as written by him.

Jonah joined Shane and the Clarks in singing "Happy Birthday." There were enough candles on the cake to burn the place down. And, of course, no matter how many times Emily huffed and puffed, the candles relit.

Priceless.

Franny took pity on the birthday girl, removed the trick candles and doused them in a bowl of water.

"I get Aunty Em's frosting." Adam scurried out of the kitchen and sat on his knees in the chair next to Jonah, elbows on the table. "She promised."

"She can have Jonah's frosting." Shane smirked at Jonah. "And his cake."

Emily eyed Jonah as if he was one of those bucking bulls she helped train and couldn't be trusted. "I thought you said carrot cake was your favorite."

"And it's homemade." Gertie took a seat at the head of the table. "By Emily. She insisted. She can cook up a storm."

"The most bestest cake-maker in the whole wide world," Charlie said, spearing a bite of cake.

Shane quirked an eyebrow at Jonah.

Jonah quirked one right back. "Wouldn't want to hurt anyone's feelings by not eating the cake of the most bestest cake-maker in the whole wide world." Even if he paid for it later. His digestive system didn't process fats easily, but if it won him favor with Emily…

"Don't push your luck, Jonah." Shane slid an arm around Franny's waist and returned to his agenda. "When will that script of yours be done?"

"When I write the end." Jonah held back an eye roll. "Didn't we just have this conversation?"

"Oh, to have the luxury of wealth and leisure." Emily rolled her eyes at Jonah. "Imagine if we, the Clarks, got around to training our bulls *whenever. Nothing would get done.*"

This woman.

Jonah sighed contentedly.

Her dialogue.

If he could only harness that special quality in a script. Jonah leaned forward in his chair. "The creative process doesn't keep a schedule, although Shane would prefer it to— if he had his way, I'd hack it up. Transcribe my notes and say done deal." Never. He had too much pride.

Emily chuckled. "The reason for a secretary becomes clear. Transcription."

"I need an *assistant*, not a secretary," Jonah said without taking his eyes off Emily.

"You need help?" There was a frown in Shane's voice, but there often was. He considered himself a fixer.

"I need an *assistant*," Jonah repeated, reluctantly taking his gaze from Emily to scowl at Shane. "I want to capture some of the flavor of Western life. I want to hire someone—" *Emily* "—to take me on the trails Mike Moody would have traveled on horseback."

"You're looking for an out-of-work cowboy." Shane frowned again, but it was his there's-a-problem-that-I-need-to-solve frown, not his I-don't-understand-you frown. "Remind me, Franny. What's the name of that old man out by Remington Creek?"

Jonah didn't want an old man and his cowboy wisdom. He wanted Emily and her take-no-prisoners attitude. He wrote his best scenes after their sparring matches. The rest went in his scrap file. Frankly, most had been going in his scrap file, quality or not, because he couldn't figure out the angle to take to tell Mike Moody's tale. It was Emily or nothing.

Jonah transferred his frosting onto Adam's slice of cake and then discretely slid his plate to the floor under the table where Bolt inhaled his portion of the celebratory dessert.

Later, when Jonah carried his plate to the kitchen with Bolt at his heels, Emily took one look at it and snorted. "Finally. We get some decent carbs in front of you and you polish the plate clean."

Bolt gazed adoringly at Jonah and licked his chops.

CHAPTER TWO

"I'M OFFICIALLY OVER THE HILL." Emily stared at the flames in the backyard firepit, one hand resting on Bolt's broad forehead. She gave him a pat. "At least I'm not alone, fella. In dog years, you've got decades on me."

They were aging, but nothing was changing around them. Behind her stood the family home, which had weathered more than a hundred winters and still looked solid. A circle of gravel surrounded the concrete firepit, built for permanence. Above her, the inky sky was dotted with bright stars. Tall, slender pines reached for their brightness, reminding her of tall, slender Jonah and his need for an assistant.

She wasn't the type of cowgirl who took greenhorns on trail rides. Emily chased down bulls on Razzy, her cutting horse. In her spare time—*ha, like she had any*—she rode Deadly until he was spent.

If Kyle was alive, he'd have laughed off Jonah's request, end of story. And she should do the same.

A crunch of quick footsteps and Franny sat down in a webbed chair next to her. She wore Kyle's thick denim jacket and Shane's large engagement ring. "There's nothing like a birthday to wind my boys up. I had to threaten to bathe them in the horse trough behind the barn just to make them take their showers."

Em rubbed Bolt's velvety ear. She loved her nephews. But she wanted some stubborn little cowpokes of her own. "I've been thinking…"

"About leaving the ranch?" Franny had been her best friend since Em had been in kindergarten. Of course she'd know Em was restless.

"It's time." Emily's chest constricted. She didn't want to leave. But there were her aging eggs and…dreaming of Bo falling in love with her was just that—a dream.

"I appreciate you staying and helping after Kyle died." Franny reached over and gently squeezed Emily's arm. "I couldn't have trained our new Buttercup for the rodeo circuit so quickly without you." Buttercup was what they named every signature bull, the one that would carry the fortunes of the ranch on his back for the next decade or so—tossing cowboys to the dirt and earning exorbitant breeder fees. They'd just sent Buttercup Five out for his professional rodeo debut. "I've leaned on you these past two years. Everyone has. It's time you thought of yourself and found a place of your own. We've got Shane now."

Replaced. Em couldn't breathe.

It was one thing to think about leaving and another to hear Franny talk about Emily's new reality. A week ago, she'd been training her nephews to rope, a skill they often worked on. She'd challenged the three boys to rope her. Three stiff lariats around her chest later and she'd been bursting with pride.

Replaced. Emily drew in a deep breath.

The week before her brother died, Emily had accepted a job with the stock distributor who bought their bucking bulls for the rodeo. After the accident, there was no way she'd have left Franny and the boys until they were settled again.

Replaced. Em drew another lungful of air.

She'd put her life on hold for her family, for this place. She'd been like the old farmhouse and sturdy trees—an unchanging fixture. And now… It was as if she was turning over the family reins to Shane, the reins she'd grabbed hold of after Kyle died. From this point on, Shane would be Franny's rock. He'd be there for Granny and the boys. He wasn't a true rancher, not yet anyway, but he made Franny happy.

She had to trust that was enough.

"I won't leave right away." Emily covered Franny's hand, feeling the bulky shape of her engagement ring, feeling the distance grow between them. "I'm coaching a junior rodeo queen for the next few weeks and I haven't even begun to ask around to see who might be hiring."

"You aren't going to work for a rodeo, are you?" Franny used her motherly voice. "That's a gypsy life. Cowboys on the circuit are like tumbleweeds and you're looking to set down roots."

"I can't get picky. Few ranchers have separate rooms for female cowhands." Emily had enough saved to buy a horse trailer with a camper feature up front. She could live in it until winter. "There's a cowboy out there for me. I just need to find him."

"Mom!" Adam called from the second-story window. "Mom, come read me another story."

"Please?" Franny prompted, turning in her chair.

"Plea-eeeeze!"

Adam was so darn cute. And yet, the chill evening air cut into the back of Em's throat. She missed him already.

Franny stood, wrapping the ends of Kyle's large jacket around her. "I'll be glad when they're teenagers and sleeping more."

"No. You won't be." Em laughed.

"No. I won't be," Franny agreed, hugging Emily before she headed inside.

The fire crackled. The wind blew gently through the treetops. A star streaked across the sky.

Emily made a wish. It was the same wish she'd been making for years: *please, let me find a tall, strong, handsome cowboy who'll love me like Kyle used to love Franny.*

Bolt lifted his head. Slow footsteps crossed the gravel.

"Another birthday." Granny Gertie settled into the chair vacated by Franny, resting both hands on top of her cane. "Congratulations." She peered at Emily's face. "Or should I say, 'My condolences'? You look grim."

"It's nothing." Emily put another log on the fire that sent sparks into the dark night.

"If it was nothing, you'd be watching television inside with me." Granny sighed. "This fire has become your television for some time now."

"Yes," she admitted. Emily eased back in her chair, fingers finding the soft, comforting ruff around Bolt's neck.

"Thirty is a powerful age." Gertie's thin voice carried on the crisp night air.

Powerful? "I haven't done anything."

"You have a trophy case that says different. Barrel racing. Team roping. Rodeo queen."

"You know what I mean. Those trophies… they mark my teens and early twenties." All that her past activities had gotten her were occasional jobs as a rodeo queen coach. On the rodeo circuit, she was known as one of the Clarks from the Bucking Bull Ranch. She was sometimes referred to as Kyle Clark's little sister. She was willing to bet most folks didn't even know her first name. "I've done nothing important."

"Like fall in love?" Gertie was in fine form tonight.

"That and…" Emily didn't want to admit there was more. "I have nothing important ahead of me." Even if she accepted a position on another ranch somewhere, it wouldn't be a job with a future. It'd be a job that could end any day.

Granny harrumphed. "You have a family legacy, nephews who look up to you, a share in that gold we found as soon as it's sold."

That isn't enough.

She couldn't say the words out loud. She didn't own the ranch. Her parents had sold it to Kyle and Franny, and moved to Padre Island in Texas. She didn't have her own cowpokes, much as she loved Franny's. And the gold would take years to liquidate. Even then, her share wouldn't be enough to buy a spread large enough to compare to the Bucking Bull.

"I understand," Gertie said in a soft voice. "You think you have nothing on the horizon that's going to impact this family, this ranch, this town...or you."

Emily pulled her gaze from the fire and stared at her grandmother, her wise and wonderful grandmother. "Yes."

"Your grandfather, Jonah's grandfather and I made a decision decades ago after the men found Merciless Mike Moody's gold. We vowed to keep it a secret. Your grandfather and I considered ourselves the protectors of the myth since it was part of our past and the Clark legacy. After so many deaths—your grandfather, your brother Kyle, Harlan Monroe—and then my stroke, I realized it was time to pass the mantle and let others decide how to move forward. Franny and Kyle may have bought the ranch..." She handed Emily a gold coin. "But that doesn't mean there isn't a Clark legacy to protect in Second Chance."

"You're talking about helping Jonah." Every fiber of Emily's being rebelled.

Correction. Every fiber but her eggs. They didn't rebel. They were gleeful.

Granny Gertie pounded the end of her cane in the gravel. "I'm talking about making sure Jebediah Clark is well represented in that story the Monroes want to tell. He's a hero."

Emily pressed the coin against her palm. "This isn't the kind of important thing I was looking for."

Gertie stood, leaning over to cup Emily's chin in her palm. "Child, good trackers pay attention to broken branches before they find a clear footprint to pursue." She straightened and began slowly traversing the gravel and then the large stone pavers leading back to the ranch house.

"That's a terrible analogy," Emily called after her.

"That may be." Gertie didn't turn. "But it's hit the bullseye."

EXTERIOR. THE STAGE ROAD. Merciless Mike Moody is hiding behind two boulders watching the stage road. We don't see what he sees yet.

"AND SO BEGINS every Western about every bandit." At the Lodgepole Inn, Jonah hit the delete key, ignoring the growing ache between his shoulder blades. He'd been hitting that key a lot lately or cutting paragraphs of Emily-inspired scenes and pasting them in a separate document, so much so that tonight his movie script was down to just the title page.

Emily would know how the story begins.

He was putting too much hope on Emily. He'd have to come up with another plan. It'd been more than twenty-four hours since his offer to work for him and…nothing. Same as his script. Maybe he shouldn't move into the Clark bunkhouse.

"Jonah!" Downstairs, someone called his name with more than a trace of impatience. It sounded like Shane.

Jonah chose to ignore him, drumming his fingers on the keyboard. Surely he could write a killer opening for his murderous antihero? His fingers continued to drum without any words making it onto the page.

"Jonah!" Shane shouted once more.

The Lodgepole Inn in Second Chance was a very large log structure with most guest bedrooms on the second floor. Jonah's room had a name, no number—the Yarrow room. Not that there was anything blooming in his room. But it faced east, giving him a clear view of the valley with its abundant wildflowers, including bouquets of yellow yarrow, and the majestic Sawtooth Mountains.

"Jonah!"

His cousin would be coming upstairs to get him if Jonah didn't answer him soon.

Jonah refused to budge without writing at least one sentence.

A buzzard lands on a nearby tree. An omen of things to come.

A quick file save and Jonah fled the room. He descended the creaky old stairs, listening to the unexpected symphony of competing voices.

"Tell me again why we need a meeting?" Cousin Bo was asking Shane. He sat on a chair near the check-in desk, as far away from the rest of those gathered as he could get and still be in the room.

Jonah's gaze and tentative smile bounced off Bo as if his cousin had erected a force field around himself. Bo's expression was darker than his hair.

Jonah's steps slowed and he wished... He wished for more than beautiful words on a page. He wished for fences mended within the family.

"Is this that town meeting you've been

talking about having, Shane?" Jonah crossed the landing, testing the welcome in the room. No one else was glowering at him, always a good sign. "Seems like you're missing some of the critical players."

Only three Second Chance business representatives were gathered around the large fireplace and its small fire—Ivy from the diner, Mitch from the inn, Mackenzie from the general store. They were outnumbered by five Monroes—Jonah and his sister Laurel, Bo, Shane and his sister Sophie. The tone of the assembled was businesslike. Jonah paused. Business meetings tended to give him hives.

From his chair, Bo made a sound like a long-suffering caged animal. He had even less patience for business than Jonah.

Out of habit, Jonah went to stand near him, testing the force field. Of all the Monroe siblings and cousins in his generation, Jonah was closest to Bo. Bo had been like an older brother to Jonah, a best friend, a sometimes rival. In a way, Bo still was, as long as his force field wasn't up and they didn't talk about the events of the past year or say anything about weddings that might prod open wounds. Meanwhile, gold had been found in Second Chance, and ever since then, something else seemed to be bothering Bo, something that closed him off to Jonah more than—

"There's a reason I've invited each of you here." Shane, the meeting organizer, had on his serious CEO face, hence the group's somberness. His measured words, the short, crisp cut of his brown hair and his wrinkle-resistant khakis would clue anyone into his need for control. "You're either a part owner of Second Chance or are invested in its success."

Part owner of a town. That's something I never aspired to.

Harlan Monroe had left Second Chance to his twelve grandchildren, which would've been fine in Jonah's book if they hadn't all been fired from their jobs at Monroe Industries as a condition for their fathers to inherit Harlan's millions. When given the choice between love and money, their four fathers had chosen money. A sobering situation, especially for a guy like Jonah, who'd made a living off story lines with laughter and happy endings.

For the past decade, Jonah had enjoyed writing sitcoms for tweens and teens for the family's production studio. He'd milked the fun out of being a kid. Write what you know, right?

I know nothing about being a cowboy who robs a stage.

An image of Emily walking confidently in her cowboy boots came to mind. He was sure she had something to teach him.

"I've invited you here today—" Shane paced in front of the fire like a general giving his troops a prebattle pep talk "—to discuss the future of Second Chance."

Jonah stifled a groan. This could take all night. In fact, on previous occasions, it had.

Merciless Mike Moody would've shot to his feet, hand resting on his notched six-shooter, and said, *"Enough talk!"*

"But before that, we need to know where we are and where we've been." Shane kept on talking, doing the slow build that business types preferred in presentations. "How is business this spring compared to last?" He glanced at Ivy, Mitch and Mackenzie, the ones who'd sold their land to Grandpa Harlan and leased it back for one dollar a year. Not exactly the self-made man's savviest business move, but Harlan had always been sentimental, and this was his hometown.

While the trio reported in, Jonah glanced at

the thick, round logs that made up the Lodgepole Inn's walls.

Had Mike Moody ever stepped foot in here?

The inn had been around in some shape or
form for close to one hundred and fifty years.
First as a barracks and stable for the cavalry,
later as a house of ill repute, then a rooming
house and a motor lodge.

Jonah drummed his fingers on his thighs.
It was hard to write about a character with
no moral fiber when he was surrounded by
happy, well-adjusted humans, Bo notwith-
standing. His favorite cousin had his arms
crossed and his expression closed off.

"We need reasons for visitors to stay longer in town." Shane was in summary mode.
He came to stand next to Jonah. "I'm going
to open up Davey's Camp for Cowboys and
Cowgirls for a few weeks this summer on a
trial basis." His camp for kids with missing
or incompletely formed limbs, like Davey, a
venture he was financing so kids and their
families didn't have to pay. "I'm opening the
campground to the public the rest of summer,
that ought to get some business in town."

"Sure, it will." Bo peeled the label from
a beer bottle. "If I can get your cabins fixed
before June."

"We'll be fine." Shane didn't move from

his spot mere feet from Jonah. "We'll come out to help you this week."

"We? As in you and me?" Jonah stopped drumming his fingers, stopped slouching and stopped being a tool of Shane's. "I don't know how to use power tools."

"We'll learn together." Shane clapped a hand on Jonah's shoulder.

"Awesome." Jonah gave Shane's hand a disparaging glance. "Not."

Bo grinned, dropping his force field. That grin. It was the same expression he'd given Jonah when they were kids and decided their three-hour card game of War a draw. Grandpa Harlan had called their battle epic and found other ways to pit them against each other— board games, word puzzles, chores—all of which had made them closer. That grin of Bo's? It said everything was going to be all right.

Jonah attempted a smile of his own because the mistakes of the past would soon be forgotten. They'd return to their easy camaraderie. He'd tell Bo he'd written a script about the events of last year as a way to flex his writing muscle and Bo wouldn't stare at Jonah as if he'd crossed a line.

Or…

Bo's grin faded. The force field returned.

Cue reality.

Shane was oblivious to their tension. "Getting back to the future of Second Chance, our most important efforts will be to milk the legend of Merciless Mike Moody." He warmed to what Jonah hoped would be his climax, even as Jonah dreaded hearing what came next. "I'll arrange summer tours up the last trail our bandit took before he died. Mack, you'll order souvenirs and T-shirts to spread awareness of his legend and Second Chance. And then the pièce de résistance—a reenactment of the bandit's story to be performed at a local festival." Shane squeezed Jonah's shoulder. "Which we'll need a script for."

Two scripts? One for a theatrical release and one for street consumption?

"The request for my presence becomes clear." Jonah eased his shoulder free, wishing he could just as easily extricate himself from Shane's master plan.

"Tours? A reenactment? A festival?" Bo didn't like to beat around the bush. "Folks in costume? Open-air market stalls? Food trucks and hot-air balloon rides?"

"Yes." Shane seemed pleased Bo understood his vision, regardless of his opinion.

"Those festivals are a dime a dozen." Bo stood, annoyance punching his words. "Honestly, I agreed to contribute to getting the town back on its feet, which I'm doing. But let's be clear, I'm rehabbing camp cabins for a couple of weeks, not staying months to build festival booths."

"Who said anything about building booths?" A veteran of the boardroom, Shane wasn't rattled. In fact, he seemed energized by Bo's challenge. "Forget booths. Think about all those tourists. People love these festivals. And ours will be unique."

Bo didn't look convinced. Frankly, Jonah wasn't convinced, either.

"Our festival will be unique?" Jonah's sister Laurel asked in a chirpy voice that said more about her happy state than that broad smile on her face and her big baby bump. "Because we're in the mountains?"

"Or because we're Monroes?" Cousin Sophie pushed her glasses up her thin nose and managed to look sophisticated despite her rumpled jeans and the stretched cuffs of her blue sweater.

"No," Jonah choked out. He had an idea where this was going. Live performances required actors.

"No." Shane beamed at Jonah. "Ours will be unique because Jonah's going to write a blockbuster movie script and people are going to want to connect with the story and its characters by coming here and by experiencing a reenactment at our annual festival, also written by Jonah." Shane took a seat on the hearth and dropped an imaginary mic.

His plan hinges on my talent.

Bo turned to Jonah, raising his dark brows.

Jonah said nothing. He wasn't excited about the burden of saving Second Chance being on his shoulders. His shoulders had enough to carry just trying to advance his career out of tweenie-teenie fare.

But Shane was like a dog with a bone. He wouldn't let Jonah back out of this. And he never did anything by half-measures. If he asked for a script, he'd expect it to be award-winning. He'd expect it to be made instantly. Shane needed facts to temper his enthusiasm and expectations. So Jonah gave him some.

"Let's be realistic about the filmmaking process. Good scripts can get made right away, but that's the exception in Hollywood, not the norm. Scripts—even good ones—can languish in development for years as a producer pulls together the right cast and director with the same vision, and then finds a studio willing to invest in distribution and marketing."

"You know, Ashley started her own production company recently." Predictably, Laurel brought up their very famous, former child-star sister, the actress Jonah had spent most of his career writing for. "I know she's looking for material. And if Jonah wrote a role with Ashley in mind…" Laurel let the idea float out there, waiting for others to grab hold and carry that banner forward.

Which they did, much to Jonah's chagrin.

"Mike Moody could've had a normal life somewhere." Sophie leaned forward, caught up in Laurel's vision. "A wife and kids."

No. Jonah shook his head. *No kids.*

Laurel picked up the thread. "He could've lied to her about who he was and how he earned a living."

No. In Jonah's mind, Mike Moody was undatable. He might not even have all his teeth!

"There'd be a young boy who looked up to his father." Even Shane was in on it now. "It'd be heartbreaking when he discovered the truth."

Inwardly, Jonah cringed in an I-might-vomit kind of way. "This is a story about Mike Moody, thief and killer."

"Everybody comes from somewhere." Laurel sniffed the way she did when her feelings were hurt. "Everyone has family. You're so talented, Jonah. You capture emotion so well.

You can work this into your story. You can give it heart."

"And kids," Bo murmured, earning a scowl from Jonah.

Only if I scrap everything I've imagined about Mike Moody.

"But…" Jonah tried not to howl his displeasure. "This story is *based on true events*."

Sophie waved away his argument. "Everyone knows that phrase means loosely based on a fact or two."

Jonah ground his teeth.

"You could write in a love interest for a supporting character," Sophie went on, a dreamy expression on her face. "Jeb Clark was a key figure in Mike Moody's final days. Jeb courted the schoolteacher, and together they started the Bucking Bull." Jonah remembered that Sophie's husband, Zeke, had proposed the same way Jeb Clark had done—by gifting his love a horse.

Gag.

"There is no romance in this script." Jonah's voice rose to the panic octave. "Mike Moody was evil, *despicable*." And Jonah planned to keep him that way. "Besides, Jeb Clark's story line happened long after Merciless Mike Moody died." It wasn't going in his script. "No romance. No kids."

"But you do kids so well," Bo murmured, force field back in place.

Jonah did what he should've done earlier. He fled the scene.

He wasn't going to turn Merciless Mike Moody's bloody, gritty tale into a cheesy family picture just because the town he owned needed good press.

CHAPTER THREE

"YOU'RE IN CHARGE, Tina. Not the horse." Two days after Jonah had offered her a job, Emily hopped down from the top rail of the Bucking Bull's arena, landing with both boots on the ground. She'd been hired by Randall Reilly to coach his daughter on the finer points of winning a rodeo queen title. "Do it again."

Sixteen-year-old Tina Reilly brought her plodding palomino gelding to a sloppy stop. Tina's attitude was sharper than her skill on horseback, at least given what she was showing today. The young brunette had promise, if she could focus on her strengths and be comfortable in her own skin. But with the competition around the corner and Tina's unwillingness to listen, Emily would much rather have been working for Jonah.

Emily crossed the arena and leaned on a rail near Tina's father, who sat on the small set of bleachers near the middle of the ring.

Randall owned a spread north of Second Chance. He was a rugged, no-nonsense cowboy with a soft spot for his daughter, hence the pretty horse and rodeo queen lessons.

"How are things over at the Flying R?" Em asked, watching Tina guide her horse around the ring.

"Looking good. My wife had me build a large greenhouse last year." Beneath his straw cowboy hat, Randall's face was leathery and lined, his hair gray. "We've been growing organic vegetables. Helps supplement the bottom line."

Emily made a noise she hoped indicated she was impressed. "Are you hiring ranch hands?"

"No. My two boys are full-time now. Another two years and I'll need to expand the business again just to give Tina a salary." He propped his forearms on his legs. "You lookin'?"

"Yeah."

"I'll keep my ears open."

"I'd appreciate it."

His daughter wasn't doing much better on her form this time around.

"Tina, your horse knows every bit of that pattern," Emily said as kindly as she could manage. Every rodeo competition had a pattern to memorize. Contestants rode that routine in the ring where they were judged on horsemanship, often on horses that weren't their own. "You've over-practiced."

Tina rolled her pretty green eyes. "If I don't practice, I can't remember the pattern. And if I don't remember the pattern, I can't win."

"Get down and hand over those reins." When she did, Emily swung into the saddle and rode Button over to the starting point. "Watch what happens when I give him free rein." She dropped the reins to his neck.

Without guidance, Button trotted to the center of the arena and began to circle to the left, slowing to a walk before continuing into a figure eight.

"I'm not cueing him." Emily pulled the gelding up short and swung back down, ready to call this session and any further sessions to a halt. "I gave no commands. Not with my legs and not with the reins. He's a smart horse, but he's not going to win this for you. When you compete, you have to use all your skill so any horse you ride shines."

Tina hugged herself. "What am I supposed to do? Practice without practicing?"

Jonah would like her and that sass.

Heck, Emily liked her and that sass. It was better than her sullen performance. But that didn't make her fun to coach.

"Tina." Randall's tone would have been

enough of a scolding, but he added, "We're here because you want to win, not because you want to whine."

More teenage eye rolls, accompanied by a strong sense that Tina didn't want to be here, much less be a rodeo queen, period.

A lack of competitive spirit was a solid reason for Emily to call it quits. But Tina averted her gaze and wiped away a tear, giving Emily pause.

"Hey." Emily handed back the reins and said in a voice too soft for Randall to hear, "Why do you want to do this?"

Tina's chin jutted and she sniffed.

"The rodeo queen competition is hard work." Emily wasn't going to let her question go unanswered but she wasn't going to stand there waiting, either. "To compete, you have to want to be better than other girls but still be their friend. You have to study important issues, like what's happening in Idaho, in rodeo, and what's the latest in horse breeding and training practices. You have to understand the rodeo sponsor's business, plus be able to ride like you were born in the saddle. And you have to raise money for a charity. No one's going to be mad if you decide you'd rather help your mother with her organic farm."

"I'm not a quitter." Tina stared at her fancy black boots.

"I didn't say you were. Or that you should quit." Emily shrugged. "I'm asking you *why* you want that crown so badly. You can be honest with me."

"I want it because…" Tina faltered, sneaking a peek at her father before dropping her voice to a whisper. "I want to be rodeo queen because some girl at school said I wasn't pretty enough to be one."

Emily sucked in air. She hated bullies. She studied Tina's face. Her round, sweetly stubborn, pretty-in-its-own-way face. She wanted to hug her and reassure the girl she was beautiful and rodeo queen material.

"I hate it when people tell me I can't do something." Tina wiped at another tear. "Especially when girls like *her* tell me." Tina didn't have to elaborate on the kind of girls who were telling her their negative opinions.

"I hear you." There was more than a title at stake here. There was pride in taking a stand and trying to shut up a bully by saying, "You're wrong."

"So…" Tina blew out a long breath as if relieved. "What you're saying is I've practiced too much, I'm trying too hard and I've ruined my chances to win."

Emily patted Button's neck. "How mean is this girl at school?"

"She's the worst." Tina grimaced, pressing her black felt cowboy hat more firmly on her head. "She's competing, too, which is why I made Dad call you. No one knows you. *I* didn't even know you or that you'd won until I searched online for local coaches. I mean, seriously, I had no idea that Second Chance and the Bucking Bull existed."

Emily smiled as if she strived to achieve anonymity and had succeeded. But really...

Out of the mouths of babes.

She was a rodeo queen has-been. No wonder she couldn't attract Brawny Bo's attention.

"I'm taking your silence to mean I should give up and let Madison win." Tina's face pinched and she blinked back more tears.

"Actually..." Emily had been thinking that before Tina's first tears fell. But there was something about the teen she liked, an inner strength hidden within all that defeatist talk. And then there were all the obstacles ahead of Tina that Emily had faced when she'd run for rodeo queen—the full figure, not being classically beautiful, wearing her heart on her sleeve. "... I was thinking you have everything to take a run at the prize. You just need a smile that never falters, the proper coaching and motivation."

Tina smirked. "Beating Madison isn't enough motivation?"

"You have to want to win for you, not to beat someone else."

"You sound like my mom." Heavy sigh. Eye roll. Boot shuffle.

"I heard that saying from my grandmother long ago," Emily admitted. "She got on my case because I wanted to beat my best friend." Franny. "I wanted to win because my best friend won everything." In a way, Franny was still winning—three kids, barreling toward loving marriage number two, saving the ranch by capturing one large, dangerous bull and finding long-lost gold. Not that Em resented Franny anything. But envy her? Yes. "Unlike Madison, though, my best friend was kind."

"Everything okay out there?" Randall stood up on the bleachers.

"We're fine," Emily reassured him. "I'm just giving Tina her homework."

"You're taking me on?" At Em's nod, Tina threw her arms around her.

"I'm taking you on." Emily held her student at arm's length. "But you have to study."

Vigorous head nod.

"And find something to wear to dazzle the judges."

Vigorous head nod.

"And find something you like about Madison."

"Ugh." Tina pulled a face.

EXTERIOR. A PITTED DIRT ROAD WINDING THROUGH A NARROW RAVINE. Mike removes his wedding ring.

THE DAY AFTER Shane's meeting, Jonah made a sound of disgust as he browsed the back aisles at the general store and muttered, "Mike isn't married."

"Talking to yourself again?" Bo rounded the corner by the bread display. He wasn't smiling but he didn't have his force field in place, either.

"Guilty," Jonah admitted. No point denying it. "There's a reason Mike Moody earned the moniker *Merciless*. He wasn't married."

"Do you know what a habit is?" Bo perused a small display of peanut butter.

"Of course." Their banter felt familiar, like a broken-in pair of blue jeans.

Bo plucked a jar of smooth peanut butter from the stack and read the label. "You have a habit of writing about precocious kids. It's your thing. It's what you're known for."

"I was paid to write kid coms." Jonah scowled. "I'm moving past that now." Hopefully. His father still hadn't gotten back to him with feedback on the story treatment for Mike Moody's film.

Bo shook his head. "You're pegged as the guy to call for kid-friendly media. Embrace who you are."

"I've written other things." Jonah stopped short of telling Bo what. "I've written unhappy endings." He snagged the jar of peanut butter from Bo's hand and put it in his own basket. "I can do this."

"So do it." Bo gave Jonah a look that dared him to try. "Write about a murderous bad guy who died in a rockslide. A man who had no one to grieve for him. Not a wife. Not a kid."

"Sounds perfect to me." Jonah grabbed a loaf of white bread. "I'm okay writing a—"

"Gritty Western. So you've said." Bo smirked.

"Gritty and graphic doesn't mean it shouldn't be smart and well motivated." In fact, that was exactly what it needed to be, which was why Jonah needed Emily. Retracing the bandit's steps would help fill in those blanks.

"Hey, Jonah. The rice cooker and steamer

you ordered both came in." Mackenzie came out from the stock room with two boxes.

The general store had everything a person might need to enjoy Second Chance—produce, beer, fishing poles, bait, motor oil, hammers, pajamas and more. All crammed into a tight space. And whatever wasn't on the shelf could be ordered through Mack. He'd ordered the items in anticipation of moving into the Bucking Bull's bunkhouse. A decision had to be made.

Jonah was about to turn away from Bo when his cousin said, "Aria's five months pregnant."

Was there an earthquake? A rockslide? Jonah's footing felt unsteady. He did a quick calculation. "It's not mine." And then he did another, studying Bo's stone face. "It's—"

"Not mine, either."

"Oh." Jonah was going to need more than a moment to process that fact. He planted his running shoes more firmly on the floor.

A loud engine announced Emily was pulling up outside in the big gray truck with the Bucking Bull logo on the door.

Jonah wanted to talk to Emily, wanted to take another shot at hiring her, but this...

Aria's pregnant.

"When did you find out?" he asked Bo, still watching Emily.

The three Clark boys had spent the morning with their independent study teacher, who liked to hang out in the diner on weekdays, giving kids a chance to come by for help, to turn in homework or to take a test. But they'd gone home hours ago with Shane.

Bo stepped into Jonah's field of vision. "Aria told me a few weeks ago. After we found Mike Moody's gold." Bo's voice sounded flat, but that couldn't be. He had to be floored. Aria had left Jonah to be with Bo, but then… This explained so much. The grouchiness… The force field…

Was Bo considering getting back together with Aria or walking away from the situation once and for all? His cousin was no help when it came to revealing his intentions. Bo headed toward the seasonal aisle, disappearing behind a tall rack of sweatshirts that said If You Missed Your Last Chance, Make a Stop at Second Chance.

Emily entered the store and conducted a quick survey. Her gaze stopped on Bo. Her expression softened with longing.

No woman had ever looked at Jonah that way, not even Aria.

"Hey, I'm right here." Jonah stepped in the

cowgirl's path. "Have you decided to accept my job offer?"

"I have not." Emily slipped around Jonah and toward the back of the store. "I'm here to pick up my grocery order and add a pint of ice cream. Any interesting flavors come in, Mack?"

Not one to be deterred, and having had a horrible morning writing-wise, Jonah followed. "The Greek yogurt selection has much more variety and is healthier."

Half turning but still walking, Emily gave him the stink-eye. "When a woman wants ice cream, it has nothing to do with being healthy."

Bo chuckled from somewhere nearby.

"Ah," Jonah said before Emily could locate Bo again. "You're sending out a signal—*Aunty Em's had a bad day.*" He could almost picture little Adam hopping around and chanting the phrase.

Emily propped her hands on her hips, Bo and ice cream temporarily forgotten. "Can't a woman have what she wants without explanation?"

Jonah waited a beat to say, "By all means."

She slid him a sharp look that seemed to say, "Mind your own business."

Bo paid for his purchases and left, taking Emily's anger and hopes with him.

Her hands dropped to her sides. Her shoulders sagged. Even her expression seemed to fall.

A little bit of Jonah fell with her. "I... Uh..." He couldn't escape an unexpected thought—he wanted Emily to look lost when he left the room, which was ridiculous because he only wanted to have her near so he could get some decent words on the page. But it seemed the only way to get Emily to spend time with him was if Bo was around or...

A reprehensible idea entered his head. It was the kind of plan he'd give a villain in a script.

Villains sometimes do bad things with the best of intentions.

A ripple of maniacal laughter escaped his throat.

Emily's lost, floundering expression disappeared, replaced by a cold stare. She spun away from him. "Ice cream is the only reason I'm still standing here."

"I can help you," he said.

She held herself perfectly still. "I can pick out my own ice cream."

"I can help you catch Bo's eye." Jonah dared to move closer, to test the waters the way he wrote a scene when he was changing a character's motivation. "I know what kind of woman he likes." He swallowed, unable to believe he'd said the words out loud.

Still with her back to him, Emily opened the freezer door. But then she just stood there. Not moving. Not saying a word.

Jonah cleared his throat and took a few steps nearer. "Bo has a type."

"How do you know?" In profile, Emily didn't look so stubborn. Her nose was pert. Her chin delicate.

"I'll make you a deal." Jonah shut the freezer door. "I'll give you some tips on how to capture Bo's attention and in return you'll help me with the Mike Moody research."

"You'll coach me…" She stared at the pints of ice cream and gave one short, wry laugh. And then she turned, gaze fixed on his clavicle. "How do you know what Bo likes in a woman?"

Oh, what that question must have cost her. She delivered it with a raw voice that hinted at regret and defeat.

Jonah swallowed thickly, knowing he could only answer in kind. "Because I lost my fiancée to him."

CHAPTER FOUR

EMILY COULDN'T SPEAK. Not after what Jonah had said.

She couldn't speak. But she could think.

Of the day she'd first talked to Jonah. He and Bo had driven into town together. Shortly thereafter, a group of college-age female tourists had stopped and only had eyes for Bo, ignoring Jonah.

Of the day he'd come in to the Bent Nickel when she'd been having breakfast. He'd noticed she'd been staring at Bo, ignoring Jonah.

It'd been tough to grow up in Franny's shadow—in some ways it was still challenging—but apparently it hadn't been a picnic for Jonah to live in Bo's shadow, either.

Bo...

Her eggs heaved a regretful sigh.

The Texan was a gorgeous display of manliness. He'd probably been making ladies of all ages sigh from the day he was born. But that didn't give him license to take Jonah's fiancée.

Disappointment coursed through her. She

hadn't wanted Bo to be one of those men, the kind who only had to smile to get their way. The handsome kind who cut corners because life gave them so much and they unapologetically took what was offered.

And yet...

Some piece of Jonah's story didn't fit. "I thought Bo was single." And if he was, why was Jonah offering to help her garner his attention?

A moment ago, Jonah's gaze had been laid bare, his pain visible in the crease between his brows and the firm line of his mouth. At her words, he almost seemed to draw back, as if pulling within himself. "Bo's not married or engaged."

It hadn't worked out for any of them—not Jonah, not Bo and not the fiancée.

"Consider the subject closed," Jonah added, although he didn't turn away from her.

Emily was used to Jonah's sarcasm. It could be annoying, but it was never mean in nature. She wasn't used to his vulnerability. Here was a man who'd trusted, who'd loved, who'd been hurt.

He needs a hug.

Emily shifted, resisting the impulse to do just that. She looked him in the eye, noted his closed-off expression and realized he was waiting for her to respond to his offer. "What exactly are you expecting your assistant to do?"

"I want you…" He faltered, drew a deep breath and started again. "I have a map of the old stagecoach and Pony Express routes. I want to see if I can find them. I want to walk in Merciless Mike Moody's shoes—"

"Boots," Emily corrected.

"—and get in his head." Jonah passed a hand between them, disregarding semantics. "I need someone to guide me to places. I want to know if Mike could see the old roads from his hideout. If I see what he did, I'll know what tempted him to a life of crime, I'll know where he'd have ambushed the stage. I'd understand how hard it was to execute his plan."

What he wanted sounded easy, a couple of simple trail rides. Straightforward, like Tina running her sweet palomino in figure eights in the arena. But there were tricks to everything and, like the way she'd noticed Button was cutting corners, Emily could tell Jonah wasn't telling her something.

Besides the story behind his lost fiancée.

"I'm going to pass." She preferred to work with people who were honest. And if she was being honest with herself, there was no way Jonah could help her appeal to Bo. Jonah was too sharp-edged to play matchmaker, especially with someone who'd taken so much away from him. "You can find the roads alone on someone's borrowed ATV. You don't need me." Frankly, most of the time Jonah didn't appear to need anyone. "The lands across the river are nationally protected, but public. And that's where I've heard the old stage line ran."

"No motorized vehicles." Jonah ran a hand over his red goatee, swept his gaze over her. "I want to see it by horseback, the way Mike Moody would have. I've been to the smithy a couple of times, trying to get a feel for that fight Mike had with Old Jeb the last day of his life."

Old Jeb. Emily's ancestor. The man Granny Gertie wanted her to make sure was well represented in Jonah's script.

There's a reason to agree.

She was lying to herself. There was only one reason to agree: Bo.

Her eggs sighed again, transgressions with another man's fiancée forgotten. Like her, they found it hard to believe he'd stolen Jonah's bride. There had to be more to the story. The two cousins were friendly with each other.

And yet, knowing what she did, Emily couldn't agree to the terms. The probability of failure was too high.

Jonah waited before her with more patience than she'd expected.

It struck her then. There was another reason to agree: Jonah. He deserved help after what he'd been through. And if she learned more about Bo and his moral fiber… If she learned Bo regretted all that had happened…

"I sense your hesitation." Jonah opened the freezer door and selected a pint of fudge chunk. It was the flavor of ice cream she'd been considering when he'd dropped his proposition. "I'm offering you options in a place where you don't have many. I'm offering you strategy, not a makeover, although a new look wouldn't hurt." His smile was apologetic as he handed her the ice cream.

Emily glanced down at her pink checked button-down shirt and dirty blue jeans.

"Women chase after Bo like hungry bloodhounds on the scent of a fox." Jonah tipped the brim of her cowboy hat up. "You have to be different. You have to act like he *isn't* the most handsome man in the room."

"Is that how it was with your fiancée?" Had that woman treated Bo like he was no different than any other man?

Jonah turned his back on Emily and started walking. "You have to earn that information."

She followed him. "I could just ask Bo."

If she could actually form words when the hunky Texan was near. That had always been a problem in the past, hence her invisibility.

Jonah shook his head. "Asking about Aria won't get you a coveted date."

"I'm not looking for a date. I'm looking for something long-term."

Jonah chose that moment to face her. He stood in front of an entire shelf of chocolate. Big bags in exotic flavors left over from Easter. It was amazing she registered the chocolate behind him when his eyes were upon her. They were so blue and full of regret that she held her breath.

"I'm moving into your bunkhouse today." Gone was the sarcasm, the snark, the attitude that implied Jonah was smarter than everyone in the room. She didn't recognize this man. "Tomorrow afternoon. You bring the horses. I'll provide the map." He turned, grabbing a yellow bag of chocolate with a large, happy Easter bunny on the front. He handed it to her. "For your nephews."

He'd selected two items to please her, but the contents of his basket held nothing as decadent—vegetables, tofu patties, yogurt, peanut butter, white bread.

"Are you vegetarian?"

"No."

She didn't believe him. He was so thin. Although he could be recovering from some illness. There wasn't anything in his basket that a doctor wouldn't approve of, except maybe white bread. Was that why he'd lost his fiancée to Bo? Because he'd had cancer or a brain tumor or some other health scare?

She was suddenly Team Jonah, at least where the other woman was concerned.

While she'd been wondering about Jonah's health, he'd gone to the checkout counter. "Bring me my horse, Aunty Em, and leave the questions to me." Jonah paid for his groceries and moved to the door, juggling his bags and two boxes of small kitchen appliances. "Enjoy that ice cream."

Emily added the ice cream and chocolate to her grocery order, knowing when she got around to eating her pint, she wasn't going to enjoy it, not the way she usually did.

Because she was going to think of Jonah with every spoonful.

EXTERIOR. SECOND CHANCE BLACK-SMITH SHOP. Mike and Jeb face off over the forge. Mike's guns are holstered.

MIKE: I'm taking your horse.

JEB: No.

Mike shakes a small bag of gold.

MIKE: You can buy a better horse.

"BLECH. NO BLOOD. No guts. So much for trying to write the ending first." Jonah rubbed his forehead and stared at the peeling rose wallpaper in the bunkhouse. He'd moved to the Bucking Bull Ranch after talking to Emily in town. His steamer and rice cooker sat on the counter in the kitchenette. The one-room shack had a minimalist Western atmosphere, if he overlooked the feature wall. "Who puts wallpaper in a bunkhouse?"

He'd been trying to write for hours but had very little to show for it. Moving out here was supposed to help him with that. He was closer to real cowboys this way—or in the case of the Clarks, real cowgirls. The sounds of livestock, the smell of leather… It should've all been inspiring. And it might've been if Emily had agreed to be his assistant.

Don't blame someone else for your failures.

That was Grandpa Harlan's voice, gruff and disapproving.

Jonah turned from the wallpaper and stared at a small watercolor he'd hung on the refrigerator with a magnet. It was a portrait Aria had done of him right before he'd proposed.

She'd captured his face in cynical lines, everything from the slant of his eyes to the lowered eyebrows.

"There's a man who doesn't trust the world," Jonah had told Aria when she'd shown it to him, thinking she'd captured the side of himself that he didn't like. He wondered if that was the way she saw him.

"You're not looking deep enough," she'd told him, staring at his portrait with love in her eyes.

He'd proposed then. The words coming clumsily out of his mouth because they hadn't been rehearsed. If he'd delved deeper into his reason for popping the question, he'd have known it was too soon and for the wrong reasons. He'd have realized where their romance was headed.

Later, he'd plotted it out, written it up, complete with sparkling dialogue, painful, tense moments and a tearful romantic ending. For Bo. Later still, he'd put the project away, certain his father and agent would laugh at it. Getting movies made in Hollywood required a certain amount of clout. Jonah had none, which made writing in a different genre difficult.

He may have nailed Bo and Aria's script, but he was floundering with Mike Moody and more was at stake with the Western. Every word, every action he detailed on the page could let Shane and Second Chance down. He got to his feet, needing to get out of the small cabin, wanting to talk to Bo but assuming he'd be rebuffed. Did it matter whose baby it was if it wasn't his or Bo's? Bo's force field seemed to indicate that it did.

The sky above the ranch was an endless black dotted with bright stars. Crickets chirped. In the barn, a horse whinnied. There was no traffic noise. No sirens. Not even creaking timbers from the Lodgepole Inn.

It was after 9:00 p.m. The farmhouse across the ranch yard was dark. The Clarks were in bed. Moving here might have been a mistake. The writing wasn't coming any easier just because he was in these authentic, wide-open Idaho spaces.

The mistake was telling Emily about my failed engagement.

Like Jonah, Emily wasn't the most trusting type. And he'd given her a reason to look beneath Bo's pretty veneer. That weakened Jonah's bargaining power.

Jonah blew out a breath and breathed in… woodsmoke.

That was odd. No smoke came from the farmhouse chimney.

Curious, and in need of a distraction from

the dreadful script, Jonah walked around to the back of the house, telling himself he wasn't snooping. The backyard wasn't fenced.

Emily sat at a circular firepit while eating her fudge chunk ice cream. For once, she was outside without her cowboy hat. The firelight made her hair seem a richer brown.

"Evenin', neighbor." Jonah's spirits immediately lightened. His running shoes crunched over gravel as he entered the circle around the pit. He claimed a webbed folding chair next to her.

"Jonah, I don't want to sound rude but—" she put a spoonful of ice cream in her mouth, pausing until she'd swallowed "—I live in a house full of people and this is the only time I can be alone."

"Hmm." That wasn't the type of statement he could let slide. "Aren't you alone when you ride out to check on the cattle?"

She dug her spoon into the carton and said nothing.

"Or when you drive into town to get groceries or pick up the boys?"

Emily indelicately shoved a spoonful of ice cream into her mouth and stared at the fire.

"I came here to see if you'd been considering my offer." An outright lie, but he needed inspiration, and one of her snappy lines could be used as inspiration for a new scene.

"Your job offer?"

Jonah nodded. "About helping you attract Bo's attention."

She scraped her spoon around the inside of the carton, seemingly not sold on his proposition. Or perhaps his confession had turned her off Bo.

Jonah had been in enough pitch meetings in Hollywood to recognize that she needed a teaser. "Here's some free insight. Bo's parents were Texas-Philly snowbirds. Migrating whenever a business Uncle Darrell ran needed his presence for more than a few days at a time. His branch of the Monroe family is in oil and yacht building. Contrast that to me. I was born and raised in Hollywood. My dad runs Monroe Studios and my mom is my sister Ashley's momager."

Growing up, Jonah had been the overlooked older child. Not an actor. Not an athlete. And later, not even healthy.

Emily stared into the depths of the empty container and shifted her feet as if getting ready to leave, which was odd. Most people liked to know they had less than six degrees of separation between them and actress Ashley Monroe.

Jonah turned the conversation back to his cousin. "Bo likes women with a bit of polish." That was because of his cousin's Philly roots. "Independent women who might occasionally find themselves in a bind." Bo had a serious rescue complex. He'd take on the cause of any damsel in distress. "And women with contradictory layers." They had to be intriguing.

Emily was intriguing, although she didn't seem to know it.

She tossed her ice cream carton in the fire and then set her spoon on her chair's plastic armrest. "Did you just describe your former fiancée?"

Now it was Jonah's turn to go silent.

"You're not doing a very good job of selling Bo as the man for me." Emily slouched in her chair, burying her hands in her jacket pockets. "I'll forget for a moment he was involved in a messy love triangle if you'll answer me this. Does your description fit me? Do I have a bit of polish? Am I independent but perhaps not completely self-sufficient? Do I have contradictory layers?"

Yes. Yes to everything.

Emily's laughter lacked humor. "I'll take your silence as a no. No on all counts." Sober again, she asked, "Are you trying to fix me up with Bo so you can win your fiancée back?"

"No!" The word burst forth at a volume that had her studying him.

"Then why try and fix me up with Bo?"

He couldn't tell her the truth—that the matchmaking was just a carrot to draw her into his sphere. Guilt prickled along his skin. He was no better than the legions of females who'd pretended to like him in an effort to further their acting careers. Although he supposed there was a possibility that Bo might fall for Emily and get over Aria for good, so the deal between them could be mutually beneficial. "If I explain about my engagement, will you take me on a trail ride?"

A log on the fire collapsed in on itself.

"Curiosity was the cat's downfall." Emily slanted a glance at him. "But in this case, if you tell me about your engagement, I'll give you one trail ride."

"Sure." Jonah was certain he could turn one ride into another. "Long story short..." Because the full story was messy. "Bo and I are close. We met Aria at a fund-raiser in Houston a year ago. I was on location for a movie. We both dated her." It had become a competition to see who would win her heart first. Not Jonah's proudest moment, to be sure. But relying on hindsight could be harsh and judgmental. "After a few months, she accepted my proposal and shortly thereafter admitted she also had feelings for Bo."

She'd stood in front of Jonah and handed his ring back. "I can't marry you if I love Bo."

Bo had stood nearby, stone-faced.

"And all I could think in those first few seconds was there's something wrong here." He'd taken a breath and realized something important. "My heart wasn't broken." He'd taken another breath and realized Bo's had been. "It all happened so fast."

"Like a traffic accident," Emily noted.

The tofu patty Jonah had had for dinner churned at the memory of a once-innocent rivalry gone wrong.

"She loved two men at the same time." Jonah hardly recognized his voice. It was flat and emotionless, the way Bo's had been earlier in the store. "And now she's pregnant with someone else's baby."

"She's..." Emily laid a hand on Jonah's shoulder, bridging the distance between them. Just one brief touch before she retreated. "How do you feel about that? Are you okay?"

He blinked. Not even his mother had asked him how he was doing after his engagement fell apart. "Shocked at the speed of her rebound, obviously. Although given the whirlwind courtship I had with her, I shouldn't be."

But Bo was. Bo seemed devastated.

Emily blew out a breath. "So you're saying Bo's *not* a homewrecker."

"Not in the slightest," Jonah was quick to say, turning the subject to safer waters. "And afterward… It took a few months but we're back to doing things together—like coming here—but our relationship isn't the same." It felt more like an obligation than a fondness for one another's company.

Emily stirred the fire with a poker. "You do realize you're in a broken bromance with your cousin?"

"Technically, I don't think family relationships can be bromances." But her slant on the situation was clever, he'd give her that.

Emily made a dismissive noise. "You have bigger problems than writing the story of Mike Moody's life. I'm not sure I want to get tied up in all this."

Jonah bristled.

But Emily wasn't done. "I'm not going to mend Bo's broken heart."

"We'll never know if we don't try. Are you in or out?" He crossed his arms over his chest. "I sense out."

"I didn't say…" Her head wobbled, along with her resolve. "I shouldn't be…"

Ah, the longing for a husband of her own.

Jonah leaned into the space between them. "Bo's a good man. If you're interested, I can get you a shot. He can't resist lending a hand to a woman in her time of need."

She half turned in her chair, gripping the plastic armrest that didn't hold her spoon. "You want me to pretend to twist my ankle and fall into his arms?"

"Oh, good." Jonah grinned, choosing to ignore her sarcasm. "You've read this story before."

Emily stomped her bootheel on gravel. "I'm not the woman that men rush to rescue."

"No. I imagine you're the kind of woman who rescues her man." Jonah sat back and stared into the flames, distracted by an idea. He needed to open the script with Mr. Merciless saying something clever to a stagecoach driver during a robbery. Not just clever. Cold-hearted *and* clever.

"No." Emily got to her feet.

"No?" Jonah glanced up at her, having lost the trail of their conversation.

"I have my pride. I'm rejecting your job offer."

He captured Emily's hand to keep her near, at least long enough to ask, "What do you think Mike Moody said to stop the stage that last time?"

Emily didn't hesitate. "'Stop or I'll add another murder to my Most Wanted poster.'"

She was quick, but it still wasn't right. "That feels incomplete."

Emily tugged her hand, but not with much force. She was smart. She probably enjoyed crosswords and other puzzles. She probably found his question intriguing. "He'd say, 'What's your name? I want everyone to remember so they can add it to my wanted poster.'"

"Better." But not quite right. His thumb brushed along the soft skin of Emily's inner wrist, finding her pulse. It was strong and rapid.

Maybe she'll trip and fall into my lap.

Emily snatched her hand back. "The day he died, Mike Moody shot the guard sitting next to the stage driver. And then he probably said something like, 'You remember to tell the sheriff his name. Wouldn't want it left off my wanted poster.'"

Jonah curled his fingers into his palm, trying to save the heat from her touch.

Quit being a sentimental idiot. Focus on the script. This is a great opening.

Jonah extended his fingers, releasing her warmth. "He'd want the passengers on the stagecoach to know his name." Because a successful thief would have a reputation and the fear he'd have instilled in others would have fed his brazenness. "He'd squint up at the driver and say, 'State your name! Wouldn't want it left off MY wanted poster. That's right. I'm Mike Moody!'"

Oh, that was good.

Emily didn't let on if she was impressed or not. She gestured toward a bucket of water near his feet. "Douse the fire when you're through." And then she scooped up her spoon.

"You're leaving?" Jonah shifted in the chair to watch her walk away. "But that's a great line." It conveyed attitude and a history of killing. "We could come up with some other ones."

"I'm a rancher, not your assistant." That was a nose-in-the-air tone if he'd ever heard one.

And yet, Jonah couldn't shake the idea that she'd enjoyed tossing lines back and forth. "I'll see you tomorrow and we'll go on a trail ride. Just two friends enjoying the day." After all, she'd promised to take him.

She slammed the back door behind her.

Jonah faced the fire, running possible lines of dialogue in his head as he ran the palm of his hand—the hand that had held her wrist—across his jaw.

Toss down that strong box like it holds your granny's pearls.

I'll take that fancy purse of yours, pretty lady.

That's what the last coach driver said before I put a bullet between his eyes.

The lines weren't as clever as the wanted poster line, but the ideas were flowing. It was time to get in front of his laptop. He'd write a couple robbery scenes. Maybe they'd give him ideas about what happened in between.

A window opened behind him. "I have conditions."

Jonah took in Emily's silhouette in a window on the bottom floor. Was she talking about the script? "That's not what Mike Moody would say."

"I'm talking about me. *If* I work for you, I have conditions." She shut the window, latching it closed without divulging what her stipulations were.

Jonah bet he'd never agree to whatever terms Emily came up with. He doused the fire, waiting to make sure it was out before walking back to the bunkhouse where he spent the next few hours drafting scenes that weren't half bad.

CHAPTER FIVE

JONAH MONROE WAS INCONVENIENT.

It was creeping up on noon. He'd be expecting his trail ride soon.

Emily had a dozen things to do around the ranch and her body ached. Earlier, she and Franny had been working with some of their younger bulls, getting them used to being taken in and out of the stock trailer. Emily had been stepped on and had bull snot blown on her chest. And then one nervous yearling slammed her against the metal wall.

She was willing to bet bull snot didn't count as the polish Jonah referenced she'd need to capture Bo's eye.

Franny was in a far stall, checking an abscess in her horse's mouth. Her soft voice drifted through the barn. "Just a little more of this peroxide mixture, Danger, honey."

As if sensing his brother's distress, Deadly poked his head over his stall wall and nickered.

"You baby that horse, Franny." Em finished disinfecting feed buckets and wiped her hands dry.

"That's what Kyle used to say." Sadness no longer dragged from her syllables when Franny talked about Kyle. "But surely everyone needs to be babied when they have a toothache. Isn't that right, Danger, honey?"

Deadly huffed, wanting some attention.

Emily stopped at his stall door to oblige, scratching between his ears. "Don't expect baby talk from me, fella."

"No baby talk?" Jonah appeared in the barn doorway. He wore relaxed blue jeans, a neon yellow T-shirt and a blue baseball cap. The sun glinted off his fringe of bright red hair. "Ever?"

"Ever," Emily said firmly, heat creeping up her cheeks.

In the history of bad ideas, Emily receiving love advice from Jonah had to rank pretty high. She needed to establish some rules today, because despite Jonah being annoying, there was the little matter of a slight attraction to him. And there was no way she was getting involved with a city slicker. She had her sights firmly targeted once more on Brawny Bo.

"The lack of baby talk is for the best since you're working for me now." Jonah closed the distance between them, looking as pleased as punch. He scratched the beatnik hair on his chin. "How about that ride?"

"Go on." Franny chose that moment to come out of Danger's stall. "It's a beautiful day outside."

"Beautiful." Jonah stopped a few feet away, looking nowhere but at Em. "My thoughts exactly."

Is he flirting with me?

Emily's head felt muddled. "About those rules…" She couldn't think of one.

"I thought we'd ride up to Mike Moody's hideout and see what he could see of the valley." Jonah didn't let Emily collect her thoughts. There were those clear blue eyes and that handsome grin. "You know, we'll follow the path Mike took after he stabbed Old Jeb at the smithy. I just know the blacksmith was no threat to Mike."

"What makes you say that?" Emily snapped. After all, Jonah was talking about her five-times-great-grandpa.

"If he was a big threat, Mike would've just shot him." Jonah sounded so certain. "Why risk injury to himself confronting Jeb with a knife?"

Emily frowned, not liking that Jonah made sense. "That trail you want to take starts in the heart of Second Chance proper." A couple miles as the crow flies. A couple of ridges between them on horseback.

"Is that a problem?" Jonah's smile dwindled away.

"It's not a quick trail ride and it's my day to pick up the boys in town." This was why they needed rules, so he'd know when she had other obligations.

"I can get the boys." Franny joined them in front of Deadly's stall, giving Jonah a welcome smile.

"On second thought…" Emily marched toward the tack room, a new course of action planned. "I've been promising the boys a special outing. We'll take the horses over to town and then the lot of us can ride back by way of the bandit's trail." Locals enjoyed taking the trail for hikes, mountain bike and horse rides. Her nephews would be tickled. It would just leave a lot on her plate around the ranch tomorrow but she was leaving town soon and wouldn't have many more opportunities for moments like these with her nephews.

Franny followed her. "Can you make sure that Adam—"

"Goes to the bathroom before we leave town? Yes." Emily was way ahead of her sister-in-law.

"And check that Charlie—"

"Brings home all his schoolbooks." Franny's middle son was notorious for leaving them behind. Emily turned, waiting.

"And that Davey…" Franny arched a brow at Em, daring her to complete that sentence.

"Davey is the least of your worries."

"I know." Franny grinned. Her oldest took the role of the man of the house seriously, perhaps more so since Shane had proposed to Franny.

"No Popsicles for the boys today, I guess." Jonah came to stand behind Franny. "Where's Shane?"

"He's working on the cabins with Bo at the camp by the lake." Franny scooped up Adam's saddle and tack. "He was expecting you to help today, Jonah."

"My helping would not be very helpful. I'm not handy when it comes to fixing things."

Sliding her arm under Davey's saddle blanket, Emily exchanged an arched-brow look with Franny, unable to resist a tease. "Where does your handiness lie, Jonah?"

"With the written word." He grinned unapologetically.

"I guess words would come in handy—" Emily smirked at Jonah on her way to Yoda's stall "—if I was writing an email."

"Or an online review," Franny added, moving toward Taffy's enclosure.

"Or a social media post." Which Emily had no use for. Having lost her brother in a horrible way, she valued her privacy too much.

"Oh, ladies." Jonah was unfazed by their ribbing. "Don't you know it's dangerous to poke fun at a scriptwriter?" He tsked. "You could end up dead on the screen someday."

"Gruesomely murdered." Emily chuckled.

"Stabbed in the back." Franny laughed.

"I'm so glad the Clark women *get me*." Jonah patted Deadly's neck. "Can I ride this one? He seems gentle."

"No," Franny and Emily chorused, both immediately solemn.

"Deadly's a handful." Emily entered Yoda's stall. "You'll ride my horse, Razzy."

"I appreciate you taking me out." There was something wrong with Jonah's tone. He was too confident. "Take me for another ride and we'll get this *My Fair Lady* thing working."

"What's he talking about?" Franny caught Em's eye across the breezeway.

"I'm going to help Emily land a date with my cousin." Jonah rubbed his hands together.

Again, Emily's cheeks heated. "I haven't agreed to anything."

"You said you had conditions." Jonah was

enjoying this too much. He stroked the well-trimmed whiskers on his chin. "That implies we have a deal."

She hadn't wanted their agreement to be public. Emily saddled Davey's mustang. "Here are my conditions. For your safety, you must obey my commands when we're riding."

"Oh, I like that one." Franny was busy saddling Adam's pony and didn't look up. Surprisingly, she wasn't questioning the wisdom of Em considering Jonah's deal, either.

"And you have to check your wardrobe advice at the door." Emily gestured to her dusty, dirty clothes. "Because this is me."

"Yeah," Franny agreed. "Guys shouldn't tell women how to dress."

"Um…wait." As usual, Jonah had a differing opinion. "I think there should be a rule about the number of conditions you can set. It should be three, like the number of wishes you get from Aladdin's lamp. It sounds like you're gearing up for more than that. Plus, I'd like to negotiate the scope of the wardrobe condition because you'd look fabulous in—"

"There's no negotiation when it comes to my clothing." Emily drowned out his voice with hers. If he had his way, he'd have her floating through a cattle pasture in a glamorous gown. "My third and final condition is that you have to be up-front with me and your advice has to work or all deals are off."

"That's two terms in one." Jonah frowned.

"Not really." Franny cinched up Taffy's saddle. "It all boils down to trust."

Jonah looked from one woman to the other. "Do all your tag-team negotiations box your opponent in a corner?"

"Yes," Franny and Em chorused, like-minded from decades of friendship.

Jonah held his hands up in surrender. "Then I suppose I've got no choice but to say yes."

Emily snuck a glance at Jonah—all half grin, relaxed shoulders. And yet, she had the distinct impression that she was the one who'd been boxed in and bamboozled.

Jonah drifted into the tack room.

"You know, I'm pulling for Jonah to succeed in this bargain." Franny tied Taffy to a hook in the breezeway.

"You mean, you hope he gets more trail rides?" Emily fastened Yoda's reins to a similar hook on her side of the barn.

"No." Franny didn't grin, didn't tease. "I hope Bo falls for you so you'll stay in Second Chance with me."

"It's just a shot in the dark," Emily said

gruffly, wishing the same thing. "Don't get your hopes up."

In short order, she and Jonah were ready to ride. Emily had Davey's mustang and the younger boys' ponies on a stringer. Jonah brought up the rear on Razzy. Franny bade them farewell, closing the barn door behind them.

Predictably, Deadly required her full attention until he'd burned off some energy. He pranced sideways, tossed his head, gave a half-hearted kick at Yoda when the mustang followed too closely.

"What's wrong with your horse?" Jonah called, worry in his tone.

"He's rambunctious and not a team player." And they were riding through thick brush, similar to the situation where Deadly and Kyle had been ambushed. "I've got your back, buddy," she muttered, with a steady seat and firm hand on the reins.

The brush thinned and Deadly settled down to a fast pace, making the ponies work hard to keep up.

The ride into Second Chance took nearly an hour. There was little opportunity for conversation, given Jonah was four horses back. Emily was fine with that. The warmth of the sun. The smell of the pines. The solid thump of horse hooves on dirt. This was what she loved about being a cowgirl.

When little Adam saw them cross the highway toward the Bent Nickel diner, he hopped out the door and across the parking lot on two feet like a bunny. "Aunty Em brought the horses!" Hop-hop-hop. He bounced in a circle.

Emily dismounted and handed Deadly's reins to Jonah so she could take the horse and ponies off her stringer. After sending Adam back inside to the potty and Charlie back inside for his schoolbooks, she charged her nephews with securing their backpacks on their saddles.

Egbert emerged from the diner with a cup of coffee in one hand and his cane in the other, looking like Santa in the off-season with his white, flowing locks and full white beard. The unofficial town historian raised his mug in salute to Jonah. "Finally following Mike Moody's trail, are you?"

"Yes." Jonah leaned his forearm on his saddle horn, as if he'd been raised a cowboy. "Any words of wisdom?"

The old man gestured with his coffee mug. "By all accounts, Mike Moody galloped into those trees like the devil himself was on his tail. You should do the same."

"He galloped?" Jonah gazed across the road, brows drawn low. "That hill's pretty steep." He was a greenhorn having second thoughts.

"We're going to go fast but not ride at top speed." Emily caught Adam's eye and winked. "You can get a flavor for Mike Moody's escape without galloping."

Her nephews were vocal in their disappointment. They wanted to ride like the posse was hot on their heels.

"Can't we run on ahead?" Charlie climbed on top of Buff, a stocky brown pony he claimed looked like a buffalo. "You can stay with the city Monroe, Aunty Em."

"I feel so unappreciated." Jonah's blue eyes twinkled, contradicting his words. "As if I'd be left on the trail if I were shot and would slow Mr. Merciless down."

"You got that right." Egbert waved farewell. "That desperado didn't love anyone but himself."

Once all five horses and riders were safely across the two-lane highway, Emily led them toward a deer track in the trees. She turned and assessed Jonah, who was behind her. His seat was too casual. He wasn't a natural rider. He was a passenger out for a ride. "Are you up for this?"

"Never let it be said that a Monroe was afraid of a little speed." Jonah glanced up the mountain, a rare, grim expression on his face. "Besides, if Mr. Merciless did it, so can I."

"Hold on to your saddle horn." Emily gave Deadly free rein and a squeeze of her heels. The gelding surged forward in big, choppy strides until he found his rhythm. The re-enactment of Mike Moody's escape was on.

Her nephews hooted and hollered like a bunch of cowhands headed into town on a Saturday night. Another voice joined their enthusiastic cries, a deeper, booming voice.

Darn if Jonah wasn't enjoying himself.

Grinning, Emily reached the next rise and pulled up to a walk, turning Deadly so she could watch her merry band catch up.

Jonah had one hand on the saddle horn and was laughing. She'd never seen him so free and gleeful. His joy filled her chest, too, as if they were connected. She was sure she had a goofy grin on her face, one that mirrored his.

Davey passed Jonah coming up the last few feet. "Can I lead?"

"Only if you give the horses a breather." Emily waited for Charlie and Adam to reach her, letting them continue on after Davey. "Follow the trail up to Rocky Point and then take the north fork toward the Bucking Bull."

"We know," Davey called back.

"I've been meaning to ask." Jonah gestured toward Deadly's chest. "Where did your horse get that scar?"

The lightness in Emily dimmed. She explained about Kyle's death. "This poor guy showed up in the ranch yard all bloody and shaking. But once the vet had him sewn up, he kept trying to bolt from his stall, almost as if he wanted to rush back to Kyle's side." Em swallowed thickly. Kyle and Deadly shared a special bond, one that hadn't transferred completely to Emily. "He's always been a handful. My brother used to say some horses are like fast cars. You have to know how to drive or both you and the horse are going to end up in a wreck." She patted the gelding's neck. "But since that day, Deadly's been skittish when he doesn't have a clear view of his surroundings. When I take him out alone, I like to stick to open land."

"And what about you?" Jonah's gaze searched her face. "Since the day your brother died, you've been..."

"Moving forward." Sometimes blindly. Sometimes when she'd have preferred to stay in bed. Only now, as Emily admitted what she thought she'd been doing, did she realize that she'd been moving on a big hamster wheel. "Except... I haven't really gone anywhere."

Jonah nodded. She knew he understood. It was there in the way they didn't have to say anything or look away as if they'd accidentally invaded each other's space.

The moment stretched until it rang in her ears. She almost wished it wouldn't end.

This is what I'm looking for.

Not Jonah specifically, but that feeling of unity and acceptance.

A bird squawked in a nearby tree.

Jonah seemed to shake off their bond the way Deadly shook off a persistent fly. "We've gone a long way today. Forward progress, I'd say."

The sense of connection was broken.

Emily squared her shoulders, ready to carry on alone again. She breathed in trail dust and the scent of pine. "No use whining, then."

"Nope." Jonah turned Razzy so he could look back down the trail. "We're barely a quarter mile from the highway and I can't see a thing. It's good cover up here. Do you think our bandit was a local? Did he know this route or was it luck?"

"He had to have known." Emily guided Deadly up the trail, leaning forward in her saddle as the ground grew steeper. "He hid his gold before then. And he'd need supplies. Egbert is supposed to have the blacksmith's journal. Have you read it? Did it have any clues?"

"Oh, I read it. It was bedtime material. Put me right to sleep a couple of nights. A couple of days, too, if I'm honest." Jonah told his horse to giddyap, giving commands like the tenderfoot he was. "It was more like the smithy's ledger than a journal, detailing business transactions. And then when Jeb married the schoolmarm, he barely kept any records at all." Jonah chuckled.

"What's so funny?"

"He probably had other things to occupy his time."

"He was happily married." Em guided Deadly around a patch of eroding ground, coming to her ancestor's defense. "Don't forget, if not for Old Jeb, Mike Moody would have gotten away."

"How do you figure?"

She wanted to stop and argue with Jonah, but they were midmountain, so she kept going. "Mike and Jeb fought. That slowed Mike down. Think about it. Mike Moody robbed a lot of stages. No one had come close to catching him before."

"Rumor has it he was riding a horse that threw a shoe. That slowed him down, more than the blacksmith. And then the rockslide got him."

"Are you writing Old Jeb out of your movie? He was a hero." A beloved local icon.

"I'm sure he was comforted in his hero status while he nearly bled to death from a stab wound."

Gertie was right to worry about the portrayal of their ancestor. Jonah only paid him lip service. He'd be a forgotten footnote in Hollywood's version of the story.

"Why do you want to date Bo?" Jonah's unexpected question drove concern for her ancestor out of her mind.

The boys were ahead of them now, chattering but so far away Emily couldn't hear what was being said. The same would be true of her nephews and her conversation with Jonah. Whatever they discussed would be private. "I'm thirty. It's time I set down roots of my own somewhere."

"Yes, but why Bo?"

She glanced at Jonah over her shoulder, prepared to fire a quip back at him, starting with "It's none of your business."

Jonah wasn't grinning. His expression was the same as it had been the other day in the general store, the expression of a man who'd been jilted and who knew what unrequited love was.

Emily focused on the trail ahead and spoke plainly. "Bo's a cowboy."

"He's not a cowboy," Jonah scoffed. "He's a Texan. There's a difference."

"Potato-Potahtoe. He wears boots. He knows how to ride." Bo would help her raise her little cowpokes. "Besides, there aren't many single men in town my age." This could be her last chance to stay in her hometown.

Jonah stopped talking, which was always unnerving because he wasn't like anyone she'd ever met before. He had little to no filter and seemed to consider no topic off-limits.

Except when it came to details about his fiancée.

His silence meant he was thinking about something.

Me?

She whistled softly. Deadly swiveled his ears back and forth, no doubt wondering what signal she was sending.

After a few more minutes without talking, Jonah cleared his throat. "First off, you need to compliment Bo on something no one else would, like his way with animals."

"How would I know that? I haven't seen him with any animals."

"He has a dog," Jonah said in a tone that implied Emily hadn't done her homework. "You should clean up and visit the camp he's working on. He's handy with a hammer."

"You do remember my second condition," Em said, because his advice was sounding hokey. "About clothing?"

"Trust me. A little style goes a long way."

Although Emily was starting to like Jonah, she didn't trust him.

Ahead, the boys followed the north fork in the trail. Emily and Jonah reached Rocky Point not long after.

"Hang on." Jonah brought Razzy next to her. "This view is spectacular. Would Mr. Merciless have stopped here to see how close the posse was?" He rose up in his stirrups. "I can see the entire valley, but not the town proper. Could he have watched for an approaching stage from here? Galloped down the mountainside and—"

"Broken his neck?" Emily snorted. She gestured back the way they'd come. "You saw how steep that was. And the stages had schedules. He could wait much closer to the road."

"The stage road was across the river in the

valley. I want to go there tomorrow. Maybe there was a narrow ravine they passed through. A place he could set a trap."

"If you want to go on horseback you'll need to live up to your end of the bargain first." Emily couldn't see the boys. She urged her horse after them.

"I gave you gems about Bo," Jonah grumbled.

Gems? Not hardly. He wanted her to talk to Bo about dogs and power tools. Anyone could do that.

Emily left Jonah to eat her dirt.

EXTERIOR. MIKE'S HIDEOUT. Mike is cooking beans over a small campfire on a sad hill.

A ROUGH PATCH of land on a sad hill.

That was what Merciless Mike Moody's hideout was.

Of course, back then Mr. Merciless didn't have the Clark family cemetery on the doorstep of his small man cave. Still, it was an isolated, lonely place, requiring a hard man to stay.

Jonah slid off Razzy's back, landing on shaky ground. Or, at least, his legs felt like the ground shook. "Hold still, fella, until I get my bearings." He clung to the saddle horn.

Razzy swung his head around, nudged Jonah in the hip hard, and blew a raspberry as if he was one of the Clark boys and found Jonah's sore muscles hilarious.

"Hey. Not funny." Jonah turned sideways, still clinging to the saddle.

The horse whinnied and shook his head.

"And that's why I call him Razzy. He's a comedian." Emily hopped down and checked to make sure her nephews had their mounts secured to the low wrought iron cemetery fence. Her honey-brown hair fell in a loose braid over one shoulder, but she was otherwise none the worse for wear after that long ride. "I had high hopes for you, Tenderfoot. Walk it off."

Jonah took a step away from Razzy, pleased he didn't falter or receive another horsey nudge. "Ha. Like you wouldn't have unsteady legs after taking a spin class."

"Spin class? Is that where they ride bicycles that go nowhere?" Emily scoffed, giving him attitude from beneath her hat brim. "City folk."

Jonah opened his mouth to fire back a retort when his gaze snagged on Emily's face. A sly smile. A crinkle of big brown eyes against the glare of the sun. His mouth went dry and he forgot what he'd been about to say.

I need to write about her.

About the love she has for her home and her yearning for a romantic love of her own, a desire so great she'd make a deal with the devil to find a husband. She was settling for Bo because he was convenient. Jonah bet that normally she was picky about her men. He bet few could live up to her high expectations.

Emily caught him staring.

Jonah glanced away, wrapping his horse's reins around the cemetery fence rail as he'd seen her do. Emily wasn't going to be a character in a script any more than his sister was going to land a role in Mike Moody's tale. He was here to soak up the inspiring atmosphere, to look for traces of the rockslide that had killed the infamous bandit. But it was hard to put together the story pieces when the bigger boulders had been cleared away a month ago to allow better access to Mike Moody's loot.

Laughing, the Clark boys swarmed the area like ants on patrol, just the way the Monroe kids used to do when Grandpa Harlan took them on his biannual family trips. It was amusing, but it wasn't the kind of atmosphere he'd been hoping to find.

Taking a protein bar from his pocket, Jonah scanned the area as he ate, finding nothing but unsettling memories of an angry bull as large as a tank and the sickening, repeated crunch of metal as the animal rammed them.

Like him, the Clark boys remembered that day. Unlike him, they chattered enthusiastically, reliving it as a grand adventure.

"I haven't been up here since we came to your rescue," Jonah told them, recalling the wild time in Shane's SUV.

"And then Mom and Zeke caught our new Buttercup!" Adam played hopscotch on the flat grave markers, as if catching feral bulls was an everyday occurrence.

"And we found Mike Moody's gold." Davey followed his little brother at a slower pace.

There was nothing strategic about the location of the cave, other than it was a natural shelter on a ridge separating two valleys. The trees blocked the view in either direction. How had Mike found this place? And why had he hidden his gold here?

"What are you doing, Charlie?" Emily asked as the boy disappeared into the bandit's cave, a fissure in the rock that had been blocked by boulders for decades before Grandpa Harlan and the others found it.

"I'm just making sure we didn't miss any gold, Aunty Em." Charlie poked around the cave.

"Are you going to do that every time we

come here?" Emily stayed close to her mischievous nephew.

"Yep," Charlie said.

"Who's this?" Adam pointed to the granite square beneath his feet.

"Shove off and I'll read it," Davey said. When his little brother moved, he knelt and brushed the dirt off the flat marker. "Jeb-ah… Jeb-ah… Jebediah Clark!"

The pair oohed and then proceeded to read the name on every marker. Clarks, the lot of them.

Jonah wandered over to read Jeb's headstone. "Old Jeb lived up to his name. *Old.*" He'd been nearly ninety when he died.

The boys chortled.

"Surely, that's worth mentioning in your movie's epilogue." Emily leaned against the cave's entrance, looking like she was ready for a bold, local cowboy to walk over and kiss her.

Jonah took a step her way before stopping himself. He was wrong for her on both counts.

Not a cowboy. Not setting down roots here.

Adam knelt by a marker nearest the cave and brushed the dirt off. He turned to his older brother. "Who's this?"

"Let… Let-ty. Who's Letty?" Davey wiped away more debris covering the stone. "She doesn't have a last name."

"Is there a date?" Jonah wound his way through the markers to join the boys.

Davey read off the years framing her life.

"Letty was a young woman. She died a year before Mike Moody did." Jonah removed his sunglasses and bent, running his fingers over the professionally engraved letters. "She died when only Mike knew about this place."

"So he must have known her," Emily said with a certainty Jonah didn't like. "But who was she?"

"Not another mystery." Adam fell back on his bottom.

Jonah's gut rebelled against Emily's implication. "He didn't have to know her. He could've found this spot after Letty died here."

"But then why only one name on the stone?" Emily shook her head as she studied Jonah. "You don't care about who she was, just like you don't care about Old Jeb."

"No." Jonah shook a finger at the heavens. "I don't want her to be part of Mike Moody's past." Or to have given him any children. "Merciless men don't bury anyone. That's why they're merciless. And if they cared enough to bury someone, they'd have added her last name to the stone."

"I know who she is. Letty was his horse." Charlie hopped over the low fence to weigh in. "Don't look at me like that, Davey." He gave his older brother a small shove. "When Buff dies, I'm gonna bury him on the ranch."

"I bet Granny Gertie knows who Letty is," Davey said solemnly. "She knows everything about Mike Moody."

The old woman knew everything because her husband, along with Grandpa Harlan, and his brother Hobart had researched the myth and found the gold, only to consider it unlucky and put it back where they'd found it.

Jonah didn't believe in luck. But he was stuck on the first act of his script and the very last thing he needed was this Letty person to have been important to Mr. Merciless. To have been sweet and kind, a woman the bandit cared for, a woman who wouldn't approve of the man's ruthlessness.

"Let's head back." Jonah had plot points to figure out. "Maybe Gertie will know something about Letty."

Something that wouldn't undermine his impression of cold-blooded Mike Moody.

CHAPTER SIX

"WHAT DO YOU THINK?" Tina had several different outfits spread across Emily's bed—all black. The teen was at the ranch when Emily, Jonah and the boys returned from their ride. "I need to pick some outfits for the rodeo queen competition or go shopping. The event is in a week and it takes me forever to find something that fits."

Emily studied the clothes Tina had brought. Granny Gertie was baking. The smell of oatmeal cookies filled the air. It should have comforted Emily, but these clothes…

"What you've got here is nice, Tina." Black jeans. Long-sleeved black shirts with pearly snaps. Safe. Predictable. Slimming, at least in theory, because they were black. Nothing Tina brought stood out like Jonah with his sharp blue eyes and city clothes. Not that Emily should be giving Jonah more than a passing thought. He was vinegar. She was oil. She went to her closet and dug around for some color. "A lot of girls wear outfits like that. But we want to stand out."

"No. We don't," Tina blurted. "I try very hard to blend in. It's my mission in life."

Emily gave the teen a critical once-over. "That outfit you're wearing doesn't blend in."

Tina had on a bright red T-shirt with braided blue handkerchiefs sewn on the sleeves with silver threads. Her jeans were gray. Her shoes yellow with white polka dots.

"I wore this because…" Tina hesitated and then pressed on. "I wore this because I…" Her round cheeks pinkened before words spilled out of her nonstop. "I wanted to show off to you because I made this. I mean, not the whole T-shirt. I sewed the trim on the sleeves. I like to take ordinary things and make them different. Which is dorky, I know. But maybe I'm a little bit of a dork." Her fingers twisted in the hem of her T-shirt. "Nobody cool sews. And if they did, they wouldn't wear what they made, at least not to school. That would be the crowning achievement of dorkdom."

Smiling wanly, Emily fingered the woven strips of material attached to Tina's sleeves. "I take it you didn't wear this to school today?"

"No. *Gah*." Tina tossed her thick brown hair over her shoulder. "Madison would eat me alive."

Emily wanted to tell Madison a thing or two. "Do you love sewing?"

Tina nodded, squirming as if she'd never admitted a love of her hobby to anyone before.

"Then you should sew your own blouses and jackets to compete in." The embroidery, the beading, the sequins. It would take her hours. "Not that there's time for that now. But if you compete later, it earns you respect with the judges. Now, the clothes you choose should be a bright color that complements Button's gold coat."

The teen sat abruptly on Emily's bed, a defeated expression on her face. "All due respect, Miss Emily, the only person who compliments me on my sewing skill is my mother."

"Is that because you never show anyone, apart from your mother, what you've made?" At the teenager's reluctant nod, Em gestured to Tina's customized T-shirt. "Well, I've seen it and I'm complimenting you. There are easily twenty to thirty girls going to compete for the rodeo queen crown and you can bet they'll all be wearing the same thing."

"But..." Tina's shoulders were creeping downward. "People will look at me if I dress different."

"You're beautiful. Why wouldn't they look

at you?" Tina made a strangled noise that Emily ignored. She turned back to her closet, digging around until she found what she was looking for—a fitted, red denim jacket with a black velvet horse appliqued on the back. "I wore this when I won the crown. It was—"

"Really? You won wearing that?" Jonah stood in the doorway, looking like he was ready to take a meeting in Hollywood in his white chinos, pink polo and leather loafers without socks.

"Yes, really." Emily flushed with heat. Jonah always managed to make her feel like a country bumpkin. "Can I help you?"

"Yes." Jonah beamed at Tina and introduced himself. His hair was wet, as if he'd showered. "I thought we'd ask Gertie about Letty."

"After dinner." Emily shooed him away.

Jonah didn't budge. "But I need to figure out my plot and—"

"I'm working now. With Tina." Emily mustered a smile for the teen's benefit, which was challenging considering she wanted to scowl at Jonah until he left the room. "I'm coaching Tina in her efforts to be a rodeo queen. We're discussing wardrobe choices for the various events." She huffed and, to Tina, said, "You have an evening gown, right?"

Tina nodded, although she hadn't brought it.

Emily reached deep in her closet for a zippered bag. She hung it from a hook and opened it up. "If you don't have fancy chaps, you can borrow mine." Hers were white with red fringe and lined with red sequins. "This was the evening gown I wore when I won." It was yellow. Emily spread the skirt wide, revealing ombré shades of yellow in the train.

"It's leather." Jonah sounded shocked.

"Rodeo queen competition dresses often are." She'd sold off most of her other gowns and fancy jackets. "And I wore a belt and a huge buckle." Emily rummaged around in the bottom of the bag until she found it.

Charlie hurried in carrying a plate of cookies with both hands. He practically dropped them on Emily's dresser and then ran out. Tina and Emily each took a cookie. They were warm and wonderful.

Jonah ignored the cookies, his expression curious. "Ah." He moved toward Emily and her closet with the jerky movements of a man who wasn't accustomed to riding. "I believe the issue is how Tina should dress to convey sophistication and yet be able to do her cowboying. Cowgirling." He stopped his perusal of Emily's closet to face them and raise a finger. *"Rodeoing!"*

"Jonah isn't actually qualified to dress anyone for a rodeo competition." Emily pointed at his pink polo. In her wildest imaginings, the man she married would never wear pink. That just wasn't the cowboy way. And yet, he made pink look good on a man, although she'd rather not admit it.

Tina struggled to contain a smile.

"Au contraire." Jonah tilted his head as he stared at the clothes laid across Emily's bed. "I'm qualified to give fashion advice because my sister is Ashley Monroe." He smiled at Tina. *"The* Ashley Monroe, beloved former child actress and style icon."

"Name dropper," Emily murmured. He was stealing her credibility with Tina. "Hollywood has a completely different style of fashion."

Jonah ignored Em. "And my other sister Laurel was Ashley's stylist for years. I couldn't block out their clothes conversations with my earbuds in and the volume on as loud as it would go. Trust me, I tried. I'm painfully familiar with styling a look for every occasion."

"But not the rodeo, Hollywood man." Emily laid her hands on his shoulders. Despite him being slender, they were broad, strong shoulders. When she tried to turn him, he didn't budge. "Leave the Western styling to the former rodeo queen. Everything about the competition is larger than life."

"I would, but..." Jonah patted one of her hands, gaze drifting toward the wardrobe options on the bed. "Desperate times call for desperate measures."

"I can't say this any clearer," Emily spoke through gritted teeth. *"Leave."*

He didn't.

"You two are about the same size." Moving past her, Jonah made quick work of Emily's closet, one hanger at a time. "No. No. No. No." His hand paused on the dress Emily had worn to his cousin's wedding last month, the one Franny said brought out the highlights in her hair. "We can do better. Do you have anything in a rich purple color that would go with your red horsey jacket and those fancy white chaps?" He didn't wait for her answer. He continued his rejection of Emily's wardrobe. "What about this?" He drew out a lavender button-down and held it up to Tina, who'd been as silent and still as a cornered mouse since he'd mentioned his famous sister.

"I like it," Tina said in a voice that sounded as if she hadn't spoken in a hundred years.

"It does warm up the brown in your hair." Conceding the fact, Emily took the hanger from Jonah. Her fingers curled around the hook the way she'd like to curl them around the neckline of his polo as she dragged him out the door.

"This look…" Jonah wasn't through. "It says sophistication. It says wisdom. It says I belong to this horse posse."

"The point is *not* to conform, but to be yourself." Emily couldn't stress that enough to Tina. "To show people who you are and what makes you special."

"Which version of herself should she show?" Jonah scanned Emily's closet once more. "Everyone has different sides to themselves. Tina, you strike me as a down-to-earth, friend-to-all type of person."

"Thank you for that assessment," Emily began.

Jonah nodded. "Though I suspect you've got a stubborn streak, like this one." He nodded toward Em. "A rich, royal purple is the way to go. And avoid ruffles." He shuddered.

"A lot of Western wear has ruffles." Emily bumped him aside with her hip.

Jonah gave her an incredulous look. "You're in the arena to show off your skill, not your ruffles."

"He's got a point," Tina said meekly.

He did. Emily blew out a breath.

"Now." Jonah gestured toward Emily's wardrobe. "Since I'm giving out fashion advice, if Emily's going to be dating, she needs more feminine footwear than these boots." He picked up Emily's pink boots with gold trim. "The next time we're within the radius of a decent-size mall or clothing store, we shop."

"The likelihood of us going anywhere together outside of Second Chance is never." Emily snatched her boot back. The pink boots were the one thing she owned that was fun and impractical. "If only I had my beloved boots on, I might kick you out of here." She curled her toes in her socks, and gave him a look designed to discourage. "Remember my conditions? No wardrobe changes."

"Every deal is negotiable." Jonah grinned. He was impossible, skin so thick he didn't seem to care that she wanted to get rid of him.

Emily sighed. "If I agree, will you skedaddle?"

"Skedaddle?" Jonah's grin widened. He leaned toward Tina and spoke behind the back of his hand. "In modern times, we say get lost."

"Get lost, Jonah," Emily ground out.

"Hang on." He scanned the trophies on her bookshelf. "Is that your rodeo queen trophy?"

He picked it up, blowing dust off it. "I never got more than a participation medal in soccer."

"Perhaps you'll finish that script and earn an award." Em snatched her trophy and returned it to its place of pride on the shelf among her other dusty awards.

"I'd like that." Jonah smiled at them both. "A trophy I'd never dust, just like Emily."

"Jonah," Em wound out the word.

"One more thing before I go." Jonah reached into the closet and tugged a black scoop-neck blouse free. "When you talk to Bo later, wear this."

It was the blouse she wore once a year to meet her friends in Ketchum for a night of dancing. "Wait." Emily tapped her foot impatiently as his words sank in. "I really don't have time for—"

"You do!" There was mischief in those brilliant blue eyes of his.

Emily narrowed hers. "Get lost, Jonah."

"Lady Tina. Queen Emily." Jonah bowed dramatically. "I'll be in the kitchen talking to Gertie if you need me."

Finally he left, but the annoyance of his presence lingered.

"He's related to Ashley Monroe?" Tina's voice hadn't gotten any smoother, but there was a respect in her eyes that hadn't been there before. Sadly, it was for Jonah, not Em. "What's he doing here?"

"He's writing a movie script about a local legend." And because she needed a little ego boost, Emily added, "And I've agreed to help him."

"I'M AFRAID I can't help you, Jonah." Gertie transferred oatmeal cookies from a cookie sheet to a cooling rack. She wore a gray T-shirt with sunflowers embroidered on it, as bright and cheerful as the woman herself. "I have no idea who Letty is."

"I know she's dead," Adam piped up from the kitchen floor, where he was sitting, eating a cookie under the watchful eye of Bolt. "We found her in the cemetery."

The Clark kitchen was in need of an update. The oak cabinets had seen better days. They were water stained and banged up. Jonah leaned against a counter near the kitchen sink, enjoying the welcoming smells of sweet cookies and the nostalgic feeling of inclusion in a large, bustling family.

Davey and Charlie darted in to steal a couple of cookies and then ran back to their video game. Carrying a handful of invoices, Franny came in to fill a glass with water, muttering about the rising price of hay. Emily and Tina's laughter drifted to Jonah from the other side of the house.

Grandpa Harlan would've loved this.

He would've loved Emily and the way she stood up to Jonah, going toe to toe. Aria had always taken Jonah's sarcasm the wrong way. Looking back, it was hard to pinpoint what had drawn him to the ethereal beauty, other than the fact that she'd looked twice at him before looking twice at Bo.

"I feel sorry for the poor woman," Gertie went on. "Letty's been forgotten."

Jonah didn't know whether to be upset or relieved that Gertie knew nothing about the woman buried on the ridge.

"Who do you think she was, Jonah?" Gertie put a few cookies from an earlier batch in a small red tin, making room for more cookies on her wire rack.

"His mother. His grandmother." Jonah snapped his fingers. "Maybe a passing hermit."

"Anyone *but* a love interest?" Gertie slanted him a look that judged. "Jaded. That's what you are."

Jonah chose to ignore her observations, mainly because they were true. "Maybe Letty found the cave first."

Gertie tsked. "You don't want this Letty woman to mean anything to anyone."

Emily had said much the same up at the cemetery.

"Now, now. Like I told Emily, I care. I just don't want any little Mikes running around." Jonah made the no-no gesture by shaking his finger from side to side. "It's hard to be ruthless when you're a dad. Maybe single Mike felt he owed Letty for guarding his cache of gold while he was out robbing folks and that's why he bought her a grave marker."

"That implies he cared for her and acted with honor." Gertie was just as feisty as her granddaughter. "Why do you want to make him so irredeemable? People make mistakes all the time. That doesn't make them bad through and through or untrustworthy."

"But mistakes—yours and others—make you think twice about trusting anyone." Even yourself. Jonah frowned. The conversation wasn't giving him what he needed. "What can you tell me about the Clark cemetery?"

"Only that we stopped burying Clarks up there midcentury." Gertie extended a spatula with a cookie toward him.

Jonah politely turned her down, plucking a banana from a fruit bowl instead.

"Can I have his cookie, Granny?" Adam held out a hand, smiling for all he was worth. *"Please."*

Gertie gave him the cookie she'd offered to Jonah and then leaned her elbows on the kitchen counter and fixed Jonah with a no-excuses stare. "Emily told me you were engaged once."

"As opposed to being engaged many times?" Jonah tried to put her off with humor.

"You're a slippery one." The old woman gave Jonah a knowing smile, the careful mouth-curl of an intelligent woman who wasn't going to be put off the scent. "What happened?"

"We broke it off." Jonah shrugged as if there was no more to the story, when the opposite was true.

"Oh, young man. I'm looking at you now and getting an impression…" Gertie straightened, gripping the counter for balance until she could grab the cane leaning nearby. "You don't particularly want to be married."

"No, ma'am." But he was curious about her grandmotherly intuition. "Did you have this same feeling about Shane when he came around?" Shane had been a career-driven bachelor until he met Franny.

"Shane." Gertie tapped her cane on the worn linoleum. "Shane always gave an impression of being a good family man."

"I'm a good family man," Jonah countered,

although he wasn't sure why he was defending himself. Marriage was a subject best left untouched. "I just don't think I'd be a good daddy."

"Said every stubborn man who fights falling in love ever." She harrumphed and peered at her great-grandson on the floor. "Do you like Jonah, Adam?"

"Yes." The boy beamed at his adult audience. "He's funny sometimes." Adam held out a hand, expecting his answer to be rewarded with a cookie.

"Last one." Gertie handed Adam another treat, a small one as cookies went.

Adam didn't care. He gobbled it up and then let Bolt lick his fingers.

"You can protest fatherhood all you want." Gertie hobbled out of the kitchen. "But there'll come a day when you'll change your tune. All the best ones do." Gertie moved toward the living room. "I'm not done thinking about you, Jonah. I'll be back with more questions after my talk show is over."

Adam got to his feet. There was a hole in his sock near his big toe. "Are you in Granny school?"

"What?" Jonah didn't understand the boy's question.

"She's givin' you a test, like I get in school." He skipped out of the kitchen, Bolt at his heels.

The kid was right.

More than anything, Jonah didn't want to be around when Gertie's show was over and his test would resume.

CHAPTER SEVEN

"YOU LOOK PRESENTABLE." Jonah fiddled with Emily's hair after Tina left, arranging it over her shoulder.

Emily swatted his hands away. She'd rolled the ranch ATV out of the equipment shed and was stowing a red tin of oatmeal cookies in the storage compartment. "You're supposed to make me look better than presentable." She'd changed into the black scoop-neck blouse, swiped on some mascara and lipstick, and was anxious to get some results.

Old Man Time was marching on. She had to keep up.

"Hey, you should be wearing one of Laurel's designer dresses." Jonah studied her face. "Add more makeup maybe to get rid of your raccoon tan. And can you try not to scowl?"

Emily shoved her sunglasses in place, hoping to cover the tan lines.

"That'll do." He nodded.

They were going to ride the quad down to the camp where Bo was living and working. It was located near the entrance to the ranch near the highway. Emily was a nervous wreck. Her hands shook. This was her chance to be seen by Mr. Bodalicious. She got on the ATV and waited for Jonah.

"Hop on and let's see if you know what you're doing coaching-wise."

Jonah sat behind her, placing his hands on her hips. "I can give you advice until your cows come home. It's up to you to execute it successfully."

She noted the warmth of his hands.

I'm oil. He's vinegar.

She sighed.

"Show some restraint." Em wasn't sure who the words were meant for—herself or Jonah. She started the engine and headed down the gravel road.

A few minutes later, they left the driveway and passed through a gate. They crossed a large meadow, stopping near a cabin a few feet from the shore of a small lake that would be dried up by late September.

Bo emerged from a cabin carrying a water bottle and wiping sweat from his forehead. In a sleeveless shirt that showed all those muscles, he looked like a model from a men's cologne ad. "Are you dropping off my cousin?

I could use a spare hand now that Shane's gone."

Emily was tongue-tied. No news there.

Jonah climbed off the back of the ATV and gave Emily a searching look. When she didn't say anything, he did. "Gertie made cookies for you."

"I knew there was a reason I loved that old woman." Bo hopped off the front porch and walked toward them. "That doesn't get you out of work, Jonah."

"I was working." Jonah's chin jutted. "Don't forget Shane's plans for my scripts."

"You can daydream about stagecoach robbers while you help me cut lumber." Bo glanced at Emily, smiling politely.

Him-him-him, the eggs chanted.

Jonah poked her shoulder, raising his eyebrows.

That was Emily's cue to say something besides "I want to bear your children."

"We brought you cookies," Emily blurted. Immediately, she wanted to be swallowed by a sinkhole. She got off the quad and produced the canister of cookies.

"I already said that," Jonah said mulishly, not living up to the hype of her romance consultant, although he did turn his back to Bo and mouth to Emily, *"Fix your hair."*

"I'm sorry, I…" She handed Jonah the tin of cookies and finger-combed her windblown locks. "I couldn't hear what Jonah said. My ears were ringing from the motor." She could speak if she didn't look at Bo. Em turned her gaze to the closest cabin, which was larger than the rest. "This used to be the mess hall, I think."

"It will be again," Bo assured her. "Jonah, did you get to go on your little field trip to the bandit's lair? If so, you can help me cut two-by-fours tomorrow. We can race to see who can cut the most."

"I'm taking a hiatus from competing," Jonah grumbled.

Emily decided to barge into their conversation, risking a glance at Bo. "Don't mind Jonah," she blurted, talking faster than an auctioneer. "He's stressing about Letty and my grandmother grilled him about being a bachelor. She thinks he's afraid of kids."

Bo wasn't looking at Emily like she was annoying, but he wasn't looking at her as if he wanted a date, either.

"I'm not afraid of children. You haven't seen me running from your nephews, have you?" Jonah set his red-whiskered jaw. "Besides, I used to make a good living writing stories about impish kids."

"Wow. Yeah. My bad. I got that wrong." Em snorted and quickly put a hand up to her mouth. "Granny was asking him about being a dad. She thinks he's scared of being a father."

Talk about throwing Jonah to the wolves.

"She thought I'd make a good dad someday, when I was ready." Jonah's arms were crossed over his chest. "Not that I sought her approval. I wanted to know about Letty." Jonah smoothly changed the subject, explaining about the grave they'd found. "Gertie doesn't know who she is."

"A mystery woman." Bo waggled his dark brows, warming up to Jonah for the first time since they'd arrived. "You know what this means."

"No." Jonah shook his head and thrust the tin of cookies at Bo. "Definitely, no."

"What does it mean?" Emily asked.

Bo dug into the tin for an oatmeal cookie and took a bite. "It means Merciless Mike Moody had a wife. He had a heart. He had ki—"

"If you say *kids*, I'm never bringing you cookies again," Jonah grouched.

"But you write them so well." Bo winked at Emily, which nearly brought Em and her eggs to their knees. "Maybe Mike's gang was made up of his children." He handed Emily a cookie.

Even though she'd already eaten three cookies when they were hot out of the oven, Emily accepted his offering. "Jonah, do you want a cookie?"

Bo closed his tin of cookies and then handed Jonah his unopened bottle of water. Jonah didn't seem upset to be denied a snack. He drank water instead.

The cookie seemed to lighten Bo's mood even more. He showed them around, taking them into a few of the cabins he'd repaired. "Things would go faster—" he poked Jonah's shoulder "—with help. The kids are depending upon the Monroes to have this camp ready in time."

"Maybe I'll come by for a bit in the morning," Jonah said, finally relenting. "Is this where you're staying?"

They entered a cabin that was in better shape than the rest. A small cot sat in the corner next to a duffel and a pile of what looked like dirty clothes. A cowboy hat hung from a hook on a wall.

"Five-star accommodations." Bo sounded like he believed it, but that narrow cot didn't look comfortable.

"There's room in our bunkhouse if you

want a bed and some company." Emily blushed. "I mean if you don't mind sleeping with Jonah. Not in the same bed but—"

"He knows what you mean." Jonah headed back to the ATV. "Separate beds, Bo. Just like when we were little."

Bo laid a gentle hand on Emily's arm, holding her back.

Mr. Bodalicious is touching me!

Emily's heart tried to pound its way out of her chest.

"Was Jonah okay on the trail ride today?" Bo asked.

"Yeah. Why wouldn't he be?" Emily was reminded of her suspicion that Jonah had been sick. He might still be recovering.

Instead of answering her, Bo shuttered his gaze and released her. "Watch out for him, will you?"

"Sure. Of course." Anything for Mr. Bodalicious.

"Time to go, Aunty Em," Jonah called from the quad.

"He can be a trial," Bo told her, still using that lowered secret-keeping voice. "But he's totally worth it."

"Totally..." Bo thought she wanted to date Jonah? Emily's cheeks flushed with embarrassment.

"Aunty Em," Jonah called, saving her from the horror of trying to correct Bo's impression.

Emily got on the quad and brought the engine roaring to life. She drove too fast, letting the wind cool her cheeks. And once she was in the equipment shed, she flung herself off before Jonah could move. "I can't believe it. Bo thinks I want to date *you*." Or worse. He thought they were already dating. "This is a disaster." As soon as the words were spoken she regretted them. "I'm sorry. It's not that you're not datable."

Quite the opposite, the eggs murmured.

"Or that *I* wouldn't want to date you." Her face burned so hot sweat popped out on her forehead. She wiped it away. "Not that I want to date you... Not that I wouldn't date you if you were a cowboy." She made a strangled noise and considered making a run for the house.

"You should have quit while you were ahead." Jonah sat sideways on the quad, crossing his arms and giving her a half smile.

"You know what I mean." Emily stomped around the quad. "You're datable to city women. You don't have to enjoy this so much."

He quirked a brow. "Are you through trying to dig yourself out of that hole?"

She covered her face with her hands. "Why do you have to make everything so hard?"

"Why do you have to make it so easy to tease you?" He stood and gently pried her hands from her face, keeping hold of them. "Bo's misunderstanding about us isn't necessarily the end of the world."

"What? You think he's going to try and steal me away from you the way he stole your fiancée?" That would never happen.

"There was no stealing. And yes, we've always been competitive." He shrugged. "So... it's a possibility."

"Nobody has ever fought over me." The concept was hard to believe but also a bit of an ego boost. "Ever."

"Somebody should've," Jonah said in a thick voice.

The sentiment behind his words was so lovely Emily couldn't say anything for a moment. And then her curiosity returned. "If your fiancée loved you both and you broke it off, why didn't she and Bo end up together?"

Jonah's eyes filled with regret. "They... Aria and Bo would never do something that would hurt me." He dropped his hands to his sides.

Emily's stomach fell along with them. What an awful thing to have happened to

Jonah. Not to mention to Bo and Aria. Her heart ached for them all.

Jonah stared out at the ranch yard. "And now it seems like it's too late for them."

"I… You…" Emily drew a deep breath, trying to gather her scattered thoughts. "Tell me I'm not a pawn in this drama being played out between you and your cousin."

"Honestly?" His blue gaze hit her with a soulful intensity that pinned her in place. "Initially, I hadn't thought much beyond what I wanted out of our deal." He sighed and then brushed his hands through her hair and around to the back of her neck. "But…"

The word hung between them. It hung, like a pause before a first kiss.

Perplexed, Emily waited for the pause to end. And waited… Perhaps he didn't realize she was good at waiting.

"The more I get to know you, the more I just want you to be happy." His hands caressed the back of her neck. "Now that we've put you on the path to Bo, I really need help with some dialogue. You're good at it, you know."

"What you need help with…" *Is making a move on a woman who's practically in your arms.* Emily gasped. Her eggs had taken over the wheel for a moment. She took a step back. "I'm no help with creative writing, but if you want to give me more tips about Bo, you can find me after dinner at the firepit." She turned, heading toward the house, and then stopped. "Would you like to join us for dinner?"

"I have food in the bunkhouse."

"Rabbit food." She was amazed he was so strong given what little he ate.

Jonah nodded, looking so mournful she ran back and hugged him. His arms came around her with that surprising strength.

"I'm sorry about your fiancée." And Bo. And whatever had caused him to get so thin and worry Bo about his health. She squeezed Jonah tighter, wanting to make it all better.

"That's not why I'm bummed," he said huskily.

"Good." Emily wanted to linger. She wanted…

Jonah wasn't her ideal cowboy, but he called to something in her soul.

Help me out here, eggs.

But her eggs were silent, leaving Emily to do the responsible thing for a woman with cowboy dreams—pull away, excuse herself and escape.

EXTERIOR. MIKE'S CAMP AT NIGHT. He sits at a campfire next to a freshly dug grave. There are two horses tied to a picket line at the edge of the firelight. A lockbox sits unopened next to him, along with a child's reader.

"OH, MIKE IS moody all right." Jonah stared at the words on the page. "Just not merciless." And neither was he.

He'd hugged Emily. And it wasn't the kind of teasing hug he'd given her on her birthday. It was the kind of hug high school slow dances were made of. They'd held onto each other while they talked, barely moving.

At the time, all he had to do was pull back a little, shift a little and then give her a little kiss.

Except…

There'd be nothing little about kissing Emily. She did everything on a large scale.

Kiss Emily? It would have been an all-out adventurous expedition, full of unexpected thrills.

Kiss Emily? Jonah wanted to do no such thing. She had her heart set on Bo. Hadn't he learned anything from his engagement to Aria?

He closed his laptop, which was a mistake. He needed to keep working on the script, horrible as this first draft was turning out to be.

But all he could think about was Emily and her determination to find a cowboy.

And if he thought about Emily long enough, his thoughts circled around to the bargain they'd made. It was laughable, him giving her love advice to attract Bo. In fact, it was romantic comedy–laughable. If Jonah had any interest in writing rom-coms, this would be the perfect idea.

Cowgirl needs romantic assist from city slicker to catch a cowboy.

It didn't matter that Emily was completely wrong for Bo. It was comedy gold.

His gaze shifted toward the watercolor painting on the refrigerator. That jaded face. His face. It was the portrait of a selfish man, a writer who hadn't always lifted his head from his keyboard to make sure he was being a good person. The man in the watercolor wouldn't fit Emily's idea of a family man, cowboy or not.

Giving in to temptation, Jonah reopened his laptop and pounded out an opening of a romantic comedy where a cowgirl was over-looked by a wealthy cowboy. In no time, he wrote a complete scene that wasn't half bad. And—shocker—there weren't any adorable kids in it. It was so earth-shattering Jonah called his father.

"Yes." Lincoln Monroe sounded like he was driving, distracted and not pleased to field Jonah's call.

"Hey, Dad." Jonah forced himself to play it cool. "Just calling to check in."

"Are you still in Idaho?"

The truthful answer to that question wouldn't make him happy. "I've been working on a script and—"

"Son, I hope you haven't been working on that Western. I read the treatment and the premise is interesting, but…" His father honked the horn and swore. "If I was producing it, I wouldn't hire you. Your voice isn't a good fit for such dark material, it's young and irreverent."

Jonah felt like honking and swearing in an irreverent manner. His own father didn't believe he could do justice to Mike Moody's story.

"Play to your strengths," his dad stated in the way know-it-all dads did.

But… Does he know what my strengths are? Do I?

"Son? Are you still there?" His father's voice was laden with annoyance. "I said you should stay in your lane, focus on what you do best."

"Fifth grade fart humor, you mean." Jonah closed his eyes. "Thanks for your opinion, Dad."

"Anytime, son. Just because you're not my employee doesn't mean I don't love you. Now go out and find a project that suits your skill set."

"Love you, too, Dad." Jonah stared at the ceiling and shook his head. "Gotta go."

Father disconnected. Dreams trampled. Confidence shot. Jonah tried to look at the bright side.

"Someday, a film student is going to make a documentary of my life and spend a good five minutes on this moment." He drummed his fingers on top of the computer. "The low point in my life. When my own father didn't think I should stretch myself."

He had to get out of the bunkhouse. Not that he was going to go to the firepit behind the ranch house to see if Emily was there. But once outside, he loaded his arms with some firewood stacked near the bunkhouse door before he walked around to the back of the Clark home. If Emily was there, she'd appreciate more wood to throw on the fire. He'd just drop it off and say good-night.

Emily had a big fire burning and her boots propped on the concrete brick rim of the pit.

Jonah set down his load of firewood and

then sat down in the chair next to her as if he'd meant to do so all along. Neither one of them said anything. Like him, she probably regretted that hug.

"I haven't sat in a chair like this in twenty years." Jonah shifted his weight, causing the seat webbing to creak. "When my grandfather took us on summer trips to places like Mount Rushmore and the Adirondacks, we each had our own chair." Often, at night, those chairs had been set up in rows while they performed small plays Jonah had written.

"Sounds like fun." Emily continued staring into the flames. "We used to go on trail rides up the valley with Franny's parents, driving their cattle from the upper pastures and back."

"Did they help you move your cattle?"

"No. We have fewer in our herd to move. Maybe a hundred. Sometimes more. Franny's family runs about a thousand head. Anyway, it was during those drives that Granny Gertie would tell stories of Merciless Mike Moody."

Jonah wouldn't be going on cattle drives, wouldn't be sleeping under the stars and worrying about what might crawl or slither into his sleeping bag. "Bucking bulls, cattle drives. Your need for a cowboy makes sense." If not Bo, someone else would come along, especially if Jonah came through for Shane with that script.

"Every cowgirl needs a cowboy." Her shoulders flinched in an almost shrug, as if she was questioning her resolve.

What was going on in that head of hers? He didn't know why it was important to understand Emily. He should have been trying harder to understand Mike Moody. But Emily was there within reach and Mike Moody was just a whisper in his head. "Idaho is true cowboy country." Or so he'd been told. "Why hasn't some yahoo snapped you up before?"

"I'm inconvenient." She ground her boots against the concrete block, almost as if trying to snuff out the label.

"Inconvenient? Well, that much is clear to me." *And* thank you *for the opportunity to lighten up the mood.* "But don't forget you're outspoken and stubborn." And a spitfire. What was wrong with men in Idaho that they didn't see what a great catch she was?

Her scowl made Jonah want to add "often annoyed" to his list of descriptors for her.

"I'm inconvenient because I've been needed here," she said testily. "First, when the boys were young and then after my brother Kyle died. Most folks run their own spread or work someone else's. I'm not able to afford my own ranch. And I'm not much for taking orders. I like doing things my way. The Clark way."

The fire crackled and hissed.

"You know, Bo has a life in Texas." And not on a ranch.

"He's making a life here." There was some of that stubbornness.

Temporarily. Jonah didn't have the heart to tell her that, not after they'd shared that hug. "You were too nervous around him today."

She grimaced. "Mr. Bodalicious is an intimidating presence."

"Mr. Bodalicious?" Wait until he called Bo that. "I shudder to imagine what you call me."

That grimace turned right around. "Mr. Hollywood. City slicker. Greenhorn."

"Not Mr. Jodilicious?"

She rolled her eyes. "Let's not overanalyze what happened today. I have you in my corner. That should be enough to let nature take its course."

A cold shaft of guilt pierced his shoulder blades. Bo wasn't going to ask Emily out.

"What's wrong?" Emily turned toward him. "Are you stewing about Letty?"

Jonah wasn't going to admit he was stewing about her, which was infinitely better than stewing about his father's opinion of his talent.

"You'd better spill, city boy." Emily had a firm way of looking at a man that said she could take whatever he dished out and sling it right back. "You know I'll get it out of you eventually."

He sat back, unable to contain a grin. "The country girl has learned interrogation tactics now?"

"I'm good with a rope." She spun her arm as if twirling a lasso. "Ever heard of hog-tying?"

"That sounds like an unusual seduction technique." He sank deeper in his creaky, webbed chair, not liking where his mind was going.

Emily poked his thigh. "Hey, what was the dialogue you wanted to run by me?"

"Forget dialogue. The story is all wrong." He stared at her, at eyes that sparkled and a smile that told him he was taking everything too seriously. "In my mind, Merciless Mike Moody was a ruthless, greedy, heartless killer. And yet there's a woman buried a few feet away from his hideout."

"Don't be sexist. Letty could've been his accomplice. There were women in the Old West who broke stereotypes."

Jonah scoffed. "He'd bury a partner? Buy her a gravestone? My Mike Moody would never do any such thing."

"Your Mike Moody?" It was her turn to scoff. "Okay. Fine. What if she was a woman of ill repute he brought up there and murdered? The Lodgepole Inn used to cater to that clientele."

Jonah turned to face her, to face all that stubbornness with some of his own. "Murderers don't bury their victims. And if they did, they wouldn't mark their graves with expensive headstones."

She took a moment to process his words. "How do you know Letty wasn't a relation of Jeb's? After all, the rest of the graves up there are Clarks. Jeb picked that place as a family cemetery for a reason."

"Most homesteaders buried their dead in their backyard." Although given the number of graves up there that was clearly not the case.

"And you know this tidbit about backyard cemeteries how?" Emily raised a hand. "Don't tell me. You've seen it in the movies. That's like saying everything you read on the internet is true."

Jonah didn't know what to say.

She laughed. Like everything else about her it was loud and full.

She made him want to smile. She should be making Bo want to smile. He pulled his feet toward the chair legs, preparing to stand. "I should go." Go hide in the bunkhouse and get his head on straight. Who cared what his father thought? He'd write the Western story anyway. Shane wouldn't accept anything less. And who cared that Emily wanted Bo? Jonah wasn't looking to settle down.

"But…" Emily sat up. "We haven't solved anything about Letty."

It was probably the only thing she could have said to make him stay.

The wind kicked up, rustling the pines and making the fire dance.

"All right. Last question." He sighed. "If you were writing this script, who would Letty be?"

"She died, city boy. You're overthinking this tragedy." Emily grinned, not sad about her tragic ending at all. "Think about it. Knowing what a pain in the butt Mike Moody was, she probably came after him with a gun. It was probably him or her."

As usual, she'd thrown Jonah a curve. "And then Mike buried her, but only because he respected the fact that she'd challenged him." He let the idea gel for a moment. "I don't like it."

Em tossed her hands. "Can we talk about your cousin?" The real reason for her rushing him around the issue of Letty became clear. She caught his wrist, the same way he'd caught hers the other night, only her gaze held a hint of alarm. "Do you think I have a chance?"

No.

Don't tell her that!

"Let's have breakfast tomorrow morning," he blurted instead.

Emily rolled her eyes. "Pancakes and eggs won't help me."

"They will. At the Bent Nickel with Bo," he improvised. "And this time, try not to go all fangirl on him."

"I wasn't that bad today." She bit her lip. "Was I?"

"No." Jonah loosened her hold on him. "You were worse."

CHAPTER EIGHT

EXTERIOR. MIKE'S CAMP. Dawn reveals Letty sitting at Mike's campfire, a shotgun in her lap. A big black horse is tethered nearby.

JONAH LAY IN the bunkhouse staring at the rose wallpaper, trying to work out the weaknesses in his plot.

Moonlight streamed through the window, nearly bright as day.

Mike Moody had lived in a cave. He'd buried his loot in it. There was nothing about that hole in the mountainside that was feminine. If Mike had been married to Letty, he might have abandoned her, leaving her back east while he sought his fortune out west. It wasn't outside the realm of possibility that Letty had come looking for her husband with a grudge to bear and a loaded firearm.

Jonah grinned. Emily had looked so pleased to have come up with the idea.

He turned on his side, contemplating his characters.

He could ignore the wrinkle of Letty. She could've been a woman who died on top of that mountain, a woman found by Old Jeb and given a name, like the archeologists who found that T-Rex in Montana and had named her Sue. She could have been no one. She could have been anyone.

Except she'd been buried outside Mike's hidden cave with a marker on her resting place.

It was most likely a random tragedy, the way Emily said.

Except Jonah had written enough story lines in his time to know better. That woman had meant something to someone. Grave markers didn't come cheap in those days. And the person with the most gold to spare in this scenario was Mike Moody.

There was a knock on the bunkhouse door. One knock. And then Bo barged in carrying a sleeping bag. He turned on the light and took in the one-room shack.

"The bunkhouse has bunks." Bo closed the door behind him, taking stock of the interior. "And you chose the bottom."

"Same as always." Jonah propped himself up on one elbow. "Did I invite you for a sleepover?" He chose to ignore the fact that Emily had invited Bo to stay.

"You brought me cookies," Bo said cryptically, approaching the bunks. He removed his boots. "Hey, you have sheets."

"I'm a guest." Although Emily had told him he'd be doing his own linens.

"I'm a guest, too." Bo spread his sleeping bag on the top bunk and then climbed up.

Jonah laid back down, smiling. "What about the light?"

"You'll turn it off, just like you always do." Bo sounded like he was smiling, too. He waited for Jonah to do so and get back in bed before he said anything else. "Those were the good times, weren't they? When Grandpa Harlan took us places?"

"Yeah." When they could be just a family—good and bad, young and old, laughing, bickering and, yes, loving—and not be the Monroes of wealth, expectation and forced loyalty. "Do you remember when Grandpa Harlan took us to Yosemite?"

"And we stayed in those tent cabins? It was August and hotter than blazes." Bo's sleeping bag rustled with movement. "You wrote an awful play for us to perform around the campfire. You killed us all off."

"Don't hold a grudge. I was eleven and it

was satire." Not that Jonah had known the word for it back then.

"It was payback for us making fun of you for trying to dance your way across a creek." Bo chuckled. "You can't dance with two feet on the ground. What made you think you could dance from rock to rock?"

"It's hard to follow greatness," Jonah murmured.

"I assume you're talking about me, seeing as how I didn't fall in."

"You can assume all you want." Jonah could apply his statement just as easily to his career as to that day in Yosemite.

He wasn't a top athlete like Bo or Holden. When they'd crossed the creek with assurance and accolades, Jonah knew his would be just another ho-hum crossing. So, he'd done a jig on each rock he landed on until he lost his balance and fell in the creek. The cold mountain water couldn't cool off his heated embarrassment, not when his fall was the joke of the day.

To get even, his eleven-year-old brain had written the day's vignette starring himself as a highly skilled villain who called each Monroe out on their discretions, right before pushing them in the creek. It had been more monologue than play and he'd considered it the best thing he'd ever written.

At the end, before he'd taken a bow to a chorus of boos, Grandpa Harlan joined him. His grandfather took the pages of Jonah's script and threw them into the campfire. "There's room for snark in storytelling, Jonah, if your characters have heart and learn their lesson. What lesson did you learn today?"

Jonah hadn't known what to say.

"I learned he's a jerk who hurts people's feelings," Holden had said in that lofty voice of his.

Grandpa Harlan had held up a hand to stop more commentary. "He's upset because you boxed him into a corner and made him feel small. People who are cornered do desperate things. Uncharacteristic things." Grandpa Harlan hugged Jonah. "We can all learn something from what happened today."

Looking back on it, Jonah had learned many things, but mostly, he'd learned not to write himself into a script and to give every character heart.

But as for my take on Mike Moody—

"Did you hear back from your dad?" Bo asked, interrupting Jonah's thoughts. Bo was the only one who knew Jonah had sent his father the treatment of the Mike Moody myth.

"I did."

"Oh." Bo let that sit between them for a while. "Grandpa Harlan would say the only person you need to believe in you is you."

"In Hollywood, you need a champion, someone to cheer you on when the hits come."

"I'll be your cheerleader."

Jonah nearly rolled out of his bunk in surprise. "Thanks."

Outside, an owl echoed his support.

"I didn't call Aria," Bo said.

Jonah nearly rolled out again. "Go ahead and call Aria if you want."

"She played us off each other." Bo's deep, mournful voice filled the bunkhouse. "I never saw it coming."

"We were willing participants in whatever game she was running." Jonah cleared his throat. "We can be a bit overwhelming when we're competing for something."

"We shouldn't contend for women."

"Lesson learned." Jonah cleared his throat again. "And just so you know… I never loved her, not the way a man's supposed to love a woman he proposes to." Not the way he suspected Bo loved her.

"But you still have Aria's painting." Bo's tone danced on the edge of judgmental.

"It's a reminder." Like a thick scab or a

deep scar. "Put family first. That's a must in the movie business where the divorce rate is higher than the rest of the country." Monroes, his career and then love.

The owl hooted again, almost like an amen.

Bo hung his head over the top rail. "Jonah, are you so pessimistic you won't get married for fear of divorce?"

"I have a slew of successful friends who are passionate about their work and every one of them is on their second marriage. Look at my father. He's considering trophy wife number three. Not to mention Grandpa Harlan was married four times."

"Since his final marriage lasted close to fifty years, I don't think you should include it in your case against marriage." Bo scoffed and rolled back into the bunk proper. "Is that why you had second thoughts about getting married?"

"And thirds." And he'd realized what he had with Aria wasn't true love.

An image of Emily's dirt-smudged face came to mind, contrasting against the cynical lines of Aria's painting.

"You're not as jaded as you think," Bo said.

"Really?"

"Really." Bo chuckled softly. "You write an awful lot of romance, you know."

Emily's dirt-smudged face broke into a knowing smile. He couldn't recall Aria's painting at all.

It was Jonah's turn to scoff.

Above Jonah, Bo shifted in his bunk and heaved a sigh. Knowing Bo, Jonah was sure he'd be asleep in a minute.

"You've disabled your force field," Jonah murmured.

"My…my what?" His cousin sounded sleepy. He yawned. "Shut off that clever writer brain of yours for a minute…and tell me about Emily."

Jonah's mouth went dry. He didn't want to tell Bo about his favorite rodeo queen. She was like a forgotten treasure that he'd found, one he could keep to himself.

But there was Emily's hope of finding a cowboy and there was his tentative truce with Bo.

So Jonah started talking and he didn't stop until he heard Bo snore.

"Bo's at the diner," Jonah announced when Em opened the door to the ranch house the next morning. "Let's go."

"Hold up." Emily's curiosity was fired up enough to have her bouncing on her toes. "How do I look?"

Jonah gave her a perusal she was sure didn't miss anything.

But she missed something. Gone was the flirtatious gleam in Jonah's eye from the day before.

He cleared his throat. "You look like a cowgirl ready to go on a date in town."

"You say that like I failed." Em stared down at her midcalf jeans skirt, pink cowboy boots and pink button-down.

Adam ran past them and out the door. "You look pretty, Aunty Em."

"Thank you." At least one male thought she looked good, even if Adam was only five.

"Is someone getting married?" Charlie ran out the open door next. "Aunty Em never wears a skirt 'cept at weddings."

"She's a rodeo queen." Davey shot by them, carrying a wrapped birthday present. "She's supposed to look pretty every once in a while."

Emily blew out a breath. This wasn't how she'd imagined the morning going. She'd fantasized about making Jonah's jaw drop, followed by a show-stopping entrance into the diner where Bo would do the same.

"It'll do." Jonah turned. "Let's go. Bo's there and I'm hungry."

"It'll do?" Em lifted her chin. She'd tried

on six outfits before sticking with this one. And now she had no time to change because the boys were in the ranch truck waiting for her to drive them into town for a friend's breakfast-themed birthday party.

"You look lovely. Why don't I come along?" Franny held a bucket of cleaning supplies. "Shane is due any minute. We can lend some moral support even if we're only sitting across the room."

"Thanks, but no." Emily poked Jonah's back. "Jonah's supposed to be my Bo-coach. Jonah's supposed to build me up. Jonah's supposed to—"

"Be in your corner." Jonah faced Em once more, attempting a smile. "I meant to say you look very nice." He took her arm, drawing her out the door. "I like that you're leaving your cowboy hat behind."

Several minutes and very little adult conversation later, Emily had dropped her nephews at Nate Ritter's house and was entering the Bent Nickel diner with Jonah. The restaurant was a midcentury classic—checkerboard linoleum, green pleather booths, chrome stools at the lunch counter and town gossip around a large community coffeepot.

And there he was. His Bo-Highness.

Bo sat at a booth to the side, every strand of

thick, dark hair in place. His chiseled cheek-bones were illuminated by the fluorescent lights. His breakfast had already been served—a large omelet, a side of plump sausages, strips of thick bacon and a plate of toast. Her kind of meal. He gestured them over.

An invitation to breakfast with Mr. Bodilicious?

Emily's heart beat faster.

Ivy waved at Jonah and Emily from behind the counter. "The usual for you two?"

"Uh…" Emily wasn't aware she had a usual.

Ivy took out her order pad. "When you were stranded in town a few weeks ago, Emily, you ordered the two-egg breakfast every morning. Over easy, crisp bacon, English muffin?" Without waiting for Em's assent, Ivy turned her attention to Jonah. "Green tea and Greek yogurt?" When Jonah nodded yes, she disappeared into the kitchen.

Jonah guided Em into the booth seat across from Bo. She scooted over to make room for him next to her.

"Morning." Bo cut into a sausage. "We didn't talk about your schedule this morning, Jonah. I've got wall framing to do today."

This morning? Emily slanted a glance at

Jonah. He'd seen Bo already this morning? "I'm sure Jonah or I can—"

"Busy today. Sorry." Jonah waved to the elderly man coming through the front door, and slid to the edge of the booth, as far away from Emily as he could get. "Egbert! I've got a question for you."

Bo continued to eat, but was frowning at his plate.

And since he wasn't looking at Em, she could ask, "Did you guys see each other earlier?"

"I slept in the bunkhouse," Bo said between bites. "I saw you in the henhouse collecting eggs when I left."

He saw me with bedhead and a slouchy pair of sweats?

"Oh." Emily hadn't noticed Bo because her earbuds had been blasting country music. She'd worn her stall-mucking, egg-collecting, ugly plastic boots, too, which were so *not* polished or sophisticated. And... Em's mind circled back to the earbuds because her playlist was designed to make her move in the morning.

He could have...

She peeked at Brawny Bo from under her lashes. Was he smiling as he ate?

He saw me dancing?

Which was worse than him seeing her

with bedhead and wearing a slouchy pair of sweats.

Emily stifled a groan and sank lower in her seat. As discreetly as possible, she nudged Jonah beneath the table and whispered, "Help me out here."

"Huh?" Jonah had his back to Emily and his feet in the aisle. He was waiting for Egbert to get his coffee, although not patiently. What was wrong with Jonah? He was twitchier than a wood tick looking for a home. It was as if he'd forgotten their purpose this morning. Or...

Her eyes narrowed. Or his purpose had been different than hers all along. He'd wanted to chat with Egbert, whose head was full of Second Chance history.

She leaned close and whispered to the back of his neck, "You're a horrible Bo-coach."

Jonah jerked and slapped his palm to the back of his neck, as if swatting a mosquito.

"What was that?" Bo asked.

"Nothing. I..." Without the aid of her redheaded Bo-whisperer, a sweaty-palmed Emily returned her attention to the man seated across from her. She had to go it alone. "I like to make sure there are fresh eggs for the family in the fridge every morning." And she was a light sleeper. One rooster crow and she was awake. "Are you...moving into the bunkhouse?" Em's brain whirled through the personal implications of the Texan moving to the Bucking Bull—ironing her grubbies, flatironing her hair, fixing her makeup...er, actually *putting on* makeup *and then* fixing it throughout the day to ensure she was polished 24/7.

She did groan this time.

In the scheme of things, Mr. Bodilicious was becoming more inconvenient than Jonah!

"I hadn't really thought about it." Bo reached for a small container of jam and applied it sparingly to his toast. "Although the mattress was a nice change, I like to get up early and start working since I don't have much help and the days are getting warmer."

Emily was getting warmer. Heated. Along the band of her fancy bra. Beneath her armpits. Up her neck. Her internal thermostat seemed unsure if she was freezing with fear or needing to warm muscles for a quick escape from this potentially mortifying situation. She prodded Jonah in the back before pressing on. "I can bring the boys out to the lake to swim this afternoon and lend you a hand with the camp." Having been raised on a ranch, she knew her way around a toolbox.

Bo shook his head vigorously. "I know

you've got a lot of work to do on your spread. I don't want to impose."

"It wouldn't be—"

Mr. Bodilicious glanced at her directly, dark eyebrows raised in challenge as if to say, "Don't lie to me. It would be an imposition to abandon your chores on the Bucking Bull."

Em held her breath. Was she reading Bo's mind now? Or at least projecting what he might be thinking? Could a date without Jonah tagging along be far behind?

She swallowed back her nerves and resisted the impulse to grab hold of her top button and air herself out. "The camp is Shane's pet project and he's almost family. Plus, Davey's going to benefit. I'll make time to help."

"That's neighborly of you." Mr. Bodilicious gave her a half smile, as if he knew she couldn't handle full wattage.

She couldn't, of course. She might pass out if he beamed at her. Which might work to her advantage because then he'd come to her rescue…as he dragged her limp body from beneath the table. Her Bo-coach was supposed to prevent disasters like that. She nudged Jonah once more.

He glanced at her over his shoulder and whispered, "Don't faint."

What a help he was. She rolled her eyes.

Egbert pulled up a chair and smoothed his whiskers so he could drink coffee without staining his Santa beard.

Jonah explained about Letty and presented the theories that she could have been a beloved wife or a scorned wife or a woman of ill repute. If he hadn't been infringing on her Bo-time, she'd have respected his dedication to his work.

"What do you think?" Jonah asked Egbert.

"I vote married and scorned," Bo said without looking up as he continued to demolish his food. He'd be done soon and off to begin framing cabin walls.

"You don't have a vote," Jonah told Bo in an uncharacteristically ill-tempered tone of voice. "You're not the expert on Mike Moody, Bo. Go on, Egbert."

"Well, I... I'm not sure which explanation might be the right one." Egbert sipped his coffee. "I might need a bit more caffeine to think this through. Takes a while for this old brain to get up to speed, especially in the morning."

Jonah barely paused to let the old man think. "You know how Old Jeb's ledger recorded purchases? Do you remember if he bought a gravestone marker? Or do you know who the local gravestone maker was?"

Egbert stroked his white whiskers. "Back

then, the folks who could afford them ordered headstones from the quarry in Ketchum. It was closest."

"Would the quarry have records?" With a sigh that seemed to anticipate a negative answer, Jonah tucked his feet beneath the table and began taking over more of the booth. His elbows extended. He set his feet wider. Even his shoulders seemed to unfurl. "Forget I asked. Why would a quarry keep records that far back?"

"I don't know why it's a big deal, Jonah." Having inhaled his breakfast, Bo pushed his large, empty plate away and dug out his wallet.

Mr. Bodilicious was leaving?

They hadn't even gotten their food yet! Emily put her hand on Jonah's knee and gave it a gentle shake.

Jonah looked at his leg and then at her.

Emily fought against the mesmerizing power of his gaze. Those blue eyes weren't going to distract her this morning. She curled her fingers around his knee and shook it again.

Bo put some bills on the table. "Jonah can get lost in his head sometimes, researching too much when he should be writing."

Without looking at his cousin, Jonah made the shooing motion at him with one hand.

"You stick to your wheelhouse and I'll stick to mine."

Jonah was encouraging Bo to leave?

Bo stuffed his wallet back in his pocket. "I suppose this means you aren't helping me frame this morning."

Trapped in the corner, Emily released Jonah's knee, grabbed hold of his arm and mouthed, "What about me?"

"Don't panic," Jonah whispered.

"I am not panicking," she whispered back, truly hot and panicking. "I'm angry."

"What are you two whispering about?" Bo grinned at Emily, full wattage.

All that beauty… Emily's mouth hung open and went dry. Her anger evaporated.

A car backfired as it pulled out of the parking lot. Egbert announced to no one in particular that he was planning an excursion to see Letty's tombstone. Franny entered with Shane and they found seats across the diner.

All around her, people were moving, making plans. And as was typical, Emily was standing still, overthinking, not reaching for what she wanted.

"Tell him we were talking about carrot cake," Jonah whispered.

Talk to Whoa Bo about cake? She couldn't. Her tongue stuck to the roof of her mouth. And oh, gosh. Emily was fangirling. Another minute under that grin and she'd melt, sliding to the floor like room temperature cream cheese.

Bo arched one beautiful brow.

Emily slid an inch.

Scowling, Jonah grabbed her arm, holding her in place. "We're arguing about Mike Moody."

"Do tell." Bo stood, still grinning. He wasn't leaving without an answer. "Seriously, do tell."

Jonah pinched Em's arm.

"Ow." Emily swatted Jonah and then held up a hand, blocking out Bo's perfectly chiseled face. True to form, she could speak when not looking into the sun. "He's right. My nephew Charlie thinks Letty was Mike Moody's horse. I think the headstone marks where Mike hid more gold. I'm so fascinated, I could talk about Mike Moody forever." Or sink beneath the diner table.

This was horrible. She risked a glance at her Texas crush.

Bo was no longer grinning like he had a secret. He was looking at Emily like she had a cold and he was a germaphobe. He patted Egbert on the back. "The topic of Letty will split households and divide friends. I'm out." With a nod, Bo headed toward the door.

"He's right. I need a refill before I weigh

in on Letty." Egbert ambled over to the coffeepot.

"Congratulations," Jonah said, obviously fighting a grin. "You've just turned off Bo and made Egbert's head explode. Treasure beneath the headstone? Where'd that come from?"

"I don't do well on the fly." Emily swatted Jonah again. "You promised to help me."

"Bo is just a guy," Jonah stated matter-of-factly. "You can't hope to have a future with him if you can't look him in the eye."

Emily glared at Jonah, looking him in the eye. Something she hadn't been able to do with Bo. And then the meaning of his words sank in.

"Oh, of all the luck." She swatted Jonah's arm again without glancing away. "You're right."

"As usual," Jonah said in his most superior voice, no longer trying to hide his grin.

Emily wanted to laugh because she'd practically made a fool of herself over a man she could never have. Whereas she wanted to stare into Jonah's eyes and laugh and laugh…

Except…

Em sobered, stopped by a thought.

One singular, unexpected thought.

She might be falling for the wrong man.

CHAPTER NINE

EXTERIOR. OUTSIDE MIKE'S HIDE-OUT. Merciless Mike Moody finishes leveling the marker that hides his gold.

"WHAT A DISASTER." Jonah stopped grinning and rubbed his forehead. If Emily's theory spread, everyone would come from miles around to dig beneath Letty's headstone.

"I'll say." Next to him, Emily jabbed him with her elbow. She'd been prodding him a lot this morning. "Bo either thinks I'm painfully shy or…"

"He doesn't think about you in the way you want." Which was perplexing given his interest in Emily last night.

"Exactly." Emily pushed him with her hands this time. "Shove over. I need coffee and Ivy's busy making our breakfast."

He let her out of the booth and slid back in while she went to the large community coffeepot set up on a side table. Egbert finished filling his mug and took it over to greet Shane and Franny.

"We need to regroup," Jonah told Em.

"No." Emily's shoulders were slumped. Her tone taut. "I'm going to look for a cowboy elsewhere."

"You're giving up?" She didn't seem the type. "You don't give up on your dreams when the going gets tough. You might whine a little, but give up? No."

She doctored her coffee, shaking her head. "Landing a man like your cousin isn't a dream. It's a fantasy."

"I assure you that Bo's heart is attainable. Don't give up on your dream so easily."

"Like you know anything about chasing dreams. As a Monroe, all you had to do was ask for something and it probably appeared."

"Not true. I'm chasing my dreams." Jonah tilted his head back until it rested on the top of the bench seat and stared at a crack in the ceiling. "Every year growing up, my family threw a party for the Emmy Awards because television was our bread and butter. Every year, we were in the running to win." Because his father submitted entries in every category to which he was allowed. "We didn't make a big deal of the Academy Awards." Monroe Studios produced low-budget children's and teenage fare. Popcorn flicks. "But I watched the Oscars anyway, dreaming that some-day I'd be on that stage. That someday I'd be holding a statue and everyone would know I had talent, especially my parents. That's my dream." Too bad his father thought it was a fantasy.

Emily came to stand at the edge of the booth, cradling her coffee mug in both hands. "Didn't you work as a scriptwriter in Holly-wood?"

He nodded. "Employed and managed by my father."

"If you were paid, someone had to realize you had talent."

"Not necessarily. I haven't won any award."

"But you're closer to your dreams than I am." Emily's cheeks had a rosy hue that brought out the rich brown in her eyes. She'd straightened her hair. It fell in a natural wave over her shoulders. She arched a brow as if daring him to continue to bemoan the achievements of his career so far.

"Maybe, but…" Jonah sat up. "My father, who fired me, thinks I'm a hack. A rom-com, sit-com writer who shouldn't stretch to be anything more. But my grandfather would say no one should tell you what your dreams should be. So, go ahead, Ms. Rodeo Queen, and dream."

"As I understand it, your dad fired you as a condition of his inheritance. I'm discounting his opinion." She set down her coffee on the white Formica, sending the liquid sloshing over the lip of her cup. "The fact that you've had your words spoken in television and in movies means you're on your way to those awards you cherish." She stacked Bo's plates and silverware, tossing his used napkin on top before transferring his dirty dishes to the next table over. "You think you're not qualified to write the tale of Mike Moody because you can't decide how to tell Mike's story? Or is it because of your father?"

"Yes." He let the one word answer both questions. "You think what happened this morning with Bo means you don't have a chance with him?"

"Yes." Her brown eyes flashed.

A part of Jonah was glad. But a part of him wanted her to be happy, deal or no deal.

The Ritters entered the diner, herding in a troop of boys, including the Clark kids. The group headed for the larger tables at the back.

Little Adam stopped to hug Em's leg. "We're having our pancake party here because Miz Ritter ran out of milk and pancake batter." He skipped off to join his friends.

"Let's hit the pause button," Jonah said. "Just because I'm not be the best Bo-coach, doesn't mean—"

"I invoke the third condition of our agreement." Emily sat down across from him. "You aren't being up front with me. You know I don't stand a chance with Bo. Our deal is off."

"Let's not be hasty. You have a shot. I can—"

"I'm going to be leaving town soon anyway." The disappointment in her eyes was cooling, shifting to resignation. She slid into the booth and brought her coffee mug to her lips. "I have a lot to do and not a lot of time to waste on bodalicious dudes."

Jonah sat back. "What about turning thirty? What about your ticking clock?" *What about me?*

Strike that.

He wasn't part of her dreams or her fantasies, nor should he be. Jonah wanted her to be happy living her own dream.

"Time has a way of marching on." She sipped her coffee, dropping her gaze to the empty tabletop. "Which is good. I should move on so I don't get distracted by the wrong things."

Jonah had to assume that Bo was the wrong

thing in her example, which would have been fine—excellent, even—if it hadn't meant an end to their agreement.

Ivy brought their food and then scooped up the money Bo had left as well as the plates Emily had deposited. "Can I get either of you anything else?"

"I think we can make do." Emily sighed.

"Aunty Em…" Adam skidded up next to them. He was just tall enough to rest his chin on the table and smart enough to smile like an angel. "Can I have a piece of bacon? Please?"

Emily turned her plate so he could pick his piece.

The little bugger chose two, leaving Emily none. He scampered back to his place with the birthday party.

"Ah." Charlie scurried over. His brown hair had been properly combed when he got into the truck earlier. Now it was wild and out of place, as if he'd thrust his hands through it. "Adam stole all your bacon." He picked up half her English muffin, took a bite and then asked, "Can I have this, Aunty Em?"

She nodded, reaching for the other half, which she held out to Davey when he showed up.

"I guess you're having eggs for breakfast." Jonah sipped his tea, gauging her expression to see if she was upset.

She wasn't. She seemed…happy.

Ivy hurried out of the kitchen carrying a plate with another English muffin. She set it near Emily and gave the Clark children a stay-away stare.

"I guess I'm having eggs and a muffin." Emily smiled for the first time since they'd entered the diner, but it was a conditional smile, an I-always-come-last-but-that's-okay smile.

Emily shouldn't be used to last place. Someone should be spoiling this generous, warm-hearted woman. It was a mystery why no one hadn't applied for the role already.

Jonah sipped more tea, registering the chatter about Letty and Mike Moody circulating the diner. "Hey, I know things didn't work out this morning as planned." He ignored her put-upon sigh. "But can you take me along the stagecoach road this afternoon?"

Her expression didn't change. "The pursuit of your dream continues."

"Yes. My intuition tells me there's something good here." He stirred his yogurt. "It's my head that keeps telling me it's a mess."

Emily considered Jonah more carefully than she'd considered which flavor of ice cream to buy several days ago. "My grandfather used to say sometimes you have to follow your gut."

"Mine, too." Jonah nodded.

"They were friends." Emily still seemed to be taking in his expression; hers was a closed-off one. "I suppose they'd have shared a lot of similar words of wisdom."

"I suppose they'd have helped each other out from time to time." Other than on their quest to find Merciless Mike Moody's stolen gold. "We could do that, too." He could continue to push her agenda with Bo and push his fascination with her aside.

Emily nodded. "I suppose we could. But I can't take you today." She pushed her eggs around her plate. "Tina's coming over to practice. Perhaps tomorrow…"

Jonah readily agreed.

Though he couldn't shake the feeling that there was something out of kilter in her mood, something he'd missed, something that might come back later to bite him in his crisp new blue jeans.

"How was your breakfast date?" Granny Gertie glanced up from her knitting when Emily returned from breakfast. She closed her music box, halting the strains of "You Are My Sunshine."

"It wasn't a date." Em sat on the bench in the foyer and tugged off her fancy pink boots. She wished she could shed her foul mood as easily. "I watched Bo eat breakfast and then he left."

"And then you had breakfast with Jonah, I bet." Gertie chuckled, examining her stitches. "You've been spending a lot of time with him lately."

Emily went into her room, which was just off the foyer. "We had an agreement," she called back, before realizing she didn't want to admit to her grandmother what their deal had been. "But that's over now." She changed into a pair of stained blue jeans and a T-shirt from the tractor supply store in Ketchum and crumpled her date clothes in her dirty-laundry basket. She stared at her trophies.

Dreams. Once upon a time, she'd had many. But none of her dreams had ever involved taking a big chance. Not like Jonah, who was challenging his reputation and his self-image. He wasn't just moving forward, he was switching tracks. And despite the obstacles in his way, he wasn't giving up. He was reaching for more.

Em took down the trophy she'd won when she was crowned rodeo queen, wiping away the dust Jonah had missed.

Gertie appeared in the doorway, leaning on her cane. "I remember the day you won that. We were all so proud."

Em returned the prize to the shelf. "When I won these trophies, I felt they were worth more than the cost of their parts. Like they meant something important and lasting." She grimaced. "You know, Kyle used to laugh at me when he caught me staring at these." He'd known the truth—that wood and plastic trophies meant nothing long-term. Just look at how unimpressed Jonah had been.

"Your brother was a good man," Gertie said solemnly. "But that didn't mean he could resist teasing his little sister every once in a while. Don't make light of awards earned for being good at your profession."

Emily waved that aside. "Kyle was a good cowboy with big dreams for this place." She felt his presence surround them. "And he was an excellent rancher."

"He knew it, too." Gertie shifted her feet and stared about the room, as if she, too, sensed Kyle was near. "But pride drives us to make choices we regret later. Dangerous choices." She frowned. "He shouldn't have gone looking for that gold alone."

"Kyle liked to do things his own way." Em dug in her drawer for a pair of socks.

"As do you." Gertie executed a careful turn. "He and that horse of his had swagger, but they could back it up most times. His pride didn't make me love him any less, same as your itch to find a place you belong doesn't change my love for you."

Emily followed Gertie to the foyer where she slid into her work boots while her grandmother returned to her chair and her knitting.

"That Jonah Monroe has swagger," Gertie said slyly, flipping open her music box. "Why don't you swallow your pride and ask him out?"

"Uh… Because he lives in California? Because he wears sneakers and city jeans?" Em stomped her heels in her boots.

"Because he's skinnier than you?"

"No." *Yes.* "I'm comfortable with my body. We're different, that's all. And when he's done writing this script we'll live in different states." Plus, he had drive. He'd keep reaching for loftier dreams. While she wanted to settle for a ranch and family of her own. How small he must think her.

"You can't pull one over on me." Gertie slid a pair of readers on her nose and stared at Emily over the rim. "People aren't like the molded couple you see on top of a wedding cake. Not real people. Look at me. I'm short.

Your grandfather was tall. You're built sturdy. Davey has one hand. No one is going to love us any less because of our physical differences."

It wasn't her body image that had doused her in reality at the Bent Nickel. It was her drive. Or lack thereof. "I'm going to the barn now." Emily opened the front door.

"Because you disagree that opposites attract?"

"Nope." She was attracted to Jonah, yet they were as different as could be. Em stepped onto the porch. "Because I've got equipment to mend and animals to train."

She knew her place. It was time to stop dreaming.

JONAH SHOULD BE WRITING.

Instead, he'd spent an hour since breakfast at the Bent Nickel searching online. But he hadn't been able to identify who Letty was, which was too bad since conditions were perfect to write. The Clark boys were still in town. Whatever Franny and Emily were doing around the ranch wasn't loud. Bo was down at the lake camp, presumably framing. There was peace in the bunkhouse. All that was missing was a connection to the mysterious Letty.

Rather than waste time not writing, Jonah faced his laptop and opened the document containing the script about Emily's search for love. Like the romance he'd written last year about Bo and Aria, he wouldn't try to sell this one. Romance and rom-coms weren't going to gain his father's respect or advance his career in the right direction.

A few hours later and he had four scenes roughed out. The flexing of writing muscles gave him a boost of confidence.

He shut down his laptop, planning to make lunch, but wound up staring at Aria's watercolor of him on the fridge.

"There's a man who doesn't look like a romance hero," he muttered, turning the portrait over. He set about making a tuna sandwich.

A truck pulled into the ranch yard. Tina hopped out carrying a stuffed backpack. She hurried over to the arena.

It was safe money to assume Emily was at the arena, too.

The sun was out and the birds were singing. It was a good time to take a break and mingle with humanity. Jonah finished the last bite of his sandwich, grabbed his blue baseball cap and headed toward the arena.

Emily and Tina sat in the bleachers.

"What are the arguments animal activists present against the rodeo?" Em asked.

That sounded as dry and boring as day-old toast. There was no reason his heart should beat faster upon hearing them. No cause for his mouth to curl in a grin at the sight of Em's brown hair dancing in the breeze. What was going on here? Jonah's steps slowed.

Bo walked up the driveway toward him, a welcome interruption.

"Welcome back, Mr. Bodilicious," Jonah said, still thinking of Emily. "Rough day at work?" he added when Bo scowled.

"Call me bodilicious again and you'll be having a rough day." Bo came to a stop near Jonah, wiping the sweat from his forehead with his arm. "This isn't a social call. I need a drill press."

"I have no idea what that means." Thankfully.

"It drills uniform holes in wood." Bo glanced toward the arena and then back to Jonah. "Let me clarify. It drills uniform holes in wood, which are useful when you're building a stair or porch railing with round dowels."

"That makes complete and total sense." Jonah filed that information away for use in a script someday. "Where do you plan to get one of these press drills?"

"Drill press," Bo corrected. "Shane said Franny had one in the equipment shed. I'm supposed to meet him here."

"Shane's going to show you this piece of equipment?" Shane? The former CEO? Jonah scoffed.

The two men stared at each other for a moment and then chuckled.

"Yeah." Bo slapped Jonah affectionately on the back. "It's almost as unbelievable as you knowing what a drill press is and where it'd be stored."

Shane pulled up in a new black SUV. "Oh, Jonah. You have the entire town guessing who Letty is."

"If only someone knew for sure." Bo grinned. "They could put Jonah out of his misery."

Shane checked his cell phone. "I think it's great that people are talking about her."

"You would," Jonah and Bo said at the same time. They high-fived.

The part of Jonah that had been tentative around Bo the past month had relaxed. The episode with Aria had been forgiven and forgotten.

Jonah glanced over at the rodeo queen and her protégé. They were walking through the arena, kicking up dust.

"Buzz like this can be replicated for the film," Shane continued as if his cousins hadn't made a joke at his expense. He led them toward the equipment shed.

"You might need to have a film filmed first." Bo gave Jonah a sly look, tossing him the conversational ball.

Which Jonah would have taken if he had something worth sharing that he'd written.

Shane stopped, turned and frowned. "Do I want to know how that script is coming?"

Jonah shook his head. "Here's the thing about a plot not coming together. It's like having a mystery ingredient you need to add to a cake to give it flavor, but you don't know which flavor or how much flavor is too much or too little." Which seemed to justify his interest in Emily, the bestest cake-maker in the world.

"You don't even eat cake. Keep in mind the town's relying on you," Shane grumbled, opening the shed. "Okay. Where is this thing? Franny said it was tall." He peered around the ATV.

"Step aside. I'm the drill press expert." Bo pushed past Shane and Jonah, poking around the various boxes, plastic bins and oddly shaped surprises under canvas covers.

"Seriously, step back in case I disturb a rat or something."

Shane arched a brow at Jonah, who shrugged. If there was a critter in the shed, he hadn't seen one the other day when Em had hugged him.

Bo found the drill press, which was about the height of two microwaves stacked on top of each other. He carried it to Shane's SUV for transporting to the lake camp.

"Faster, Tina." Emily's voice drifted to Jonah. "You only have ninety seconds to get through your routine."

What routine? "That's our cue..." Jonah nodded toward the arena. "We must investigate."

The three Monroe men walked over to the arena.

Tina was riding Davey's mustang. She guided him in ever-tightening circles, pulled him to a halt and then backed him up about ten feet. "I never thought about practicing on other people's horses. How was that?"

"You're ten seconds too long." Emily mashed her hat firmly on her head as if preparing for a faster ride, not that she was on horseback.

"Good thing I won't be competing on Yoda." Tina dismounted. "He's a plodder. Which horse do you want me to ride next?"

"Razzy." Emily led her own horse into the ring and then brought Yoda out, tying his reins to a rail. "Don't ever blame your performance on your horse. This is a test of *your* skill. A good cowboy can ride anything."

"Are you a good cowboy?" Jonah teased Bo.

"I'm a Texan." Bo put his hands on his hips. "Nobody would call me a cowboy. I don't have professional skills on horseback. I just get by."

Was it wrong to be glad Bo had just unchecked an important box on Emily's romantic wish list? Jonah grinned.

"Bo's no wrangler. Remember when he tried to ride a bull?" Shane found this exceedingly funny.

"Near-death experiences aren't humorous," Emily chastised, without looking away from her charge.

Jonah tended to agree. Bo had been thrown and gotten the wind knocked out of him. He was lucky he hadn't been trampled.

Tina mounted Razzy and rode him faster than she'd ridden Yoda.

Jonah tried to watch but his gaze kept drifting to Emily.

"You didn't get him to change leads on that last turn." Emily stood on a railing on the op-

posite side of the arena, as far from Jonah and
Bo as she could get.

Tina sat up straighter in the saddle. "I forgot."

Em tsked. "You can't forget. The competition will be here before you know it."

"I know." Tina brought Razzy to a stop.
"Let me start again."

The pair did better that time. Coming in
on time and without Emily pointing out any
mistakes.

The Monroe men applauded. Even if he
didn't understand the rodeo queen competition, Jonah was happy for Emily that her student had done well.

"Don't let their applause go to your head,"
Emily told Tina. "If you assume you're going
to win, you'll lose. You have to earn everything. Because your horsemanship is worth
the majority of possible points, the winner
of the riding competition usually takes the
crown."

Tina nodded.

Shane and Bo left, making the drive to
the camp. Jonah headed back to the bunkhouse, one phrase Emily had said sticking
in his head.

If you assume…

If Mike Moody assumed anything, he'd be

dead. To be a successful desperado, he had to be methodical and detail-oriented. He had to be focused.

EXTERIOR. THE STAGE ROAD. Mike picks wildflowers for Letty.

Jonah groaned. Increasingly, his attraction to Emily was becoming tangled with his storytelling voice.

This wasn't good. This wasn't good at all.

CHAPTER TEN

"WHAT? NO ICE CREAM?" Jonah joined Em at the firepit that night. He gave her a curt nod and claimed his usual webbed chair. By the weight of his sigh, he still hadn't figured out who Letty was.

"I had a yen for muffins," Em told him. She'd baked chocolate chip mini-muffins after dinner. Em held one out to him. She'd brought a few out with her.

"No, thanks."

The wind ruffled Em's hair, the same way his rejection of her cooking riled her inside. "Are you sure? They're good for what ails you."

"Do I look like I'm ailing?" Jonah didn't look at Emily when he said it.

"Yep." Emily smiled. In the scheme of things, she'd had a good day. Productive around the ranch. Successful with Tina and competition training.

The owl that lived in the pine north of the house hooted.

Sure, there'd been her breakfast fail with

Bo. And yes, there'd been a moment when she'd allowed loneliness to latch onto the idea of Jonah as the compromised answer to her falling star wishes. But she'd talked herself out of it. Why wouldn't she? Emily thought Arabians were a beautiful, smart breed. Didn't mean she had to have one. She could appreciate Jonah's wit and pretty eyes without trying to make him into her dream man.

"Is baking your hobby?" Jonah continued to pout in his chair, sinking into his jacket.

"Sort of. What's your hobby? Spin class?" Emily broke off a small piece of muffin and popped it into her mouth.

"My hobby is script writing."

Emily swallowed. "You can't have a hobby that's the same thing as your job." She brushed muffin crumbs from her lap. "That'd be like me saying my hobby is ranching."

"That's my pillow," Charlie yelled from inside the house. "Mom!"

"Are you saying I can't have a hobby in the same field as my work?" And there it was—the playful glint in Jonah's eyes that had been missing when she'd opened the door this morning.

"Correct, sir." Emily shook her head, trying to shake off the attraction, as well. "For years, my grandmother's hobby has been knitting. She used to knit everyone a scarf or mittens or a sweater for Christmas." Of course, their family was so big she'd start in January.

"Has been?" Jonah's brow wrinkled. "I see her knitting all the time."

"Yep." Em nodded. "Your sister Laurel said she'd buy some of her knitted goods to sell at the Mercantile. My grandmother no longer has a hobby. She knits for profit."

"Mom! Charlie used my toothbrush." Davey sounded mortified.

"On accident," Charlie shouted back.

"On purpose," Davey countered.

She and Jonah exchanged glances and laughed. Soon, their laughter died out, but their gazes remained fixed on each other.

He wasn't as pretty as Bo, but he was easy on the eyes. The eggs were mesmerized.

Jonah broke the connection and stroked his goatee. "I see your point about hobbies and work, and the separation of feelings."

She hadn't mentioned feelings at all. "Have you ever sold a script you wrote in your spare time?"

He hesitated.

"You have!" Emily pounced. "You're trying to deny it, but you have."

"I haven't," Jonah said in a surprisingly

firm voice, staring at the crackling fire. "But I've considered it."

Emily angled toward him, drawing her knee up on the armrest, waiting for him to say more.

After a moment, he did. "I write stories when I'm stressed."

"Really?" Such a small revelation. But it said a lot about him. And the way he said it— like a blurted confession—made her think he didn't tell many people about his habit.

Jonah nodded. "I don't just pluck an idea from the sky and run with it. I write stories that are more personal."

Emily picked a chunk of muffin with a melted layer of chocolate chips. "There's personal, like buddies going on a fishing trip. And then there's personal, like your failed engagement to Aria." She took a bite of the muffin crown and let the chocolate melt in her mouth, waiting to see if he'd be offended by her probe, wondering if it would be better if he was. There was danger in this fireside intimacy, peril to a heart on the lookout for love.

"All writing is personal," he said, answering nothing. He knew it, too. Jonah's eyes flashed with a tease. "I can't remember how old I was when I started writing. I know there was a smart remark made by me and a punishment involved. And then I was scribbling the scene in my math notebook. I've been scribbling ever since."

"Ah. Your hobby is to right wrongs. On paper." She liked that.

"And to flex my writing muscles." He squirmed a little at her sharp glance. "Or to vent. As the older brother of a budding superstar, you can imagine how boring it was to be dragged around like one of Ashley's entourage." For all that sounded like torture for a kid, he looked rather pleased with himself. "I wasn't always the most well-behaved child on the set."

The source of his sharp humor became clear—his family.

"And that behavior wasn't tolerated, not from the son of Lincoln Monroe, studio head." Jonah sobered. "As a kid, I didn't always have the right comeback in the moment. But when I wrote a script, I was brilliant. I brought peace to the family and love to the world. I created characters who weren't as bitter or as gullible as…" He paused. "Writing made those childhood years bearable."

"Oh." Emily's chest ached with worry for the hurts suffered by a little redheaded boy.

"It wasn't all bad," he was quick to clarify. "My grandfather was a gift. To all us kids."

She took his hand.

He looked at it, saying nothing, doing nothing.

And yet, the feel of his warm skin next to hers was doing something. Deep in her chest, deep in her heart, emotions stirred.

A whisper in her head tried to halt the stirring: *city fella, vinegar, Arabians.*

Em should listen to that whisper. She wasn't a lofty dreamer like he was.

But like yeast set in a warm bowl, the process of forging a bond had begun. And she let it. Because she liked him. Because he was hurting. And like her brother's horse, she couldn't take those painful memories away. She could only help him march forward with a steady hand and the strength lent to get through a less than rosy past.

The owl took flight, sweeping across the yard on a breeze laden with shared confidences.

"Your parents were strict?" Emily gave his hand a squeeze, not going anywhere.

Jonah stared at her, wary, stoic. "Yes."

"They betrayed your trust." He'd mentioned being gullible, after all. And his parents were powerful in Hollywood.

"In some ways." There was no sign of his trademark grin. "For example, they set poor examples of conscious coupling."

He was talking about relationships.

The cautious whisper in her head grew louder. "And yet, you have a strong sense of right and wrong." Not a question.

"Yes. Back to my grandfather. He made sure of that." His gaze never wavered, never flinched, never moved from her face.

He's braver than I am.

She no longer wondered how it could be that she felt connected to Jonah and not Bo. Jonah was cynical but kindhearted. Despite him being Hollywood royalty, he wasn't on a pedestal. He befriended everyone. She was afraid he was doing more than befriending her. And that was all on her.

Jonah cleared his throat. "Emily, I—"

"Are you guys getting married?" Adam stood at the edge of the gravel circle.

"No," Emily and Jonah said at the same time, releasing their handhold and putting distance between them without moving from their folding chairs.

Adam wore cotton pajamas with cowboy hats on them and his cowboy boots. Bolt sat at his feet. "Can I have some muffin?" He didn't wait for Em's permission. He bunny-hopped over and climbed into her lap, taking one of her mini-muffins. "The boys are fighting." He tilted his head up to Em with that smile she loved so much. And then he glanced over at Jonah and said, "She's the bestest baker in the whole wide world. You should marry her."

Neither one of them protested his statement. Shouldn't they have?

CHAPTER ELEVEN

EXTERIOR. THE STAGE ROAD. Mike galloping for the hills, a sack of gold tied to his saddle horn, dodging ruts and mud puddles. Ahead of him, Letty led the way.

DID DESPERADOS DODGE mud puddles?

Jonah didn't know. Heck, he wasn't even fighting the Letty plotline. He was more interested in the logistics of stagecoach robbery and escape.

Case in point: road conditions. It probably wasn't good for a horse's health to run through mud puddles. They might be deep or filled with rocks. A lame horse was like a flat tire. Did that mean most stagecoach robberies happened in good weather?

"I sense an online research session, Razzy," Jonah said.

The horse blew a raspberry.

"What are you doing back there?" Emily had been riding ahead of Jonah on the old stage trail.

She'd been unusually quiet this morning, as if she was working something out in her head. She couldn't be thinking about Adam's teasing words at the firepit last night, the ones about them getting married.

Emily twisted in her saddle. "Jonah?"

"I'm plotting and evading mudholes." True, but Jonah had slowed Razzy down so he could eat a banana and drink some water, items he'd stowed in the inner pockets of his lightweight jacket on this cloud-filled day. Jonah had hung back because he hadn't wanted Emily to notice he was eating. She asked more questions than anyone he'd ever met.

Emily turned her scarred black horse around and headed back at a quick clip. There was nothing about the big gelding that was slow, even when he was walking.

Jonah took a bite of banana.

They'd joined the trail early in the morning where it was flanked by the Salmon River and a wildflower-strewn meadow. Farther north, the road had sharp S-turns and was crowded by trees and gentle rises, offering great spots for an ambush.

"There's no mud, Jonah." Trust Emily to poke holes in Jonah's excuses.

"There would be if it had rained recently."

She scoffed.

He cast about for a distraction. "I think I owe you an apology for that Bo-breakfast yesterday. I got all tangled up in Letty. Truth be told, I'm still tangled." But now he was tangled with Emily, too. And only Emily's knots were unraveling, revealing intriguing contradictions of vulnerability and strength.

"You're apologizing *and* lagging behind?" Em shook her head, eyes hidden behind her sunglasses and beneath the brim of her cowboy hat. "Is that a banana?"

"It's no big deal. I'm eating." Jonah waved her off. "Go on. I'll catch up."

"Seriously?" Emily kept coming toward him, starting to grin. "For a person who doesn't eat much, you sure eat often."

"I'm on a strict diet, which is why I eat often." He finished the banana and stuffed the rolled peel in the pocket of his lightweight jacket. "I have to eat several small meals a day."

"You're dieting?" Emily stopped her horse next to him, close enough that she could reach out and touch his leg, but facing the way back to the ranch. "Are you trying to keep your weight down?"

"No." Jonah hoped the clipped response would discourage Emily from prying.

No such luck.

She raised her brows. "Do you..." She stuck her finger in her throat, mimicking the actions of a self-induced vomit.

"No." He tried to think of something clever to say—normally not a problem for him. But he drew a blank, and a part of him was weary of deflecting the truth. "I have Crohn's disease." At her blank stare, he added, "Basically, ninety percent of processed food makes me ill."

You'll regret that, Grandpa Harlan used to say when Jonah was tempted to eat something he shouldn't, like greasy pizza or carrot cake.

"Oh." Emily turned Deadly around, practically without moving herself. "I'm sorry. Both for assuming you were a survivor of some dreaded disease and because I've always given you a hard time about eating." She gave a little head bobble. "Seeing as how I have no problem eating and eating well, I shouldn't cast stones on someone who can't."

"I never resented your eating habits or your teasing." He resented his condition. He resented having to think about every bite of food that passed his lips.

"Is that why you're so thin?" Emily inventoried his frame, a clinical inspection that lacked any sexual sizzle.

He shrugged off his disappointment. "I was

never as big as Bo." No Monroe had ever been as big as Bo. "I was diagnosed when I was thirteen." And mortified when he'd fainted from the cramps on one of his grandfather's family outings. It had taken a medical diagnosis for his cousins to stop ribbing him.

"The awkward teen years." Emily nudged Deadly forward.

Razzy followed along without any guidance from Jonah.

"You had cake on my birthday," she said.

He winced. "Actually, Bolt had cake on your birthday. And Adam had my frosting."

"You're that strict about what you eat?" She slanted him a look. "You don't cheat?"

"Humiliation and physical pain have a way of making me eat smart." Always. "I didn't tell you to earn your pity. I try not to make a big deal out of it. One of the things I like about living in Hollywood is that everyone is on some kind of specialty diet. No one questions what I choose to eat."

"What do you eat? What's safe?"

"Tofu. Steamed vegetables. Dairy." Luckily he wasn't allergic to dairy. "Can we talk about something else? It's all very emasculating."

Emily gave him a sideways look. "As would be any serious illness if you had a fragile ego, which you don't have."

Right. "I'll take that as a rare compliment from a most respected rodeo queen."

"I get it now." Emily guided Deadly around a big rock that seemed out of place on the trail. It would've stopped a stage from passing had a bandit rolled it from a slope above. "I always wondered why you just sat back and watched women fawn over Bo. But it's not just amusement. You don't think you're as attractive as he is. Or a real catch."

Jonah suddenly hated how smart Emily was. "Most people would agree that I'm not." He cleared his throat. "Case in point…you."

She disqualified that comment with a roll of her big brown eyes. "This is perfect. It suits your tendency toward melodrama to sit back and be ignored."

"Oh, come on, now."

"It's true. You can admit it. We're friends." Emily turned in the saddle, grinning. "But really, the exact opposite is true. You want the stage."

His head started shaking before she finished that last sentence, even though he recognized the truth in her words. "I'm not an attention-seeker. Trust me. I have a famous sister and a mother who wishes she had marketable talent. I know attention-seekers when I see them."

"Argue all you want…" Emily laughed. "But let this idea sink in, Hollywood. You slip in those little zingers, like gems waiting to be discovered by the worthy." Her voice trailed off and she gave him another sideways glance. But this time, her expression was speculative. "When did Aria know about your Crohn's?"

"What? Who's Aria?" Jonah lifted his chin and tried to pretend ignorance.

"Please." Emily tipped back her hat and shot him with a no-nonsense stare. "Your former fiancée? The woman who fell for you and all your charm, and Bo and all his muscles?"

"You fell for Bo and all his muscles." Jonah didn't want to have this conversation. His privacy and his past were being invaded. Not to mention that her infatuation with Bo bothered him more every day.

The corners of her mouth turned up a smidge. "Technically, Bo checked more boxes than just muscles."

"My bad. Let's see. The first box is cowboy." Raising his voice, Jonah ticked the points off on his fingers. "Muscles. And… why else are you so darn compatible?" The annoyance he was battling shocked him. He'd never raised his voice to Aria. Of course, he'd never confronted her directly about her attraction to Bo, either.

"Do you have to overanalyze everything and everyone *but* yourself?" Emily sat taller in the saddle and seemed to urge Deadly into a faster walk. "Sometimes there's just chemistry between a man and a woman. Plain and simple."

"I'll add chemistry to the checked boxes." Jonah held up three fingers. "Along with good-looking, because, let's be honest, he is Mr. Bodilicous." He raised a fourth finger. "Lucky Bo. You've fallen for him for all the right reasons."

Emily frowned, scanning the trail ahead. "I didn't fall for Bo. I never said I was in love with him. There's a difference between love and attraction." Tension rose from her like hot air from a summer sidewalk.

"A difference?" Jonah scoffed, too worked up to analyze anything. "Not from where I'm sitting when I watch you." When Jonah looked at Emily, like called to like. She saw too much truth the way he did. She found too much irony the way he did. "You expect that attraction to Bo will bring love to you, like ordering food from a menu and feeling full afterward. Love doesn't work like that, Em. It's a hard-fought battle on shaky ground." Too often, so-called love lost the war.

"You know, sometimes I like you better when you don't speak." Emily brought Deadly close to him. The toe of her boot touched Jonah's running shoe. She reached over to poke his thigh. "Sometimes when you don't shut up, I just want to..." She pulled Deadly to a stop and removed her sunglasses.

Razzy stopped, too.

"I just want to grab you by the shoulders..." Emily kept hold of her reins with one hand and grabbed one of Jonah's shoulders with the other. And then...

Nothing.

They stared at each other. They stared the same way they had the other day moments before she'd hugged him. Jonah looked deeply into her rich brown eyes, taking note of her pretty face and her pretty hair, taking note of the fact that he wanted to kiss her, to learn the softness of her cheek with his palm, to listen to her talk about what it took to be a rodeo queen until he drifted to sleep in the circle of her arms.

But hey. Cue reality. They were on horseback and there was no way Emily wanted to kiss him after he'd questioned her devotion to Bo and admitted he was a dude with perpetual tummy issues.

Très sexy.

If reality was calling, Emily wasn't picking up. She continued to stare, not completing her sentence.

Jonah smiled gently. "You want to grab me by the shoulders and…give me a shake?" he supplied helpfully, fully prepared for Em to slug his shoulder or poke his thigh once more.

She did neither. "Sometimes I want to…" She tugged Jonah closer, bringing him into the narrow chasm between them. And then she kissed him. She kissed him hard. She kissed him with intensity.

All too soon, she shoved him back, so abruptly he nearly fell out of the saddle.

"There," she said. "That was chemistry. And it doesn't mean I'm in love with you, either."

She shoved her sunglasses back on, urged Deadly into a gallop and left Jonah holding on for his life.

"SILLY." EMILY GALLOPED along the trail without looking back.

Why should she? Jonah wasn't going to let something as intimate as a kiss go by without dissecting it. He'd catch up. And when he did, she'd never hear the end of it.

"Stupid." Just because she found his eyes arresting, his arms surprisingly strong and his jaded heart compelling, she didn't need to take his lips for a test drive.

"Idiot." Because Jonah was staying at the ranch and she wouldn't be able to avoid him. Which meant she needed to slow down and face her mistake.

Emily stopped in the shade of a tall pine and turned to confront her blunder head-on.

Jonah and Razzy sauntered around the corner as if they had all the time in the world.

To make me suffer.

Emily squared her shoulders and prepared for her lumps. "I'm sorry," she said when Jonah was close enough to hear her without shouting. "I'm impulsive sometimes."

"Impulses like that can get you into trouble." Jonah didn't pull Razzy to a stop until he was almost past her. He sighed. "I know that kiss meant nothing."

What?

The eggs were flabbergasted. That had been some kiss.

"We were like two kids in the schoolyard, spurring each other on." He patted Razzy's neck. "Except we both know better than to throw a punch, don't we?"

"Sure?" Wasn't he going to tease her? Make stupid innuendos about her no longer wanting a cowboy?

Jonah nodded. "I was disrespecting the way you're looking for love. You have a type. Lots of people do. I should have honored what you were telling me about Bo's good points."

She turned Deadly so that they were heading in the same direction as Jonah, turning his words over in her head. "You don't like me."

"I didn't say that." Jonah nudged Razzy forward, easing up on the reins. Despite his tennis shoes, he was becoming a decent rider when he tried.

"Or you don't want me to like you." Could Jonah want her to ignore the attraction she sometimes felt for him? Why would he do that if he liked her?

"I see now why you've never married," he murmured. "You leave no emotional stone unturned."

Jonah always seemed to murmur the truths he saw in the world, speaking at half volume as if he knew it was inappropriate to voice his observations but couldn't keep them to himself.

Because that last statement…

He'd hit the nail on the head. Emily's impulsiveness and honesty were a key reason why her relationships never turned the corner into long-term territory. And, admittedly, she tended to protect her private life and had a bit of a temper to go along with a goodly dose of pride.

Emily stared at Jonah instead of the trail ahead. What kind of man was lip-bombed only to let the lip-bomber off the hook? Of course, Jonah being Jonah, he'd let her off the hook and then pointed out her flaws. But that had nothing to do with their kiss. Their kiss had been scary good.

And yet, it was almost as if he didn't think he deserved to be kissed again.

Jonah, you sly dog.

"Was this how it was with Aria?" Emily pressed on before Jonah could shut her down. "You pushed her away?"

He pressed his lips together.

"Aria," she continued. "Even her name sounds delicate. Was she too fragile for your humor or…" She reached across the gap between them and drew back on Razzy's reins while simultaneously bringing Deadly to a stop. "Was she too fragile to handle your illness?"

His lips thinned.

"She accepted your proposal and then…" Emily blinked. Something didn't add up.

"I feel like I've gone to Madam Mysterio's Palm Reading Solarium," he murmured. "If you get any messages from Letty or Mike Moody, can you let me know?"

"You pushed her away, right into the waiting arms of Bo." Emily drew her hand back as if Razzy's reins were electrified. "But…why?"

Razzy chose that moment to stomp his disapproval.

Jonah patted the horse and then heeled Razzy forward. "You should go into scriptwriting, Madam Mysterio."

"Me?" The tenor of this conversation was all wrong, like the gait of a horse pulling up lame. Emily's fingers tightened on the reins. It would be easy to wheel around and gallop home. But home to what? To lie in her bed later and stare at the ceiling, wondering why he'd pushed Aria away?

Wondering if he'd push me away if he ever admitted he was as attracted to me as I am to him?

Just because she was attracted to Jonah and intrigued by him didn't mean she was going to fall in love with him. *City fella, vinegar, Arabians.* "Answer one question for me and then I'll make sure to point out the section of trail I've always been told was where Mike robbed the stage."

"That's a bargain no man in his right mind would agree to." But he spared her a quick glance.

He wants me to ask.

One question? Emily should've said five!

She could ask something inconsequential like "Did you enjoy that kiss?" He'd roll his eyes.

She wouldn't ask, "Where is Aria now?" Because if she wasn't with Bo, who cared?

Which left her with "Did you call the wedding off? Or did you maneuver her into doing it?"

Jonah's chin worked and he wouldn't look at her. The sure signs of a man unwilling to admit a shameful secret. He'd let Aria think she was to blame for a doomed engagement. Hadn't he told her Aria confessed to being in love with both men?

"That's not very nice," Emily told Jonah. "You're the one who got cold feet. You told me your heart wasn't broken."

"You know nothing, Madam Mysterio."

I'm right.

Emily didn't know whether to shout in triumph or retreat to reconsider what this meant in the long run.

There is no long run between Jonah and me.

Suddenly, Emily didn't want to ride on the trail and make conjectures about Letty and Mike Moody. She wanted answers. And he did, too. "Where do you go when you want to research something?" She adjusted her cowboy hat more firmly on her head.

"The internet." Jonah shrugged. "No-brainer."

"You go to the library." Emily smirked.

"Why?" He sat back in the saddle, curiosity in his blue eyes.

"Because historical documents aren't always scanned." Emily couldn't believe she hadn't thought of this before. "Libraries have the resources to store diaries and ledgers, but not the resources to scan them into electronic files—hence them not being on the internet. You want to find clues about what Letty meant to Mike Moody? Let's go look at some microfilm of newspaper accounts and old birth certificates."

"Color me doubtful. I could never figure out how to find anything that was physically stored in the library."

Emily was certain he was just being cranky because he hadn't thought of it. "You'll change your tune." She heeled Deadly forward, eager to show Jonah the section of trail Mike Moody was rumored to have used. "Besides, you'll agree to go."

Jonah kept pace with her. "Why?"

She snuck a glance at his classic profile. "How often does a woman ask if you want to go for a ride?"

He didn't laugh.

But he didn't argue, either.

CHAPTER TWELVE

"I HAVEN'T BEEN inside a library since college," Jonah admitted, holding open the door of the Ketchum Community Library for Emily. They'd finished their ride and headed to the nearby town. Despite his resolve to remain skeptical, he was getting excited. "And even then, it was only because they had meeting rooms for students."

"I didn't go to college," Emily said briskly. She hadn't said much to him on the ride back to the Bucking Bull or during the hour-long drive to the larger nearby town. He was grateful for the silence. He didn't want to ruin the memory of that kiss by examining it any more than she already had.

Grandpa Harlan used to say that every man should have three things on his bucket list—learn how to drive a stick shift, revel in the achievement of an impossible dream and share a kiss with a pretty girl in the rain.

It hadn't been raining, but Grandpa Har-

Ian's intent was clear—kiss a pretty girl somewhere unexpected.

Or just be kissed unexpectedly.

Jonah sucked in a careful breath and followed Emily to the librarian's desk. A young woman with curly black hair hung up the telephone, glanced at them and smiled.

Emily leaned an elbow on the tall counter. "Jonah Monroe, scriptwriter, meet Abigail Winters, librarian."

Jonah smelled a trap. "Hi, Abigail Winters, librarian. How do you know Emily Clark, rodeo queen?"

"We went to school together." Abigail had the kind of smile that said she loved her job and a small, sparkly engagement ring that said the world was her oyster. "How've you been, Em?"

"Good." Emily reached down to admire Abigail's ring. "Can't complain."

She can't complain because she'd been thoroughly kissing a man—this man.

Jonah dutifully leaned forward to admire the librarian's sparkler. "You used to live in Second Chance?"

"Born and raised," Abigail said, still smiling.

"That's slick." Jonah fixed Emily with a stern look. "You have inside information about libraries and historical records."

"And you're lucky I do." Emily stuck her nose in the air. "Someone's got to watch out for the greater good of your script."

Jonah liked Emily. A lot. He liked her wit and her savvy and the sun-kissed highlights in her brown hair. And if he was honest with himself—which he wasn't prone to be with others—he'd admit he liked kissing her. He liked it too much. His grandfather's bucket list was filled, and yet it felt as if he hadn't accomplished anything where she was concerned.

Emily explained to Abigail about Mike Moody and the unsolved puzzle that was Letty. "We're interested in any articles about his robberies and any records you have—birth, burial site, family, marriages, children."

"You're going to have to let me down gently if they were married." Jonah ran a hand through his hair. "Or had kids."

EXTERIOR. THE STAGE ROAD. Mike Moody and his sons—none of them older than twelve—hide in the woods, eating hardtack made by Letty.

There was a story idea. Just not the one that would prove to Jonah's father once and for all that he wasn't a hack.

"Kids is your breaking point?" Emily waited a beat before turning to Abigail. "Whatever. We want to know how Mr. Moody came to be in Idaho." She shot Jonah a look, her left eyebrow raised. "Maybe he was so good at robbery and killing because he was trained to be a scout or something? Second Chance was the location of a cavalry post." Emily gave Abigail the year Mike Moody was killed.

Abigail scribbled all that and their contact information down. "I need to do some preliminary searches, but I think I know where to look first. Can you guys go to lunch or grab a coffee?"

"Lunch is fine." Emily didn't wait for Jonah to agree. She started walking toward the door.

"Oh no, you don't." Jonah caught her arm. "I said if we were ever near a mall or a clothing store, that I'd help you pick out some Bo-appropriate clothes." Who was he kidding? He wanted to see Emily in something other than jeans and a pearly-snapped button-down. Jonah was preparing his own bucket list, one that involved seeing Emily in a pretty dress, one that made her feel special.

"But—"

"Nope. No buts. It's you and me and a rack of clothes." He marched her toward the door.

"I can't wait to see what you choose. Not." Em sounded like she was rolling her eyes.

He didn't slow down to check. "Don't judge. I got the purple blouse with no ruffles right, didn't I?" The one from her closet for Tina to wear in competition.

"I hate it when you speak in truths." She let him drag her out to the parking lot.

Jonah found a promising boutique on his phone and navigated them there. Emily parked the ranch truck on the street. Keeping a safe distance between each other, they walked down a quaint shopping district housed in the old part of town.

"Hi." Jonah greeted the middle-aged store clerk as he shut the door behind Emily, making sure she didn't run away. "I want this fine young cowgirl to try on something she'd never choose for herself, something she'll fall in love with." Love. The word unsettled him so much, he plucked a black bra from where it was hanging on a nearby rack. "Here. Try this."

"Hey-hey. No." Emily tried to snatch the undergarment, but he kept it out of reach. "Bras weren't in my contract."

"They should have been." Much as he loved teasing Emily, he couldn't look at her right now. He handed the garment to the grinning sales clerk.

"The right look starts from the ground up," the sales clerk tittered, ecstatic to serve them in her otherwise customer-empty store. "If you'll just wait in the dressing room, honey, I'll bring you some ensembles to try."

"Do I really have to?" Emily's gaze darted everywhere.

"Give it a chance. Maybe it'll be fun." Jonah could tell by the way she didn't argue that she was curious about a different style of clothes.

In short order, Jonah and the store clerk had some outfits picked out, ones that Emily would never choose for herself.

"Bring her this outfit last." He laid the items across the counter.

A few minutes later, Emily stomped out of the dressing room carrying the white stilettos she was supposed to have on her bare feet. "Where would I ever wear this?" She held out her arms and turned around in a yellow sequined cocktail dress, the hem of which landed just above her knees. She looked stunning.

Instead of answering her question, Jonah pointed to the shoes.

"Why?"

"Because I need to be able to judge if it's Bo-worthy."

Because I'd selfishly like to see for myself.

Emily huffed but bent to slip on the shoes. "Don't ask me to walk in them. I don't walk in stilts." She straightened, blushing. "Well?"

"You should be at a swanky bar having drinks." His lips felt stiff and his words sounded wooden. He shouldn't be sitting here, staring at her. He should go back to the library and wait for Abigail's results. Alone.

"Did you just say *swanky*? No one says *swanky*." Emily turned to look at herself in the mirror, eyes widening. "I have a waist."

"And I have a large vocabulary," Jonah said thickly, wanting to kiss her again. "Expect me to use words like *swanky* and *glamorous*."

"This isn't me." Emily slid out of the heels and slowly returned to the dressing room, looking lost.

"I told you before, everyone has different facets of their personality." Jonah liked Emily in that dress. "That could be Emily's only-on-New-Year's-Eve-at-a-swanky-bar dress."

"No." Her voice was muffled from the dressing room. "It would only sit at the back of my closet."

"With that leather evening gown?" The one she'd won the rodeo queen competition in? He wouldn't let that happen.

When next Emily emerged, she wore a pair of loose-fitting black trousers that fell to her black platform heels and a cream-colored silk blouse that draped elegantly at her waist. She walked on the thick-soled heels like she was traversing a ship's deck at high seas. "Well?" She turned to admire herself in the mirror. And this time it was definitely pleasure in her eyes.

Jonah was sure there was pleasure in his. "That's more you." Casual sophistication. "I can see you wearing that to a white-tablecloth restaurant."

"Which we don't have in Second Chance." But Emily didn't turn her back on her reflection or stomp back to the dressing room.

"You never know when a chance at a decent meal might come up." He'd seen an advertisement for a five-star restaurant pop up on his phone on the drive over.

"I never have the opportunity to eat foofoo food." Emily disappeared inside the dressing room once more. A few minutes later she twirled out in a burgundy dress with a tulip skirt. She was succumbing to the attraction of her repressed feminine side. "I love it, but again, I don't have any place to wear it."

"You could wear it at home. No man would complain." Certainly not him. "Besides, I can tell you when you'd wear it. It's a date dress. Didn't I pick out heels for that?"

"I don't do heels." Emily tossed her hair.

"You can't wear cowboy boots with that dress," Jonah countered.

"Try these." The sales clerk produced a pair of suede beige booties. "Booties are all the rage with dresses nowadays. So comfortable and so chic."

"Love," was all Emily said when she caught a glimpse of herself with the booties on. "I mean, these are just like my pink boots."

"Not at all." Jonah was quick to disagree.

Finally, the clerk gave Em the ensemble Jonah had picked out for her to try on last.

The rodeo queen emerged with a big smile on her face and that familiar strut to her walk. He'd chosen slim-fitting jeans, a simple yellow blouse that she'd tucked into the waistband and a pair of black suede half boots. It was a city take on a cowgirl look.

INTERIOR. QUIRKY CLOTHING STORE IN A HIGH COUNTRY RESORT TOWN. MONTAGE. Jonah watches Emily trying on clothes the likes of which she'd never worn before. We see him falling in love with her by the changing expressions on his face.

Jonah frowned and rubbed his temples, trying to hit the mental delete key on the way

Em's smile broke through his cynicism, the way each breath when she was near made the world more vivid, the way his heart pounded in his chest when she kissed him. Soft, tender, warm emotions. He wasn't falling in love. That was his storytelling brain creating a linkage from what had been happening and what should happen next in a rom-com. Was this déjà vu? A repeat of what had happened while he was dating Aria? With her, he'd been distracted by his need to win and by his storytelling brain making mental notes about what a great romance was playing out before his very eyes. Then he'd proposed, and everything had gotten worse.

Don't make the same mistake twice.

Don't do that to Emily.

"Now this…this I could wear anywhere." Emily adjusted the shoulders of her blouse with gentle hands in a way that belied the strength she used to control unruly ranch animals. "Not that I'm going to buy anything. These clothes are so impractical."

"Sold." Jonah stood and caught the clerk's eye. "That outfit, head to toe, the burgundy dress and those suede booties."

"I can't let you…" Emily froze, seemingly torn between her love for the clothes and possibly her pocketbook, which she hadn't brought. He'd seen her tuck her driver's license and a ranch credit card in the glove box. "I'm going to pay for everything. I'll reimburse Franny."

He was determined she wouldn't pay. But she gave him the all-or-nothing ultimatum and won that battle, choosing the purple dress and the last outfit she'd tried on.

While her purchases were bagged, Abigail rang Emily's cell, asking if they'd be willing to pay for copies of some of the documents she'd discovered. Of course Jonah said yes. They hurried back to the library.

Abigail was bubbling with excitement when they returned. "Check out what I found." She led them to a small conference room and closed the door behind them. "Merciless Mike Moody wasn't a cowboy. He was a tailor."

Worst news ever.

Jonah rubbed his temples.

"He was originally from Philadelphia. He arrived in the territory about three years before his death." Abigail handed them a copy of his birth certificate and a list of parties traveling in a wagon train. "He wore a nice suit and tie during his robberies, along with a burlap bag over his head with eyeholes cut into it, but some witnesses thought he might have worn glasses underneath." She handed them a copy of an article in the Boise newspaper that had a sketch of the bandit wearing the bag, along with details about a few of his robberies. "At first, they called him the Dandy Robber."

A dandy? Jonah released a mournful sound. This was worse than Mike being married or a father.

Emily patted his arm. "Mike can still be merciless and wear a suit."

Not in my mind.

"Now, Letty…" Abigail stared at a sheet of paper without revealing it to them. "This was a surprise. Her last name was Moody."

"You're crushing all my hopes and dreams," Jonah murmured.

Abigail turned the paper around, revealing a birth certificate. "She was his older sister."

"What?" Jonah sucked in a breath.

"You can work with this." Emily grinned. "Older siblings are so bossy, don't you think?"

"I'd prefer he was an only child, raised in an orphanage." Jonah washed a hand over his face.

"It gets better. I promise." The librarian chuckled. "There is mention of a small man covering Mike during robberies, hiding in the trees with a shotgun. His backup is never named but was said to be the sharpshooter, the one who did the killing."

This is better?

Jonah couldn't breathe, not even enough to refute the idea. Mike Moody wasn't a merciless killer! This ruined everything.

"Isn't it funny how history has a way of forgetting the details?" Emily brought one of Abigail's articles in front of her. "A second shooter."

"None of this is funny," Jonah rasped. Shane was going to pitch a fit.

"Wait. There's more." Abigail wasn't done tormenting Jonah. "There are records of women dressing as men to avoid being accosted in the frontier. The small man could have been Letty." She slid another newspaper article across the table. "At least, that's what I thought when I saw this article about a man they tried to rob. He reported scaring them off by shooting into the woods. They found blood, but no body was ever found. That was a year before Mike was killed."

"Oh, that poor thing." Emily gasped. "She was shot. And then Mike was alone."

"That poor thing was a killer." Jonah rubbed his temples, trying to wrap his head around the pieces and make them fit into a cohesive story. "*If* she was the one in the woods."

"And you'll find this interesting." Abigail only had one more paper. "There's a reference in a report from a local judge regarding criminals and crime in the area the year after Mike died. It shows Mike Moody's crimes decreased significantly in body count after the date you said Letty died."

EXTERIOR...

Jonah couldn't visualize the scene.

He ran through the facts in his head, but his storytelling radar didn't ping, not even to create the opening lines of an improbable scene.

Something didn't fit. But what?

And then he knew. "Three years." That was where things got wonky. "You're telling me Letty lived in a cave on top of a mountain in the brutal winters of Idaho? For three years?" Jonah spread Abigail's research across the tabletop. "Murderess or not. They had to have another place to live."

"They did." Abigail hadn't stopped smiling since they came in. "There was a census in Second Chance a few years earlier that listed a Mike and Letty Moody renting a small farm south of town."

Jonah sat still, waiting for the links to form smooth connections, waiting for scene ideas to come. Nothing. Something still wasn't right.

"I'm amazed." Emily squeezed Abigail's hand. "You're awesome. How did you find this all so quickly?"

"There's a file." Abigail leaned forward, tapping a tattered manila envelope. "Someone researched everything about Mike Moody years and years ago. I found it in an old box last Christmas when I was cleaning out some storage cupboards. Being from Second Chance, I couldn't throw it away."

"Our grandfathers probably requested it," Jonah said, looking at Emily.

She nodded.

"Is there more?" Jonah had so many unanswered questions. "What drove them to crime? Who shot Letty?"

"If you give me a few days, I'm sure I can dig up more information about her." Abigail's interest was caught—on Letty Moody, not Mike. "This is so exciting."

Shane's comment yesterday about the buzz in town returned: *I think it's great that people are talking about her.*

They wouldn't talk about her for long if all the pieces didn't fit. And Jonah couldn't force the facts to flow together. At least, not for Mike Moody, eyeglass-wearing dandy and hapless face of the Merciless Moody gang.

He'd thought this was the perfect story, cut and dry. He'd been wrong.

He'd been wrong about everything.

"WHAT ARE YOU so happy about?" Jonah grumbled from the truck's passenger seat. He'd been heaving sighs and jerking about the entire drive.

Emily stopped humming, slowing to take a mountain curve as she drove them back to the Bucking Bull from the library. It had been nice to get away from the ranch and trying on clothes had been fun, even if buying them put a big dent in her savings.

And Jonah? He'd been a pleasure to be with until Abigail had shared her findings.

"Hey, happy girl." Jonah poked her shoulder.

"Who? Me?"

"Yes, you." He stretched his long legs and clipped his words. "Smiling. Humming. Glowing."

Em spared him a glance, raising her eyebrows. "Glowing?" Was he going to bring up their kiss?

He nodded. "Don't make me say *radiant* or *lustrous*."

He thinks I'm radiant? Forgetting about their differences, Emily almost started humming again.

"You know what I mean," Jonah muttered darkly.

Attention back on the road, Emily wondered if she did. Jonah wasn't always an open book. "I'm happy we finally found some information you might like for your script."

"You're humming because you're happy for *me*?" He crossed his arms and locked them down over his chest.

"I suppose I—"

"There's no supposing. *Supposing* is just another word for guess." Jonah may have been sitting next to her, but his tone put him in scorched-earth territory. "Suppose I sell this script on spec and default on the contract because the reality was that Mike Moody was a dandy of a tailor. My agent's shopping around Mike Moody's story as we speak." Jonah held up his phone. "But reality could kill the idea and my career along with it. Don't suppose, Emily. It'll keep you up at night."

He wasn't mad at her. Emily knew that. She gripped the wheel, keeping her shoulders back and her head high. "You're upset about the questions Abigail has yet to answer."

"Yes. I'm over here sulking because I still

don't have what I need to write this thing." His arms unlocked and he raised his hands in a plea to the heavens. "Everyone's relying on me to come through with something brilliant. And I can't."

"Everyone?" Jonah and his drama could be worse than the most selfish of rodeo queen candidates.

"Everyone." His hands came crashing down to slap his thighs. And then he sighed. "The entire population of Second Chance. Shane believes this film will be the advertising the town needs to keep it afloat. My sister Laurel believes it's the project Ashley needs to launch her producing career." Jonah shook his head and continued in a hard voice, "Sophie's in love with the idea of a reenactment of the entire story, condensed to twenty minutes so some local performers can recite lines at the festival celebrating Mike Moody's merciless past. As if writing a full-length film to impress my father and give my career a boost isn't hard enough."

The echo of his words died out in the cab as they reached the final ridge before their descent into Second Chance. The sky had cleared to a pristine blue. Tall pines hugged the slopes and gave way to a broad expanse of green meadow, threaded with the rippling blue of the Salmon River. In the distance, the rugged Sawtooth mountain range rose up like a medieval wall. It was beautiful. It should have inspired a quiet moment of awe.

But Jonah's words continued to resonate in Emily's head. She'd had no idea he was under so much pressure. She'd assumed he wanted to write a script and get paid, kind of like the way she trained bulls. She worked them until they were acceptable to be released into the world and then sold them and moved on. She didn't worry about how much the bulls sold for. That was Franny's concern. She didn't worry about where the next crop of bulls was coming from. That was Franny's concern. And before that, it'd been Kyle's. She'd been complacent. She and her trophies.

Jonah's annoyance lost its sting. He'd been holding in his frustration and had needed an outlet. She'd been the closest target, oblivious though she was to the intricacies of Monroe family dynamics and his Hollywood career. Everyone and everything did indeed hinge on Mike Moody and Jonah Monroe. Nothing hinged on her decisions or performance. Nothing significant that impacted anyone else.

"I don't know these people. And I'm not sure I ever will," Jonah admitted morosely.

"Mike and Letty Moody. Old Jeb. I've tried walking in their shoes—"

"Boots."

"Whatever." His fire had burned out, leaving only defeat. "Maybe it's time to face facts. I'm not the right person to do this story justice."

That couldn't be true. Em hit the brakes, bringing the truck to a stop at the narrow overlook.

"All I wanted…" Jonah stared out the window at the steep cliff and the valley below them. "All I've ever wanted—" he turned to Emily "—was to make a name for myself separate from the Monroes."

He's like me, minus the complacency.

Em couldn't let him quit. She put the truck in Park and reached for him, placing a hand to his shoulder and a palm to the whiskers on his cheek. "How can I help?"

He stared into her eyes, saying nothing.

"Jonah?" She moved her palm, learning the feel of his skin, the texture of his ginger goatee.

His gaze dropped to her lips. "There are other things I want." Jonah took her hands and returned them to her side of the truck. "Selfish things that have no place in Second Chance."

Em wanted selfish things, too. She wanted to kiss him. She wanted to let him know it was okay to kiss her. For a moment, maybe two, she stared into his electric blue eyes and tried to swallow her pride and initiate that kiss the way she had on the trail this morning.

"We should get back," he said.

Four words. They were jagged, hacking at the longing between them. She'd have preferred him to say two words.

Kiss me. Or *I want*...

She could have filled in the blanks with a touch of her lips to his. Instead, she put the truck in gear and her mind to work.

"All I ever wanted..." she recycled the words he'd used in an effort to make him see reason "...was to do something with purpose, make an impact, do something important. But I'm finding that I'm just another ranch hand at the Bucking Bull." She was replaceable and responsible for being so. "In fact, our one other ranch hand, your cousin's husband Zeke, is returning tomorrow from delivering a bull. When he's around, I have less to do."

"You feel less essential."

"Yes."

"And you don't have a cowboy or a ranch of your own to make you feel indispensable."

"No." And none of that was on the horizon. Just the hard Sawtooth Mountains.

So much open space. So many possibilities. If she could find a man to reach for, a man willing to ranch with her, a man she could love.

Emily risked a glance at Jonah, just a glance because the road was steep and the curves dangerous. But that one glance at his stony expression told her what she hadn't wanted to believe. When it came to the future, she should have been listening to her head, not her heart.

No single kiss was going to turn Jonah into the man of her dreams. He was from another world and he most definitely didn't have room for one insignificant cowgirl in his plans.

CHAPTER THIRTEEN

"No news from the librarian about Mr. Moody?" Bo dug through a plastic margarine tub filled with screws and fasteners.

"No news." Which was reason enough not to work on the script, although not to dwell on the memory of a rodeo queen's kiss. Jonah held a bathroom door in place in one of the lake cabins, waiting for Bo to find enough hinge pins that matched so they could hang it. Surprisingly, physical labor was effective in stopping images of Emily pivoting in a yellow cocktail dress from taking up too much of his metal space.

It seemed like half the population of Second Chance had descended upon the campground by the lake to help complete renovation and restoration one sunny Saturday nearly a week after Em had kissed him. The other half of town was frolicking by the lake. Children swam and shrieked gleefully, watched over by adults with no construction skill or inclination to swing a hammer or operate a power saw.

Sitting on a low footstool nearby, Shane stopped reading the door handle instructions and looked up. "You know what would be great?"

"No," Bo and Jonah said together, exchanging wry grins.

"If Mike Moody was one of our ancestors." Shane brightened, waiting for his cousins to find the same unexpected joy in this statement as he had.

"You think it'd be great to be a descendent of a murderous criminal?" Jonah smirked. "Why is it I find it hard to agree with that statement?"

"It would explain a lot about the choices our fathers made." Bo shook the two hinge pins he'd found in one hand. They clinked softly, unable to drown out the sounds of happy children outside. "They gave up family for fortune."

"It would add to the mystique of being a Monroe," Shane muttered, bending his head to the instructions once more. "And Second Chance."

"That mystique is the reason *being* a Monroe is so difficult," Jonah said, thinking about the pressure he was under. "Sometimes I wonder what it'd be like to have been raised in a family no one had ever heard of before."

A family like Emily's.

He hadn't seen Em much in the past week, certainly not today, and, if asked, wouldn't admit he'd been looking.

Her grandmother sat beneath a pop-up awning with a handful of other white-haired residents, near enough to the lake to witness the action, far enough back that they didn't get wet. Second Chance wasn't just filled with multigenerational families who continued to stay. It was a larger family, a community that watched out for one another. There was no greater evidence of that than the fact Grandpa Harlan had returned a decade earlier and tried to save the town from extinction.

Of course, he'd left the hard work of saving it to his grandchildren.

"Seriously, Bo." Jonah rested the heavy door on the top of his running shoes. "Could you not have found all three hinge pins before we got the door in place?"

"Found the third one." Bo stood and helped Jonah align the door with the hinges once more. "If you'd been a little more patient, I could have slid these right in."

Jonah huffed.

"Jonah, just the man I was looking for." Egbert walked slowly up the porch steps one at a time, leaning heavily on his cane. "Since you told me Letty was Mike's sister, I've been rereading Old Jeb's journals."

"The ledgers, you mean?" Jonah stood back while Bo swung the door open and closed.

"Yes. His ledgers." Egbert paused on the top step to catch his breath. He spotted a green plastic chair. His steps quickened with purpose, and he sank down to rest. "I think Old Jeb Clark the smithy was sweet on Letty."

Bo chuckled, propping the door open. "If it's a script Jonah's working on, it always comes back to romance."

"Hardy-har." Jonah wished his cousin would get a new joke. "Is it wrong to regret fixing the ceiling in here before it caved in on your head?"

Bo clutched his T-shirt over his heart and staggered back as if wounded.

Oblivious to their ribbing, Egbert opened a worn, leather-bound journal and read, "Long snow. Ladle made. Traded biscuits. Two weeks. L." The old man circled his finger over the page. "All of which is misspelled and in Jeb's shorthand."

Which meant it could mean anything. Jonah tried to draw on that patience Bo thought he lacked.

"I think it means Jeb traded a ladle he made for two weeks of biscuits that winter." Egbert stared at Jonah over the rim of his glasses. "This is only the first entry to reference L."

"Lloyd. Larry. Lincoln." Jonah tossed out possible men's names.

Egbert tsked. "He made things for a household, for a kitchen. For a woman. A frying pan. A coffeepot. A decorative, swivel-arm fireplace crane to hold a cooking pot over a fire."

"That could've been for any settler," Bo pointed out, scanning his to-do list for completing the cabin they were in.

"Agreed," Jonah said, swallowing back his impatience with Egbert's dead end because every trail seemed to have a roadblock.

"But…" The town historian had a flair for the dramatic. "He repaired a peddler's cart axle in exchange for a bolt of calico. And then he traded it for biscuits. Also noted for L."

That caught Jonah's attention. "Not muslin or canvas?" Material that men might use.

Egbert shook his head. "I'd be willing to bet that calico was for one Letty Moody, so she could make herself a fine dress."

"A wedding dress," Jonah murmured.

"Romance." Bo chuckled, earning him a shove from Jonah.

"There was no romance," Jonah said firmly, as much to Bo as himself. "Letty died and Old Jeb married the town schoolmarm."

Egbert wheezed and returned his attention to the journal.

"This is the biggest marketing opportunity ever." Shane abandoned the doorknob instructions to join Egbert on the porch.

Wearing cutoffs and a cowboy hat, Emily waded into the lake to break up a water fight between two boys.

Jonah sighed. In the meantime, she was a pretty sight, a welcome distraction from speculation about the Moodys.

"Don't you see?" Shane walked like a man in charge, a man who knew what his strengths were and played to them. "I know you've had your doubts, Jonah, but Ashley has to play Letty. I'll get a public relations firm to talk about the gold we found. It's marketing genius." He pounded his fist in his hand. "The movie will get that much more buzz. And Second Chance… People will flock here to visit."

Jonah lost sight of Emily. He rubbed his forehead and refrained from comment.

Egbert flipped through Old Jeb's ancient journal, looking as if he was in search of something else he considered important.

"As usual." Bo crumpled his list and shoved it into his jeans pocket. "Shane is putting the cart before the horse."

"How so?" Shane crossed his arms over his chest.

"Jonah hasn't written the script." Bo shot Jonah an apologetic glance. "Gritty isn't exactly your middle name and teenage Westerns don't exactly have broad appeal. No offense."

"None taken." It was almost a relief to get it out in the open. "Besides, Shane, much as I love my sister, have you seen Ashley act?" Jonah joined his cousin on the porch. "This is a gritty, nuanced role. She's not going to be frolicking poolside pretending to crush on a member of a boy band with a laugh track edited in later."

"You're not giving Ashley enough credit." Shane frowned and shook his head. "She's very talented."

Bo raised his brows.

"You could say the same about me, Shane." Jonah frowned right back. "Based on a large body of work on my résumé you could assume I was deeply talented." Jonah wished he was having this conversation with Emily. She'd slam him with a clever response that might take the ache out of his admission that he was a hack.

"Your writing résumé could be worse." Bo picked up a clipboard with the list of items that still needed doing for the entire camp.

"You could have spent the past ten years writing articles for a teen gossip magazine."

Instead, he'd been writing vehicles almost exclusively for his kid sister.

Shane clapped a hand on Jonah's shoulder. "On the other hand, a chance like this doesn't come along every day. Step up. We've got your back."

Jonah washed a hand over his face. He wasn't worried about his back. He was worried about the quality of story on the page. Dreck would make him unmarketable in Hollywood. No one could help him with that.

Emily's laughter drifted to him. She was wading back to shore and talking to Franny. How would she feel if she discovered he'd written a script based on her quest for love?

She'd hate me.

Jonah's stomach did a slow, sickening turn. His gaze found Bo next.

Ditto.

"Don't be so hard on yourself, Jonah. You were learning a craft." Shane plucked the doorknob from the floor and brought it to Bo, who sighed and dug a screwdriver out of his pocket. "You think I started in the management offices of our hotel chain? No, I—"

"Scrubbed toilets and made beds," the three Monroes said in harmony.

"Very funny." Shane frowned at his cousins.

"Well, you do have your standard lines." Jonah curled his fingers around the screws and stepped a few feet to the side so he could see Emily. She sat on the shore, letting Adam bury her feet with mud. "My personal preference being 'Listen to me.'"

"Usually followed by some cockamamie scheme designed to get under Holden's skin." Bo chuckled. He was allowed to laugh given Holden was his older brother.

"This isn't a cockamamie scheme." Shane, in typical Shane fashion, was raising his voice.

Fifty feet away at the shore's edge, his fiancée, Franny, turned her head their way.

"Boys." Egbert held his journal like a preacher holding an open Bible from the pulpit. "I know this won't stop your arguing, but I almost forgot to tell you." He paused. "Soon after Miss Letty's death, Jeb bartered with a stonecutter. Now, I always thought that was because he'd ordered stone for the foundation of his house on the Bucking Bull. But when I went back and checked the dates, I found he cut the stone soon after Letty died. He didn't order lumber for his home until after Mike met his sad end."

"Proof of a romantic tragedy." Bo screwed the door handle in place.

"Proof he cared," Egbert said solemnly, closing the journal. "And maybe he cared about Mike, too."

Jonah huffed. Egbert was like all the rest, attributing a heart to Mike Moody. At this rate, they'd credit one to him, as well.

"I know this script is hard for you." Shane stepped into Jonah's line of sight, blocking his view of Emily. "Grandpa Harlan would say there are more reasons *not* to try than reasons to do."

"He was like the family fortune cookie generator." Bo took another screw from Jonah's palm.

"Yeah, well, wise sayings come from people who've taken chances." Shane drew himself up, a CEO bringing his argument to a motivational close. "Wise sayings don't come to those who sit on the sidelines playing it safe." His gaze challenged. There was no frown.

Jonah silently swore.

Shane had faith in Bo. Shane had faith in Ashley. Heck, Shane had faith that Jonah could work miracles with Mike Moody's script.

"Jonah looks like he's ready to give those pages another go." Bo gave him a half smile. "And let's not forget one thing."

"What's that?" Jonah asked.

Bo stood, grinning. "We can always hire a better hack for rewrites."

"Do you suppose one of us should go over and make sure those Monroes don't kill each other?" Franny asked, brow wrinkling.

"No." Emily stood and followed Adam to the water, rinsing mud from her hands and feet. "Maybe what Second Chance needs is fewer Monroes." Her heart would be the better for it. Jonah had avoided her for days, making their outing on the trail and to Ketchum seem like it never happened. Understandable given the pressure he was under, but was he really expecting her to forget that kiss?

Emily sighed.

He was.

"Although if some Monroes leave," Em said, "I'll be without eye candy in the Bo-Department and without sharp-witted Jonah challenging everything I say." *Every feeling I have.*

Because Jonah read her too well, right down to her misplaced attraction.

We should get back.

Jonah had let her down easy with those words. In the traditional sense, she barely knew him. So why was it hard now to visualize her dream of a cowboy, a ranch and cow-pokes of her own? Where was the urgency she'd felt on her birthday to find said cowboy?

"The Monroes are family now." Franny brushed Emily's hair over her shoulder. "Or they will be when Shane and I get married." Which they'd decided to do on New Year's Eve. "Nothing much will change," Franny continued, but in a voice that swung more toward doubt than certainty. "You'll still have Jonah to joke with."

"Will I?"

"Absolutely you will." Franny turned her face to the sun. "If not every day, then at family gatherings. Shane plans to have a few of those a year."

Would time make things easier between her and Jonah? Would she forget what it was like to kiss him?

Emily didn't think so.

Her chest filled with regret, making her heart heavy.

She shouldn't have kissed Jonah. She shouldn't want to kiss him again. Bo could still be her cowboy dream, if only she wanted him.

Darn it. She didn't want perfection.

Em was always her own worst enemy when

it came to love. "Do you remember that summer I went out with Robert Stewart?"

Franny waded into the water. "Charlie, don't drown your brother." She backed up, rejoining Emily while keeping her eye on her mischievous middle child. "I remember. What a summer that was. Kyle proposed."

Emily squished her toes in the mud. "I think Robert only asked me out because you and Kyle were official." She'd wanted a date with Robert since she'd seen him trying to ride Buttercup on the rodeo circuit. "I heard he's married with four kids and a ranch north of Boise."

"Four kids. Brave man." Franny took another few steps into deeper water. *"Charlie."*

"What, Mom?" The rascal dove under water and swam away from Adam, who was bobbing in the lake as if he hadn't minded Charlie's attempts to push him under.

"As I recall…" Franny's gaze turned as sly as Charlie's. "Your date with Robert was a dud. You can't be pining over him."

"I'm not." All Robert had talked about on their date was his rodeo career, and occasionally Franny. He hadn't been interested in Emily at all. And she hadn't been interested in being his second choice. "I'm just wondering what it is I want in a man." And if the prerequisite of being a cowboy was a make-or-break condition. If it wasn't, did that mean she could give up the dream of living on a ranch?

Her stomach churned. She didn't want to.

Franny came to stand next to Emily, wrapping an arm around her waist. "You can make all the lists in the world regarding your ideal man. You can check all the boxes those magazines say make for a good spouse. You can even take compatibility tests on one of those dating apps. But sometimes the heart wants what the head wants to deny."

Emily leaned her head on Franny's shoulder. "But what if my heart doesn't know what it wants? What then?"

"You know the answer to that." Franny reached down and splashed Emily with water. "You give a toad a chance, with a kiss and an invitation to dance."

"Toss down your guns and the cash box, and no one gets hurt." Davey balanced the muzzle of a water pistol on his wrist, taking aim at the Ritter kids, who were pretending to be the stagecoach driver and guard.

Jonah sat next to Shane in the afternoon sun on the steps of a cabin. The local kids were reenacting Mike Moody's fateful last day as a prelude to a water fight.

Near the lake's edge, Emily stood next to Franny and held a blanket in her arms. She'd need a water gun in a minute.

"Are you Monroes watching Davey?" Gertie sat in a chair on the porch behind Jonah. "My goodness that boy can act."

Jonah cast a disbelieving glance over his shoulder. "I write scripts. I don't cast films."

Gertie winked. "A good word never hurt."

The Ritters tossed Davey a water gun and a duct-taped shoe box that sounded like it was loaded with pebbles.

Davey scooped it up and gave a villainous chuckle. "Now, count to ten before you collect those guns."

"Stop in the name of the law!" Gabby Kincaid ran around the corner of a cabin three doors down, a broomstick pony between her legs and a water pistol in her hand. She was followed by a passel of kids who were supposed to be the posse.

"I-eee!" Davey shrieked like a coward, eliciting a weary sigh from Jonah and chuckles from the crowd. Juggling the cash box and his gun, Davey grabbed his broomstick horse from the ground and ran toward Emily.

The posse thundered past. The younger

kids in the rear shot water, hitting the posse leaders in the back. It was a shrieking mess.

"Oh, my love." A small girl with pigtails skipped after the posse. "Run away! Run away!"

Jonah pointed to her as she passed. "Who's that supposed to be?"

Shane shrugged.

"It's Letty," Gertie explained.

"But…" Jonah tossed his hands. "That makes no sense. She died long before Mike met his fate."

"Oh, let them have their fun." Gertie applauded as Davey collapsed on the ground.

"Splat." Emily covered him with the blanket, which Jonah assumed was supposed to be a boulder and Davey's gruesome end.

The kids bounded around and cheered, even the hapless Letty.

And then Davey arose from the dead and attacked them with his water gun.

"They have no clue," Jonah grumbled.

"So?" Shane stood and looked down on him. "Neither do you."

CHAPTER FOURTEEN

"THERE YOU ARE." Abigail came up the gravel walk to the cabin where Jonah and Bo sat watching the sunset, each lost in their own thoughts. The librarian held the arm of a tall man with one hand and clutched some papers in the other. She introduced them to her fiancé. "We came out to visit our folks this weekend. I found something for you about Letty."

"Here we go," Bo murmured before taking a sip of his beer.

"Ten bucks says it's a marriage certificate," Jonah murmured back before standing to greet their visitors, setting his water bottle on the railing. "You didn't have to drop anything by. You could have emailed me." He much preferred bad news electronically so he could scowl at it without hurting anyone else's feelings.

He couldn't scowl at Abigail. She was too nice.

"I found an article about the Moodys." Abigail wasted no time getting to the point. "They were kicked out of a wagon train headed west. There were accusations of theft."

"What was stolen?" Perking up, Jonah hoped it was the wagon train's box of gold.

"Small things. A silver teaspoon. A gilded hair comb. A music box." Abigail handed Jonah her research.

"Are you sure Letty was Mike's sister?" Bo spoke up from the porch. "Those sound like gifts for a lover."

"I'm going from their birth certificates. Neither one of them show up in marriage records." Abigail spoke with certainty. "I also found a letter from around the time of Letty's death that sheds more light on the article I showed you highlighting a botched robbery. A woman who used to live here wrote about Jeb Clark being distraught after he shot one of Mike Moody's gang during an attempted robbery. Apparently, she and her husband had come upon Jeb just after it happened. She never saw Mike or Letty again. She assumed Letty finally moved on to San Francisco. This was the year before he died."

"A year before Mike stabbed Jeb?" Jonah squinted at the spidery handwriting in the failing light. Phrases jumped out at him.

Loyal to her brother up until then.

I doubt Jeb will ever be the same.

Burdened by the shooting.

It scares me to think of Mike hiding in the woods.

We never suspected a nearly blind man of such evil.

"Mike became quite the local demon." That was the first cheery thought Jonah had about Mike Moody in a long time. He shuffled the pages. "Another article?" With the copies' low contrast, it was difficult to make out more.

"That article is fantastic." Abigail's voice rose with excitement. "It details the robberies and murders of your criminal. He was such a killer early in his career. Not so much after Letty died."

"Maybe he had regrets," Bo said. "People do as they grow older."

Jonah's story meter tripped, pinged, sounded the pay-attention alarm. There was something here. Something he hadn't had before. More pieces fit together. Although he still couldn't see the entire story, he thanked Abigail and sent the couple on their way, returning to the porch.

"You can head on back to your comfy bunkhouse with its flowery wallpaper and decorative paintings." Bo was referring to

Aria's watercolor, which still hung face-to-refrigerator so Jonah couldn't look at it. "I know you're dying to study what the librarian brought and stare at that rose wallpaper in the bunkhouse while you ponder murder and mayhem."

Jonah was anxious to think the story through. But there was something about Bo's quiet mood that made him linger. Not to mention, there was the issue of Emily's discarded dream. Not that Jonah's jealous bones wanted them to find happiness together. Still, he knew he wasn't the man for Emily and neither she nor his cousin was finding happiness solo. "You've been alone here too long. Loneliness is starting to show on your face."

"I was thinking the same thing." Bo drank his beer. "Just not the face part."

The sky was turning an inky black. The moon was no longer full and bright. The solar lights they'd installed around the campground were coming on, including ones on the porch railing caps. It was enough light to get around in. Enough light to discern the disquiet in Bo's expression. He was noodling something, something he didn't much like.

Jonah drank his water, stalling. And then he just said what was on his mind. "If you're going to stay, you should ask Emily out. Lighten up. Smile a little more."

Choking, Bo sprayed beer all over the porch. He wiped his mouth and glared at Jonah. *"What?"*

"You heard me. You need to get out of your head." Said the pot calling the kettle black. "And you two have a lot in common." Inwardly, Jonah flailed about for something to prove his point. "Like…cowboy boots. You both wear them."

Bo set his beer on the porch near his cowboy boots. "We have nothing in common other than our shared annoyance with you. Don't think I haven't noticed how you two avoided each other all day long."

Jonah waved Bo's protests aside. "You both like…" Why was this so hard? "…steak."

Bo stared at Jonah the way Emily had stared at Jonah when he'd told her their kiss had meant nothing. "To be clear, when I agreed that I was lonely, I was thinking of bringing my dog up here."

"Although Spot is a character—" and an all-around great dog "—you can't exactly have a decent conversation with him."

"Speak for yourself. Spot and I get along just fine. We understand each other. And I left him with…" Bo reached for his beer. "I've been gone four weeks. That's a lifetime for a dog."

Jonah noticed the slip regarding who Bo had left his dog with. He had a sneaking suspicion he knew who was caring for the dog—his former fiancée.

What an unexpected complication.

Jonah debated digging in Bo's cooler for a beer but decided it wasn't worth risking an intestinal flare-up. But the more he thought about Aria, the more he knew he couldn't let the situation pass unremarked. "Didn't you tell me Aria was pregnant with another guy's baby?"

"Let's not do this." Bo got to his feet. "You should be taking Emily out, not me."

"I'm not what she wants," Jonah half murmured before catching himself. "The point is that Aria found someone new to take care of her. Emily doesn't have that someone. She's alone, just like you." The man who'd just admitted he wanted to bring his dog all the way to Second Chance. If that wasn't an indication that Bo was setting down roots here, Jonah didn't know what was.

"The situation with Aria is complicated." Bo leaned on the porch railing, staring out over the calm lake.

"Emotions often are."

Bo smiled. "Like you'd know. Listen to yourself. *Emotions*." He put the word in air quotes. "Just say what it is. *Love*. You write about it enough, but I don't hear it dropping from that run-on mouth of yours so often. If ever."

"I know what love is." Technically. "And I've seen first-hand how Hollywood ambition and love don't mix. But even when you know what it is and what it feels like, there's a point where you have to separate love for a person from being *in love* with a person."

Bo glared.

"You love Aria," Jonah continued, because they should have had this conversation months ago. "I get it. I loved her, too. And she loved *us*. Remember that? She loved both of us." Jonah pointed back and forth between them. "Whatever hang-ups Aria has, she has to work them out alone."

"She is alone," Bo said gruffly.

Jonah's jaw dropped. It took him a moment to gather his thoughts. "So it didn't work out for her again."

"No."

Intelligent, fragile, artistic Aria was once more alone. And Bo loved her. Present tense. Jonah could see it in his eyes.

There was trouble brewing back in Texas.

Who was Jonah kidding? It was brewing here in Second Chance.

Jonah stared up at his cousin. "Grandpa Harlan would say we love who we love." The old man had been an expert, having loved four women enough to marry them and having had three of those marriages fall apart. "But this…" It felt like Aria had built a web and snagged Bo in it.

"I'm leaving in the morning." Bo jutted his chin.

"Or you could wait," Jonah said carefully. "Test the waters with someone else. Just to see if what you feel for Aria can only be felt for Aria." To know that he loved her and only her.

What a stupid, stupid idea.

Bo didn't immediately call it out as such.

Jonah was relieved. Not because he loved Aria—*he most definitely did not*—but because Aria wasn't good enough for Bo. Not in this lifetime and not in the next.

"Maybe you're right. But I don't need to take Emily out to test for the possibility of love between us." Bo sighed. "Any guy can spot attraction if he looks for it. I'll just hang out at their place for an hour or two tomorrow and see if sparks fly. But I'm telling you, they won't."

That was a darn good idea. A darn good idea. So, why didn't Jonah like it? Maybe it was the fact that Emily's kiss banked a fire inside him, waiting to flame. So, why was he pressing the idea? Oh yeah. Em wanted a cowboy and a ranch. Bo could give both to her. So Jonah lied. "Hanging out won't cut it. I kind of promised her a week or so ago that I'd get you to take her on a date."

"What a stupid, irresponsible promise." Bo went inside the cabin and slammed the door behind him.

Selfish relief cascaded through Jonah's veins.

A second later, the door swung open. "I'll do it but from now on, keep your matchmaking in your scripts." Bo slammed the door once more.

Jonah stood, gathering his resolve and his regrets, holding his water bottle between two fingers. It fell, of course, clattering down the steps to the dirt.

Kind of like his original plans.

Which plans? you might ask.

All of them.

CHAPTER FIFTEEN

"I DON'T HAVE time to play games, Jonah."
Emily was up in the loft making room for
the ranch's regular hay delivery, sweeping out
snippets of old straw to fall to the breezeway
below.

Jonah had stayed away from her for days,
only to come back urging her to visit Bo?
Talk about adding insult to injury.

"I feel obligated to deliver on what I initially promised you." Jonah stood on the ladder beneath Emily, brushing hay from his
red hair. "You wanted a cowboy and it just
so happens there's an unmarried one in the
vicinity."

Emily bit back a groan. "I'd rather not live
through a repeat of that breakfast you set up
for me."

"It won't be like that," Jonah assured her,
staring up at Emily with a serious look on his
face. "He won't be rushing to eat in order to
finish working on those cabins. The cabins

are ninety-nine percent done. He's practically a man of leisure now."

"I'm not a woman of leisure." And Mr. Bodilicious no longer fit the framework of her dreams.

"What's thirty minutes here or there?" Jonah made a come-hither gesture. "The days are longer. It's not like you have to rush to get things done before nightfall. And Zeke's back. You said yourself that takes a load off."

"Did I hear my name?" Zeke entered the barn, leading his horse. He tilted his hat brim up with his left hand, the one flashing that new wedding ring of his.

Envy made a sour dash through her veins.

"Yes." Jonah climbed down. "I want to steal Emily away for a bit. You can cover for her, can't you?"

"He can't," Emily insisted, annoyed with Jonah. "This is his lunch break. I need to finish here and then start training some of our young bulls in the arena with Franny." Em swept hay into a pile near the top step of the ladder. "And later, Tina's coming by to practice her competition skills."

"Come on." Jonah glanced from Zeke to Emily. "You have time to take Bo some lemonade made by your grandmother. I was just inside and had a taste."

"Gertie's lemonade." Zeke tied his horse near her stall. "That'll go good with my lunch."

"See?" Jonah tried to grin.

"Oh, Jonah." Emily stared at the man, willing herself to hold his intense blue gaze and not think about kisses or hunkiness or frog princes. "I can spare a little time. It's just that with you it's never just shuttling lemonade down the road."

"This won't take long. I promise." Jonah made that come-hither gesture again with his hand and although it was lighthearted, his smile seemed forced. "You should try that new dress, maybe a little makeup, a spritz of perfume..."

"And then we're talking an hour out of my day, not just a neighborly thirty-minute jaunt." Emily tugged off her thick gloves and climbed down the ladder because it was easier to get this over with than to argue with him.

By the time she reached the ground, Zeke had left.

"Em, don't look so glum." Jonah was like Adam, running on ahead toward the house and waving at her to follow. "Do you know what my grandfather used to say about missed opportunities?"

"No." She took off her hat and dusted her blue jeans with it as she followed him.

Jonah walked backward across the ranch yard, still wearing that strained smile. How she wanted to kiss him until he grinned for real. "Sometimes a missed opportunity is the difference between five minutes and five excuses," he said.

"I don't want to offend you, Jonah, but your grandfather and his sayings are beginning to annoy me."

"You can't feel the true sting of Grandpa Harlan's insight unless he delivered one of his pearls of wisdom right after you'd embarrassed yourself." His false grin dimmed. "And since he's gone, you'll just have to humor me when I quote him. It keeps him alive here." He tapped a spot over his heart and ascended the front porch steps, pausing at the top to turn back and reach for her hand. "Now, let's get into the spirit of the exercise."

Emily sighed. "All right." She took his hand, telling herself to ignore the way it fit snugly around hers, and marched up the stairs. Her odds were much better for long-term happiness with Bo. That was her head talking.

Without another word, Jonah opened the door for her. And held on to her hand down the hall and...

Emily turned, laying a palm on his chest.

"That's as far as you're coming. I've got it from here."

He stared at her as if she was a sacrificial lamb in a flock he tended.

Impulsively, she stretched up on her toes and touched her lips to his.

"I'll be okay." Emily closed the door behind her and stared at the burgundy dress she'd bought in Ketchum. She felt so pretty in it. Confident. Capable. Attractive. She wished she was wearing it for Jonah. And then she stared at the box of shoes resting on the floor beneath it. The heels were completely impractical for walking across a meadow. Suede booties. What if there was still dew in the grass? They might be ruined. Wearing them was a risk, but reaching for dreams was risky, too.

What if Jonah's scheme worked? What if Bo asked her out?

Her heart might be ruined.

"You look…" Jonah frowned at Emily when she emerged from her room a few minutes later. "You're wearing cowboy boots?"

"I am." Hardening her resolve, Emily grabbed the keys to a ranch truck off a hook, her cowboy hat and the thermos he handed her. Her eyelashes felt stiff from too many coats of mascara and her pink boots rang like thunder on the floorboards. "I'll be back in a few, Granny."

"Don't hurry." Her grandmother winked. "Franny and the boys will be back soon. Trees are hard to come by around these parts. Best bark when you can, as loud and as long as you can."

Em groaned. Gertie and her metaphors.

"Hey, wait for me." Jonah was hot on her heels.

Emily turned once more, touched Jonah once more. This time a brief palm to shoulder—her palm, his shoulder. There was no impulsive zing to kiss him, thank heavens. "It's time to let your little birdie fly on its own."

Crash and burn on my own, too.

Emily didn't have high hopes for this fool's errand.

And by the looks of him, Jonah didn't, either. "But—"

"No buts."

Amazingly, that was the end of his argument. Jonah stood on the porch and watched her drive off.

Down at the lake camp, Emily marched across the meadow toward a cabin where she could hear country music playing.

"Hello?" She knocked on the front door frame.

"Yeah?" Bo came out of a back bedroom carrying a box of light bulbs. A frown flickered across his face so fast she thought she'd imagined it. "Oh, hey, Emily. Can I help you?"

Staring at the floorboards, Emily entered the main room and held up the thermos. "I brought you lemonade. My grandmother feels like she needs to extend her hospitality your way, even though this isn't our land." She thrust the beverage at him.

"Thanks." Bo accepted her gift and set it in a cooler.

Somewhere in the room, a large fly buzzed about his business.

Emily should be getting about her own, too. But not without a weak attempt at winning Bo. "How's it going?" She pretended to be interested in his progress, but she was concentrating on not looking him in the eye and listening for the grumble of a hay truck engine.

"Things are good," Bo said in that deep voice of his. He could have been the nighttime radio announcer on the Lonely Hearts channel. "I'm looking forward to seeing kids take over the place for a week or two. I might even stay to serve as a camp counselor."

What a nice guy.

"It's kind of you to help Shane." There was a scuff on the toe of Emily's pink boot.

Bo scoffed. "I'm more likely to consider myself Shane's blackmail victim. But since my dad fired me, I was just sitting on the beach in South Padre Island, going a little bonkers without anything to occupy my days."

This was possibly the most words Bo had spoken to Emily ever. She risked a glance at his face.

He's looking at me!

"I like to keep busy, too." Sucking in air, she half turned to the door. "Look at the time." *Shoot.* She'd left her cell phone in the truck and there was no clock on the wall. "Hey, I won't keep you any longer." She hurried out the door and down the steps.

"Emily." Bo's deep voice should've thrilled her, should've had her turning and smiling.

Emily gasped for air and looked over her shoulder, not quite meeting his gaze. "Yes?"

"Why don't we have dinner together sometime?" Bo rubbed a hand over his face as if he'd gotten the tough part of the conversation over with, the part he'd been dreading. Not exactly the sign of a man eager to have dinner with a woman. "Say tomorrow night at the Bent Nickel? I'll pick you up around five thirty?"

"Sure." Emily spun back around, marching toward her truck on shaky legs. Good thing she hadn't worn heels.

I have a date with Bo.

Her ears rang so loud she didn't hear the hay truck until it was past her and lumbering up the hill.

JONAH WAS POUNDING away on his keyboard on his practice rom-com script when a large truck stacked with hay pulled into the Bucking Bull's ranch yard, followed by Emily in her truck.

Her expression was grim as she ran into the farmhouse. He'd bet anything she'd struck out with Bo again. Poor thing. This was going to take some smoothing over. Maybe he'd borrow a ranch truck and take her into town to buy ice cream.

And if he gave her a hug of sympathy... and if that hug led to more than a quick buss of lips... And if she needed soothing today...

Jonah bolted out of his chair, prepared to make an ice cream run.

Gertie lowered her knitting to her lap when he entered the farmhouse, and then closed her music box. "What are you up to?"

Jonah pressed a finger to his lips and went to knock on Emily's closed bedroom door. "Hey, how'd it go? Wanna go into town and have an ice cream?"

"Ye of little faith." Emily flung open the door, having changed into the jeans and chambray work shirt she'd had on earlier. "Your magic worked. I have a dinner date tomorrow."

Jonah's jaw dropped.

She edged past him and beat him to the foyer where she yanked on her boots and mashed her cowboy hat on her head.

Jonah followed, leaned against the wall, trying to get a bead on her mood. There was no excitement. No gushing. No cheeks flushed with embarrassment. "You don't have to sound like you're going to a funeral."

"I'm busy, Jonah." Emily banged out the door. "My hay order is here." She marched away in that purposeful gait of hers, each step away from him like a stomp on his heart.

"Be careful what you wish for, young man," Gertie said from the living room. She'd picked up her knitting. Her needles clacked.

"This is what I wished for. It's what's best for…for both of them." But his words felt hollow.

Outside, Emily made small talk with the

driver. Zeke came out of the barn to join them. They laughed.

Jonah swallowed thickly. "Emily doesn't want a man like me." She wanted a man like Bo. Someone who could give her life a deeper meaning and purpose. Small town living. Cattle and horses. Puppies and kidlets.

"My granddaughter is perfectly capable of deciding what's best for her." Gertie smirked. "I can't say the same about you."

"I'm fine."

But would he be when he left Second Chance?

His phone rang. It was his agent. Jonah stepped outside to take the call, hurrying down the porch.

Maury didn't waste any time. "I fielded two calls today from studios looking for romantic comedies. They want scripts, but they'll take treatments. What have you got for me?"

"I'm still vested in the Western," Jonah said unconvincingly, crossing the ranch yard. "Isn't anyone interested in the treatment I wrote for that?" He grimaced. He'd written that story summary when he'd thought Mike Moody was a killer.

"Unless you're going to produce and direct that Western yourself, there's no market for it. I should know, I've asked."

"You did?" Maury had been anything but supportive of the Mike Moody project.

"Darn straight, I asked. I looked up the box office gross on the last three successful Westerns. Big money." Now Maury's interest made sense. "Not to mention they do well during awards season."

Jonah entered the bunkhouse and closed the door behind him.

"But those Westerns?" Maury paused to sip something, not that it made his gravelly voice any smoother. "They were all passion projects. Written, produced and directed by brand-name directors." He drew a noisy breath. "I gotta be honest. Your project has the stink. I told you, I don't want you to have the stink, too. Give me teenage rom-coms. I can sell those."

Jonah sat down on his bunk. Hard. "I don't want to write them anymore. I don't want to be that guy anymore."

"What guy?"

"I want to be on the list people consider for the most interesting projects." Not the studio hack who could take an okay idea and make it into a vehicle for a star to do in her spare time on summer break.

Apologies to my sister.

Because he'd done that a lot for her.

"Jonah, you gotta know. You're just not that guy." Maury was a lot of things, but he was brutally honest. "All your stuff... It's based on your experiences and those of your family. Those wacky siblings and cousins of yours. You've never written a story like this Western, one with a gritty premise. And I'd never expect you to, either."

Maury's words slammed home with cold certainty. The truth bent Jonah's shoulders. It shattered his lifelong dreams. It broke his heart.

Because it was true. Because he'd written teenage sitcoms for Ashley. Teenage movies for Ashley. He'd been casting shade on her talent, but he might just as well cast doubt on his own.

Dad was right.

"Don't get me wrong, Jonah. You're great at what you do," Maury continued. "So you should write what you know and only what you know."

The romance he'd written about Bo... The rom-com he'd written about Emily... They weren't teen fare, but he'd written them based on his experiences, his first-hand observations. And they were good. Maury and his father were right. He had a talent for this kind of thing.

"I'm turning thirty soon." Jonah was tired. Worn out. In the exact place Emily had been on her birthday. Looking around, he wanted more. "I can't do kiddie stuff much longer."

"If that's your way of saying you want out of the teen sitcom business permanently, we'll have to rethink our business relationship." Maury's words caused a ringing in Jonah's ears.

"You're dropping me?" He'd represented Jonah for years.

"Jonah, I'm a hustler. I move fast and make deals. But even I can't make deals to bring an organ grinder onto Broadway. I can't sell this Western with your name on it."

"I'm a Monroe." That ought to count for something.

"And someday you'll probably run Monroe Studios." Maury didn't sound happy about it. "Stick to your strengths. I can sell your strengths."

Two decent scripts were on his computer, but they were personal stories, practice scripts.

Jonah didn't say a word. It was one thing to write about family antics for television sitcoms. It was another to write a theatrical movie about a love you'd lost and a woman you cared for.

"I know you, Jonah. Silence means you're holding back the good stuff. Tell me." When

Jonah didn't, his agent repeated himself. "Tell me. Tell me. Tell me. What have you got hidden under your bed that isn't a Western?" Under your bed meaning manuscripts shelved for one reason or another.

"Two adult romances." Jonah hung his head. "One's a rom-com and doesn't have the third act."

"And everyone is over the age of eighteen?"

"Yes."

"A stretch from teen comedy to young adult is believable. Give me treatments or pages if you've got them. I'll expect them in my inbox first thing in the morning." Sounding positively gleeful, Maury hung up.

Jonah sat down at the table, laid his hands on his laptop and faced facts. He needed a sure thing to dig himself out of the teenage sitcom hole. Mike Moody was too big of a gamble.

He didn't move. He could barely breathe. He couldn't stand to be thought of as a teen writer anymore. He could send in what he had just to see if there was any interest. It would be validating if there was any. He didn't have to sell them.

He had to do something.

Because he couldn't go down with the stink.

"I'M GONNA DO your hair and you've got to smile the entire time." Emily stood behind Tina in the downstairs bathroom after the hay had been stacked and the invoice signed for. "And keep the conversation going."

"Sure." Tina checked her phone.

"No. No phones." Em swiped it from Tina and slipped it in her back pocket. "You can't have your phone while you're competing."

"I knew that," Tina mumbled, still looking like she'd been put in time-out.

"Smile and make small talk." Em took a brush to Tina's thick dark hair. "Seriously, smile and make small talk, starting now."

Adam squirmed into the bathroom. "What are we doing?"

"Seeing how long we can smile." Em took the upper half of Tina's hair and twisted it, puffing it high over her head.

"Is this a race?" Adam sat on the rim of the tub and bared his teeth. "When do we start?"

"We should've started two minutes ago." Emily caught Tina's eye in the mirror. "That's not a rodeo queen smile." It was more like a grimace. Em demonstrated the carefree, you-can't-bring-me-down smile the judges were looking for.

Tina smiled, but now she looked like she

was posing for her school pictures in a blouse she hated.

"Work on that smile and make small talk." Em put the brush handle between her teeth and used her free hand to grab a hair clip.

When she was done, Tina's hair looked like an Elvis pompadour. Not exactly winning rodeo queen style. Em had to find two hairstyles that complemented Tina's features and then teach her how to do them herself. Part of the competition was based on presenting yourself as put together by yourself.

"She's smiling," Adam said, grinning for all he was worth. "Not like me. I'm smiling and I could smile all day."

"Should I wave, too?" Tina cupped her hand and gave a queen's wave. She winked at Adam. "That's what queens do, right? Smile and wave."

"Time-out." Emily shook Tina's hair free and set the hairbrush on the counter. "Everyone stop smiling."

"What's not so funny?" Jonah appeared behind Em, his head visible above hers in the mirror. He looked in need of a smile. "Why aren't we smiling? Everyone should be smiling all the time."

Especially Jonah.

"Let me explain about smiling," Emily

began, trying not to worry about Jonah's lack of smile.

"There is no explaining about smiling." Jonah edged inside the room to stand between Emily and Adam. "Babies smile. It's natural. You don't need to explain."

Emily reached up and pressed her palm over Jonah's mouth. Didn't matter that it created a strong desire to kiss him. Didn't matter that his eyes blazed to life and he smiled against her palm. He'd set her up with Bo. She was moving on. Now if only her heart would get with the program. "For the next minute, the rodeo queen has the stage. Agreed?"

Jonah nodded.

Adam giggled.

Tina grinned.

"Now." Emily removed her hand from the attractive ginger and reclaimed the floor. "From the moment a rodeo queen candidate enters the rodeo grounds, she'll be watched by judges. Everything a candidate says or does is under scrutiny, which means you always have to smile genuinely, like you are the kindest, happiest person on earth and you have to be the kindest, happiest person on earth to other candidates. Like Madison."

"Uh-oh." Tina stopped smiling.

"I asked you to find something you like

about Madison." Emily retrieved the hairbrush and began sectioning off Tina's hair in a different style. "Tell me something you admire or respect about her."

"Shouldn't she be smiling while she's doing this?" Jonah asked.

"Yes." Em handed the hairbrush to him and began braiding Tina's hair in a soft, romantic side braid.

Tina drew a deep breath, smiled like she was happy, and said, "Madison, I've always admired your accent in Spanish class." She glanced at Adam. "She can really roll her *r*'s and *t*'s."

"I sense sarcasm." Jonah twirled the hairbrush in his hand. "And I'm the cynical voice in the room."

"He's right." Em hated to agree with him, but Tina had to learn. "I want you to start talking nonstop to Adam minus the sass and never drop that warm smile."

"Nobody told me this was going to be so difficult." Tina rolled her eyes.

"I believe someone did." Em paused in her braiding. "Madison said you'd never win."

Tina narrowed her green eyes.

Jonah nodded, seemingly in approval. "Revenge is best served cold. And it makes for great character motivation. Imagine the look on Madison's face when you win the crown."

Tina smiled.

"Much better," Em said. "Now we need to see how long you can keep that up and talk like the kind, loving person you are about any person and any topic."

"I bet I can beat her." Adam had his grin back on. "'Cuz I don't hate anyone."

"But, Adam..." Tina had a beauty of a smile. "I don't have a mean bone in my body. Why, just the other day when Madison said my shoes reminded her of her grandmother, I just smiled and said thank you."

"This Madison is mean." Jonah set the hairbrush back on the counter. "But my snarky meter is going off, Tina."

"Being nice is harder than it looks." Adam's head jerked to the side as if he was Bolt listening for an intruder, and then he gasped. "Someone opened a bag of chips." He raced out of the bathroom.

"How on earth did you win the crown, Aunty Em?" Jonah took Adam's place on the rim of the bathtub. "You're nearly as jaded as I am."

"I was an innocent back then," Em said loftily, using a decorated band to fasten the end of Tina's braid. "And I channeled my grandmother, who rarely has a bad word to say about anyone." She checked out Tina's reflection in the mirror. The asymmetrical style gave some length and definition to Tina's round features. "And I killed the other contestants with kindness." Emily pitched her voice high. *"Madison, those chaps are fabulous. Madison, that eyeshadow brings out the highlights in your hair. Madison, I've never seen such an even coat of glitter on a horse."*

"Whoa." Jonah leaned back and nearly fell into the bathtub. "Rodeo queens put glitter on their horses?"

"Yes, sir. Thicker than mascara." Tina continued to smile the happiest of smiles. "My mom bought a huge tub of glitter. We practiced making Button sparkly the other day. Hoof polish. Glitter. Hairspray on his mane and tail. Glitter. I think he knew how handsome he looked, because he high-stepped around the pasture."

Em realized none of the rodeo queen contestants she'd seen the past few years braided their hair. It was all ringlets and teased ponies. She undid the braid and then reached for the hairbrush. "And *when* you win, you'll get a butt bouquet placed behind Button's saddle every time you ride in a parade."

"Those are the most ridiculous things,"

Tina said, although with a big smile and without any cheek. "I've seen pictures of some that are taller than the queen in the saddle."

"There's a story here." Jonah rubbed a spot over his heart. "I can feel it."

"Oh, watch out, Mr. Gritty-Gory Western Writer," Em teased. "That sounds like rom-com material."

"We'll see." Sobering, Jonah left them to their hair devices. "We'll see."

CHAPTER SIXTEEN

JONAH WAS NOWHERE to be seen when Bo pulled into the ranch yard to take Emily to dinner.

Emily wore the casual blouse, slim-fitting jeans and suede booties from Ketchum.

The light in the bunkhouse was on. Jonah was burning a candle at both ends, writing. Always writing. She hoped he was eating well. She'd looked up the effects of Crohn's disease and had a newfound respect for Jonah's culinary regimen. Diet was the best way to avoid a flare-up.

"Are you gonna marry this one?" Adam stared out the window at Bo, wiping at his upper lip which was red from drinking punch. "Charlie says he's scary big."

"Everybody's getting married." Charlie joined him in the living room and collapsed on the couch. "We're gonna need a bigger house."

"That's not the Monroe she likes," Davey called from the kitchen.

"I'm just going to dinner, not to the marriage altar, boys." Emily grabbed her jean jacket, cheeks heating. She opened the door before Bo could knock.

His smile was grim. "Yes, just dinner."

How much of their exchange had he heard? Emily wanted to sink into the floor.

Adam ran to her side and shook Bo's hand. "My new daddy says this is how we meet new people."

"Howdy." The burly cowboy shook her nephew's hand with a straight face. "Shane knows how to make friends and influence people."

Adam glanced toward the living room. "You're wrong, Charlie. He's big but he's not so scary." He ran to the kitchen.

Cringing, Em made her escape out the door. "Sorry about that."

"No worries."

They walked in silence across the gravel drive to Bo's truck. He opened the passenger door for her and then made sure Emily was settled before closing it.

Manners. Check.

His truck had every modern convenience known to man, and then some. There were cup holders everywhere—dash, center console, door panel. Heaven forbid the occupants were without coffee, soda or water—all at the same time. There were air conditioner vents that blew on her face and on the back of her neck. Emily ran her hands over the supple leather seat and admired the computer display in the dash.

Money independent of mine. Check.

She hadn't realized she had additional prerequisites when it came to eligible bachelors.

Bo pressed a button and then told the truck's computer to play country hits. Music surrounded them.

A country fan. Check.

"I feel like I'm in the cockpit of a luxury airliner," Em admitted, although she still couldn't look at Bo directly.

"I suppose all this gadgetry keeps me in touch with the world."

"I'm happy just to keep in touch with my family and most of Second Chance." The seats were large, and sitting there next to him, Emily felt small for once.

This is how it should be with a man. He should make me feel delicate. Check.

Emily was suddenly struck with the thought that she didn't know how Jonah would rank according to these new criteria. He was taller than she was, but she probably weighed the same as him. Was that a check? He'd arrived in town in Bo's truck. She didn't even know what kind of vehicle he drove or what kind of music he listened to.

They rounded the last corner of the drive and passed the lake camp as they neared the cattle guard at the Bucking Bull's main gate. "How much more needs to be done on those cabins?"

"Staging." He slowed as they drove past. The truck barely bounced over the cattle guard grate on their way to the highway.

Bo headed toward town. Emily had expected their conversation to be a bit stilted. It was a first date, after all, plus she had a suspicion that Jonah had put Bo up to it. But they drove a few miles without saying anything. Anything.

Finally, staring straight ahead, she asked, "What is it you do? Or should I ask what you did for your family before…" He and his siblings and cousins had all been fired. Everyone in town knew that.

"When I was a kid, the plan was for me to manage the Monroe ranch in Texas, just like the plan was for Jonah to run Monroe Studios. Both are big. Our ranch is over three thousand acres."

That made the Bucking Bull's three hundred acres look like a hobby ranch.

"I didn't spend enough time there to become more than a good rider. Certainly not a ranch manager. I studied petroleum engineering in college. After graduation I ran our oil rig operations in the gulf."

An engineer? She'd barely passed biology in high school. And algebra had been a headache. But she had to say something or he'd ask her about her nonexistent college career. "I'm beginning to understand why you can't just sit back and take a vacation while you're in town. You're used to a fast-paced workday."

"As are you."

Not hardly. "My day's a bit more predictable and slower paced. I'm out riding a lot, making sure fences are up and the cattle look well."

"You have the freedom of making your own schedule."

"I would if Franny wasn't my boss. She divvies up the workload." Although at this point, Em rarely needed to be told what to do.

Bo parked in front of the Bent Nickel. She jumped down as soon as he'd shut the engine off.

"I would've come around and helped you down." Bo opened the diner door for her.

"Oh, right. I forgot."

There were a few locals having dinner and

a family that Emily didn't recognize occupying the corner booth. Ivy waved from behind the counter, where she was teaching her youngest how to fill saltshakers.

Em was blowing this. It was her big opportunity with Bo and she wasn't letting him treat her like a lady. But if she did that, he might do something that would make her freeze, like hold her hand while she climbed out of his truck or smile at her. "I'm kind of used to just charging in here to pick up my nephews."

"I like that you're independent."

So much for Jonah's assessment that she needed to act like a damsel in distress. Em risked a glance at her date.

Bo was smiling at her, a genuine smile. It reached his dark eyes.

He likes me.

She didn't feel the anticipated thrill of victory. *Because he's not Jonah.*

Emily sat down too fast in the booth.

"You okay?" Bo reached for her arm.

He was so darn polite. Jonah would've teased her about losing her balance. Jonah had manners. They just weren't the same manners Bo exhibited. Jonah didn't open doors for her. He didn't make sure she was safely seated before he sat down. He cut her off midsentence, sometimes to change the subject before she was finished with the topic. It should have been annoying, but he made her feel alive.

"This is wrong." Emily shook her head. She was right where she'd wanted to be for nearly two months and suddenly… "It can't be."

She didn't want to be here with Mr. Bodilicious.

She wanted to be back at the ranch, ribbing Jonah about his rabbit food and arguing over Merciless Mike Moody and his tough sister, Letty.

I miss Jonah.

Emily stared at the green booth seat cushion beneath her. She'd shoved over toward the wall as if making room for one more. For Jonah.

I thought I was getting over my infatuation with him.

He's so bossy, so loud, so darn…caring.

Emily rolled her eyes, wanting to deny it. But it was true. He cared about his extended family. He cared about her family. He might even care about her.

Or he could just consider her a source of amusement. He certainly laughed a lot during their conversations.

She did, too.

The need to be with Jonah became an ache

in her chest. She rubbed her breastbone and forced herself to stare at Bo, at his chiseled, handsome face. Those dark eyes that didn't look for a weakness. That fantastic dark hair that was blue-black in the right light.

This one, she told herself and her eggs, meaning Bo.

Those troublesome eggs were silent.

This one, she told herself again. Mr. Bodilicious. Bo. He was the one for her because he was...

Well, the truth was that besides being handsome, he was a bit boring, even if he was a cowboy. He wasn't a talker like Jonah or herself.

I can work with boring. Er... I can live with boring... I can love boring.

Emily rubbed her temples. She was never bored around Jonah. He kept her on her toes. And he... And he...

He had the most glorious way of looking at the world, generous and jaundiced at the same time. He laughed at her nephews' antics. He was both intrigued by Merciless Mike and horrified that the murderer had a heart.

And I kissed him. Twice.

That second peck didn't count. Or the first one, either. He'd pushed her to the brink of annoyance. She'd had no choice but to kiss him to shut him up. To make him see. To make him see *her*.

Bo was watching Emily carefully and in silence, with more patience than Jonah on a good day.

Emily's gaze swept the Formica tabletop as a feeling welled inside of her, gathering and solidifying until she had to give it voice. "I can't believe this but…" She crouched over the table and whispered, "I think I love Jonah."

What a disaster.

She and Jonah… They were two ships that never should have passed in the night. She and Jonah… They were headed in completely different directions.

This was bad. Really bad. This had heartbreak written all over it.

Bo's smile was a slow build that in no way acknowledged the intense disappointment he should be feeling when his date admitted she loved Jonah instead of him. "Let me be the first to congratulate you."

Emily pressed her palms to her flaming cheeks. "Don't. This is completely, utterly a mistake."

"Why?" He waved Ivy and her order pad away.

"Because he is completely and utterly wrong for me." She straightened. "And he arranged this date. Just look at me. I'm all country compared to his Hollywood flash."

"Have you listened to the two of you together?" Bo was still smiling at her and she hadn't lost her ability to speak.

"Yes," she said. "We argue all the time."

"That's not arguing. That's foreplay."

"It's a waste of time, is what it is." She wanted to take her epiphany back. The feeling. The declaration. The *L* word. Emily narrowed her eyes, trying to force herself to see Bo the way she'd seen him weeks ago—a man who represented everything she wanted in the world. "I can't believe it. You're no longer Mr. Bodilicious. Did you stop taking vitamins or something?"

Bo laughed again.

"Please don't laugh. You're making it that much worse."

"I'm imagining what Jonah's doing back at the ranch right now. Honestly, this is the best payback ever."

Emily paused. "What do you mean?"

For the first time, Bo seemed abashed. "I...uh..."

"This is about Aria." The coil in her chest that had been building a case for love suddenly whiplashed around angrily. "Are you trying to use me to get back at him?"

"No." Bo held up his hands.

"Is he still in love with Aria?"

"I'm one hundred percent certain that's a no." His dark brows dropped down.

"Are you still in love with Aria?" She didn't need to ask. It was there all over his handsome face.

Bo turned and flagged down Ivy. "We're ready to order now."

Emily tapped her chin, contemplating the situation. "Jonah won't stand in your way. He wants you to be happy, no matter who you fall for." He wanted her to be happy, too, hence this date.

"Lots of women fall for me." Bo smiled up at Ivy, twisting Emily's words. "Probably because I'm Mr. Bodilicious."

Ivy nodded. "The mythical unicorn. The prize of maidens. The apple of every female eye in Second Chance, Idaho."

Bo looked abashed again. "That's enough of that. Let's order. And then we'll plan your strategy of attack."

Emily had been about to laugh, but... "What am I attacking?"

Bo grinned. "The walls around Jonah's heart."

CHAPTER SEVENTEEN

EMILY KISSED BO'S cheek when she said good-night.

"Good luck, hon," Bo said when she looked him in the eye. He was no longer Mr. Bodilicious to her. He was just a nice guy.

The light was on in the bunkhouse.

Emily took a step in that direction as Bo drove away.

The front door opened behind her.

"If you're looking for that wrong tree," Granny Gertie said with a knowing look in her eye. "He's at the firepit. Mooning over you being out with that cowboy."

If her grandmother had made that comment earlier in the day, Emily would've scoffed about the mooning. As it was, a report of mooning was most welcome. Emily thanked her grandmother, went into her room, and changed into jeans and a hoodie.

And then she went out the back door and hesitated, filled with doubt. She sucked at poker. What if she walked out there and he saw love written across her face as if she'd written it herself with permanent marker?

"Are you going to leave me hanging?" Jonah asked without turning around. "Or come out here and spill what happened on your date? I heard Bo's truck come and go."

His chutzpah propelled her forward. "You think I'll kiss and tell with my best girl-friend?" She joined him at the firepit. "Think again."

"Look at me," Jonah demanded.

She stared into his eyes, smirking.

"There was no kiss." He returned his gaze to the fire. "I spend all this time hyping you up and you strike out."

"Nobody kisses on a first date."

"Ha! It was practically your second." He scowled.

She loved that scowl. She depended upon that scowl to keep her on her toes. But she loved that smile of his even more. She needed that smile. She needed that smile something awful.

And there was only one surefire way to get it.

"Jonah." She moved her chair right next to his and kissed him. No waiting, no hesitating.

Their first kiss had been full of frustration.

Hers. This kiss was loaded with happiness. Hers. How could it not be? She loved him.

Jonah drew back slowly, one hand resting on her waist. "You can't just surprise a man like that." He stared at her through heavily lidded eyes. And then his gaze cleared. He removed his hand and sat back in his chair. "What is this? What happened with Bo?"

"Nothing." She mirrored his position, pretended nonchalance despite the too-rapid beat of her heart and the urge to kiss him again. "We got along well, like friends."

"I knew it." He scowled. "You were relegated to the friend zone."

She ran a hand up his arm. "Is that so bad?" After all, she'd come home and kissed him.

"Yes! How am I supposed to help you?"

Em frowned. "Do I need help?"

"Clearly. I gave Bo to you on a platter."

Anger thrummed through her veins, overriding happiness and love.

Why can't he just accept the fact that he's attracted to me?

Em had to do something to make him acknowledge there was a connection between them worth pursuing. She had to...use his own advice against him. She wasn't going to lie and tell him she and Bo had hit it off. She had to be the woman who needed help, the help he was so desperately trying to give her.

"I'm sorry. I had no reason to kiss you like that. I know you don't like it. I just had all this pent-up..." she shook out her hands "...energy."

He didn't stop staring at her, but he didn't swoop in for another kiss, so...

Be sweet.

"The night got really chilly, didn't it?" She threw another log on the fire. "How's the script coming along?"

He blinked like the owl hooting in the distance. "It's going better than expected."

"Which for you is..." *Be sweet.* She switched tracks midsentence. "I'd like to read it sometime."

"I thought you said you didn't like blood and gore." He arched a brow. The firelight brought out all his red coloring.

She couldn't look away from this complex, handsome man. "It's not like you're going to have pictures of people dying on the page."

"It is." He studied her face. "Did you have something to drink tonight?"

"No. Ivy doesn't serve alcohol." He was suspicious. How could she prevent this from becoming a disaster? Her heart pounded in panic. "I wore that outfit you picked out."

"It didn't work, though, did it?" Jonah stood abruptly. "I'm going to bed. I'll try and talk to Bo about you in the morning. But honestly, catching and holding his attention is all about good execution. I gotta say, I'm disappointed."

If I wasn't in love with you, I'd be laughing right now.

Emily bid him good-night, pulled her hood over her head and sank into the chair, thinking.

Her Hollywood Cupid was going to find out what it was like to be roped by the rodeo queen.

WHAT IN THE world had Bo done to Emily?

First thing in the morning, Jonah left the bunkhouse and rode the ranch's ATV down to the lake camp to find out why Emily had returned from her date and kissed him.

I could get used to those kisses.

But wouldn't that be cruel? He'd be leaving soon and Emily deserved a good man to spend the rest of her life with. She didn't deserve a man who tested the waters for his next career move with a script based off her quest for love.

Jonah parked the ATV and marched across the knee-high grass. It was wet with morning dew. Before he was halfway across the meadow, his running shoes were soaked. "Bo! Where are you? You've got some ex-plaining to do."

Bo sat on the porch steps of the cabin he called home. He held a steaming mug. "You know, you sound just like Desi yelling at Lucy on those episodes of *I Love Lucy* that Grandpa Harlan used to watch at night."

Their grandfather's RV had been equipped with a television. No cable. No internet. They'd been forced to watch Grandpa Harlan's VHS tapes of old sitcoms.

"Don't change the subject." Jonah stomped up the stairs. "What happened last night?"

Bo handed him the mug, which contained hot green tea. "Can we sit and enjoy the morning for a minute?"

"You were expecting me?" Jonah sat down and cradled the mug in both hands.

"Please." Bo sat back in his chair and took a deep breath. "You're so predictable. Now shut up and enjoy the out-of-doors. I know you've been hiding in that cave you call a bunkhouse and pounding on those keys. Your skin is vampire pale."

"The curse of being a redhead," Jonah muttered.

Bo shushed him and picked up a coffee mug from the floor.

Jonah wanted questions answered, but he sat in silence and drank tea and took clean air into his lungs and beautiful scenery into his head. At least until he noticed Bo's half smile. "Why would anyone build a camp for kids here? It's a million-dollar view."

"You'd rather build a mansion here?" Bo bristled. "Tear down these cabins and build a vacation home some wealthy family stays in twice a year?"

Jonah grinned. "Wow. Shane slipped you the Second Chance juice, didn't he? You want to keep Second Chance. You want to become like some feudal baron, charging tenants rent to work your land."

"It's not so bad, is it?" Frowning as if he was Shane, Bo sipped his coffee. "To protect a place like this from development?"

"You haven't been here when it snows. I hear it's brutal." Jonah had read about the early settlers being trapped inside their cabins for weeks at a time. "And then there's the cell and internet connections. Dark Ages stuff. Not to mention the lifestyle. It's so slow you have to watch the grass grow because there's nothing else to do."

The sun's rays were bright and warm, making the cool mountain breeze bearable. Birds chirped in the tree line, upset at a deer that meandered through the thin brush.

"Have you gotten all your stress out of your system?" Bo's smile challenged. "Or do you need to drink more tea?"

Jonah hadn't gotten to the reason for his visit, but there was the sun and the smooth lake and the tea, which was quality. So he sat and stewed and drank some more.

Bo finished his drink first. "Finally, I understand why you've been hanging around Emily. At first, I bought into the whole I-need-a-horseback-riding-tour-guide thing, even though it's so not like you. Partners? Teams?" He scoffed. "I'd have expected you to rent an old nag and plod out into the wild, get lost and write that into your script."

So much for Maury being the only one who knew Jonah's writing process.

"And then there's how Emily isn't exactly your type." Bo smiled like he had Emily on speed dial.

Jonah glowered.

The look didn't faze Bo. "You like women who are typically willowy and well connected. Beautiful with expensive tastes. Someone who'd make a good trophy wife." Bo held up a finger. "But not someone who thinks you're the man who'll take them to the altar."

Jonah's head began to pound. "Whatever your epiphany is, I wish you'd get to it." So he could get to the bottom of Bo's behavior.

"But last night, I figured it out." His cousin grinned. "Emily's exotic, like Aria."

"She's nothing like Aria." Except in her infatuation with Bo. Except that Bo now realized what a diamond in the rough Emily was.

"Oh." Bo let out a significant ho-ho-ho which was nothing like Santa's laughter. "She's brilliant. You can't listen to her for more than a minute and not realize she's the smartest person in the room."

"She's nothing like—"

"Aria is an artist. Her work is exquisite. Have you watched Emily ride?" Bo's grin fairly split his face. "She's an artist, too. You know back in the Merciless Mike Moody days, you'd have ridden in the stagecoach and she'd have been a Pony Express rider or the stagecoach driver."

Jonah disagreed. "She'd have ridden shotgun. She'd have put a bullet between Mike Moody's eyes."

Bo chuckled. "I like her."

Jonah made a sound like a bull about to

charge. He knew more than he wanted to know about bulls. "And yet—"

"She's a breath of fresh air," Bo continued. "I never know what she's going to say next."

"And she's already here, of course," Jonah said through gritted teeth. "In your new home." Unlike Aria.

"Emily adds color to the fabric of Second Chance, doesn't she?" Bo's grin was stupidly, insanely happy.

Why did I want him to date her?

Jonah couldn't remember. "Emily doesn't add color. Emily is *the* color." There had to have been something in the tea Bo gave him. It'd loosened the hold Jonah normally kept on his feelings. "She's the kind of woman who makes you forget you're not perfect. I mean, she points out your imperfections—" *with a sharp word and a sly grin* "—but she accepts them all the same." He cast Bo a sideways glance. "She has a lot to accept about you."

"She's gutsier than most," Bo said, not put off by Jonah's ribbing. "Willing to take a chance on faith alone."

"I'll let you have this one then," Jonah allowed, although it nearly killed him to say it. "You'll be happy with Emily."

And just like that, Bo's mood changed.

"You'll let me?" Bo howled. "Like I need your permission?"

"If you didn't need my permission, you would've married Aria by now." Jonah's words echoed across the lake. They echoed up the mountain. They echoed inside Jonah's empty chest.

"Finally, the elephant marches into the room." Bo didn't look happy that it had.

"You know I…" Jonah swallowed. Now was the time to tell Bo the truth about the script he'd written from their love triangle. "The longer you keep a secret, the harder it is to put into words."

"You didn't love her." Bo had his own opinions to impart. "I get it. We were vying for her affection and we shouldn't have been. I should have told you I was serious about her."

"Yes." Jonah raised his hands in a calming motion. "I would've stepped aside for you."

Bo nodded. "I'd do the same for you."

"Good thing you don't have to," Jonah murmured.

But he did.

CHAPTER EIGHTEEN

"ARE YOU SURE I can handle him?" There was doubt in Tina's voice. Still, the teen stood in front of Deadly and stroked him gently between the ears.

"He may look like a black beast the devil might ride, but he respects a rider with skill. And you have skill." Emily handed Tina the reins. "Go on. Take a few turns on him in the arena and then put him through the pattern. This is what you're going to face on Saturday—a few minutes to get accustomed to an unknown horse. And then you'll have to put him through the paces."

Tina led Kyle's horse through the arena gate, speaking softly. Deadly's ears pitched forward attentively. There was a spring to his step, a readiness that spoke of a pent-up energy needing to be released.

"Rodeo training going well?" Jonah appeared at Emily's side, looking very Jonah-like in city jeans and a bright red polo shirt. His sneakers had lived up to their name.

Emily hadn't heard him approach. "Or is this some type of punishment for your number one student?"

"We'll see in a minute." Emily climbed up to sit on the arena's top rail, hooking the heels of her boots on a lower rail. "Tina, don't forget to smile."

Jonah clambered up to join her. "A test. I love it."

The teen stopped in the middle of the ring. The sound of her voice reached Emily but the words were spoken so low that she couldn't distinguish them. Tina's hands moved across Deadly's long neck, around his chest, along the base of his mane and back. She was loving on him the way Kyle used to, the way no one had much time to do anymore.

Emily's heart ached.

"This isn't exactly what I expected," Jonah said.

Emily shushed him. Admittedly, she was a bit worried that Tina wouldn't be able to connect with the powerful gelding. But what if she could? What if Tina was the kind of stubborn that Deadly needed? It might give her the boost she could use to win the rodeo competition. More than a ride on the mellow Button.

Emily snuck a glance at Jonah, wishing she

had the courage to steal a kiss for luck from the complicated man.

If Tina can ride Deadly, it might give me the confidence I need to go for it with Jonah.

Emily gave in to impulse and covered Jonah's hand on the rail with her own, needing the reassurance of his touch, even if it was only her palm on the back of his hand. "No one but me and Bo have ridden him since my brother died. He's a bit of a wild hair."

"Now you're scaring me." He wasn't looking at Tina and the gelding. He stared at their hands.

"You should try smiling when you say that," Emily teased. "And toning down the sarcasm. You'll earn more points."

"I hadn't realized points were up for grabs," he murmured.

Tina kept talking to the gelding, kept touching him, feet firmly planted on the ground. Deadly pawed the dirt near her boots, but not like an angry mount ready to rebel. It was more a reminder that he was saddled and ready to ride.

Jonah noticed, too. "I thought you told me that horse would chew me up and spit me out on the trail. Did you get her father to sign a permission slip?"

"Deadly loves her." Emily squeezed Jonah's hand, consumed by guilt that she hadn't given her brother's horse the attention he deserved. "I hadn't realized… I didn't know…"

"That he was just a misunderstood cream puff waiting for the right female to come along?"

"Yeah." Emily looked at Jonah, more than aware of the metaphor. Jonah was prickly and didn't want to be tamed. And she was the unlikely female who might just be able to win his heart.

"Is this a one-day thing?" Jonah stared at their hands once more. "Are you going to loan her the horse for the competition? Or sell him to her?"

The conversation continued on two levels. "That is yet to be determined." Emily could only hope for happy endings on both fronts.

"Good morning." Bo appeared at the corner of the arena, looking sly when he noted their joined hands.

Jonah pulled back.

Bo gave her an unrepentant grin. "Emily, I brought back the drill press. Do you want to show me where to put it?"

"Put it back where you found it," Jonah growled.

"I'll show you in a second," Emily said. "I'm kind of busy right now."

Tina swung into Deadly's saddle.

For a moment, everyone seemed to hold their breath, even Tina and Deadly.

And then the black gelding tried to bolt.

Tina sat back and worked a gentle rein and heel, holding him in check. She kept talking to him in that low voice meant only for Deadly to hear.

The gelding shifted his weight and pawed the ground but obeyed her commands.

"What's she waiting for?" Jonah asked.

"He's spooked her." Bo leaned his arms on the rail next to Emily.

"She's doing a preflight check," Emily said, hoping it was true. "She's making sure she's where she wants to be before she lets him run through the routine."

Tina gave Deadly a bit of slack on the reins.

The gelding tried to run. Again, Tina held him back.

"I'm familiar with that routine." Bo had ridden Deadly a few times. "Sly dog."

But he wasn't too sly for the teenager. She turned him in a tight circle at a walk and then controlled him at a slow pace around the perimeter of the ring, talking the whole time.

"She has skills," Bo noted.

Emily's chest swelled with pride.

Halfway around the arena, Tina eased him into a trot.

Deadly tossed his head, testing her control of the reins, trying to angle the bit in his mouth to a point where Tina's signals would have no effect.

"Watch him." Emily shouldn't have worried.

"I'm okay. I used to have a pony like this." Tina reined him in, slowing him back to a walk as she turned him in a tight circle.

"I don't think Deadly would appreciate being compared to a pony," Jonah said with a soft chuckle, squeezing Emily's hand.

She hadn't realized he'd taken it.

"Clearly, you haven't known a lot of ponies." Emily drew a deep breath and released it, relieved because her protégé was smiling the way rodeo queens were supposed to—as if she didn't have a care in the world. "Ponies may be small, but they can be so stubborn if not properly or consistently trained."

"Much like people," Jonah murmured. "Can't always trust them to do the right thing."

Tina put Deadly into a trot. She had a good seat, moving with the horse instead of bouncing in the saddle. Halfway around the ring, she sent the gelding into a slow gallop. Deadly continued to ply his tricks. Head toss. Neck stretch. Trying to drop into a trot and trying to steer. His hindquarters swung sideways.

Tina kept talking to him, working the reins conservatively but with authority.

"She's good," Bo repeated.

"She is," Emily agreed. With a horse like Deadly, her horsemanship skills were on full display. "Put him through the pattern, Tina."

The teen shook her head. "He needs a little more shaking out."

"You can't always get a horse completely ready in a competition." Emily leaned forward. "He'll look crisper, even if he's misbehaving."

"He'll break the pattern." Tina was a careful horsewoman.

"Try him. You might be surprised."

"Look at that smile," Jonah marveled.

Once more, Em swelled with pride. Less than two weeks ago, Tina had been rushing into a competition with no experience. Today she'd looked like a veteran competitor.

Tina brought Deadly to the center ring and made him stand still. And then she began her pattern. Tight circles alternating with ever-increasing figure eights, moving at a controlled gallop, switching leads, pacing herself.

Deadly's ears swiveled forward and back.

He held his head high. He'd always been a horse that appreciated a challenge.

"They'd make a great contender if he didn't have that scar on his chest," Bo said.

"That scar makes him interesting." Jonah gestured toward the pair. "It makes you wonder how he can look so good and move so easily. It gives you a sense of awe."

"That's how you want the judges to see you," Em said. "That scar makes them memorable." More so than Tina on her beautiful, tame palomino.

"Was this your idea all along? To make her choose Deadly?" Jonah studied the look on Emily's face. "Of course it was. You are scary brilliant."

"That she is," Bo agreed, earning him a frown from Jonah.

"You know what? I can't visualize him and all his scars with glitter." Jonah put both hands on his thighs.

"He'll be the most handsome horse of the bunch." Emily was convinced it was true.

Tina brought Deadly to a stop in the center ring. She backed him up in a straight line and then walked him forward. She brought him to a stop again, but Deadly had other ideas. He reared up. Not high, but high enough that Tina had to shift her weight.

"That's a deal-breaker," Bo predicted.

"I don't know." Emily admired how the teen had controlled the big black horse. "She smiled through the entire ride, as if she enjoyed the challenge as much as he enjoyed giving it to her."

Tina patted Deadly's neck and trotted him over to her audience. "He's a handful. I had to stay on my toes."

"You did a great job." Emily hopped down to the ground and took hold of Deadly's reins. "You did a good job, too, you big stinker." Deadly shoved Emily's shoulder with his nose. "How did that feel, Tina?"

Tina dismounted, glowing. "It was fun."

Em kept on stroking Deadly's neck, not looking at her student. "I think you should ride him in the general competition instead of Button. I think you should dress all in black and play off the fact that you are a proverbial dark horse. After all, he's the dark horse who cheated death."

"I don't know." Tina didn't immediately reject the idea. "Everyone would—"

"Look at you," Em said firmly. "They'd notice you and admire your skill. They'd remember you, too, for not just applying a coat of Worship Me lipstick and expecting to win."

"Touché," Jonah said from behind them.

"What would my dad say?" Tina's brow furrowed. "And my mom…"

"It's your choice." But Em tried to seal the deal. "If you want to win and you aren't a conventional beauty, you have to think out of the box. Embrace your uniqueness—who you truly are."

"Maybe she doesn't want to win badly enough," Jonah added fuel to Emily's motivational fire.

The teen stuck out her chin. "I want to prove everyone wrong."

Me, too.

Emily turned, smiling at Jonah.

"HEY, I'M THINKING about taking a hike up to Merciless Mike's hideout today," Jonah said to Emily when Bo and Tina had left.

They stood in the barn's breezeway, close enough to share secrets, far enough apart to avoid kisses.

"A hike?" Em looked incredulous. "You hike?"

"Walking helps me think." And Jonah desperately wanted to tie up loose ends in his head. Not just about Mike Moody, which had been percolating for days, but about Emily. Did he want to tell Bo to back off where Em was concerned? Was that fair to his rodeo queen?

"It'll take you at least an hour to get up there." Emily's gaze dropped to his running shoes. "And an hour to get back. If you leave now, that allows you time to ponder Moody Mike and get home before the sun starts setting."

"Moody Mike?" Jonah quirked his brows. "Not Letty?"

She shrugged and gave him a half smile. "I'd take you up there myself, but I've got to pick up groceries and clean out the chicken coop, not to mention call Tina's dad about the change in horse and wardrobe plans. Why don't you take the ATV down to the gate and up the fire road?"

"I can hike through the woods," Jonah insisted, feeling like his man-card was being challenged.

"I can't guarantee you won't run into feral stock." Emily frowned. "It can be dangerous on foot."

"I'll be fine." But Jonah thought about Emily's brother, the scar Deadly bore, and remembered the sound of crunching metal when the big bull had rammed Shane's Hummer. He revised his statement. "I'll be careful."

Emily came closer, almost as if she was

going to hug him. Instead, she touched his arm softly as she passed. "See you soon."

Jonah returned to the bunkhouse, where he'd used his portable printer earlier to print out both romance scripts for polishing, even though the rom-com script had no ending. Editing was relaxing. Improving his work made him feel better about himself. And right now, that was what he needed—a better self-image.

He'd been tense the past few days. Out of sorts. Restless. Emily's kisses hadn't helped, even though he wouldn't mind kissing her again to figure out why.

He put an apple, a protein bar and a couple bottles of water in his backpack and was about to leave when Maury texted him.

Two offers on those scripts, you lucky man. More later. No stink on you.

Maury was wrong. There would be stink if he made those deals. It wouldn't be clinging to his career. But it would solidify and repel Bo and Emily, two people he cared about. Two people he didn't want to push away.

Jonah stood, staring at Maury's text message, knowing he should respond right away, knowing he had to tell his agent the projects weren't really for sale. He'd give him an excuse—they weren't ready, more work was needed, I don't want to be a romance guy. He'd risk the professional stink a gap in sold projects implied.

Sometimes a man has to draw the line. Grandpa Harlan's words. But he'd been right.

The only way to career success that gave Jonah the status he wanted was to write the story of Mike and Letty Moody.

JONAH REACHED MIKE MOODY's hideout and sat on a boulder near the entrance.

It'd been a long walk, a consistent climb. With each step and each breath of crisp mountain air, Jonah had felt his head clear. Doubts. Indecision. Cowgirls. Conflicted feelings. They all drifted away.

This ridge had been used for a hundred years or more as a place to look east and west, sunrise and sunset, forward and back.

He took out his phone and reviewed his notes on Mike and Letty.

Born in Philadelphia, the siblings traveled in a wagon train until they'd been left behind somewhere south of Second Chance, accused of theft. They'd spent a year in Second Chance before the robberies began. Letty was courted by Old Jeb Clark, Emily's ancestor.

The Moodys turned to a life of theft and murder, and when they tried to rob Jeb, he'd fired back, possibly killing Letty. After that, Mike was still a greedy thief, but not such a murderous blackheart.

Had the loss of his sister reformed him? Jonah didn't think so.

He washed a hand over his face, certain he was missing something.

There was nothing remarkable about Mike, other than him hiding the gold up here.

There was nothing remarkable about Jeb, other than he'd been sweet on Letty.

There was nothing remarkable about Letty…

Oh, there was a lot remarkable about Letty. There was the theft from the wagon train—a silver teaspoon, a gilded hair comb, a music box. Those weren't items someone could sell for a lot of money. Those were things a woman coveted.

There was Mike's accomplice. A short, slight man who didn't speak but stayed far back in the woods. Oh, that had to be Letty. And then Jeb had come across the siblings as they waited for a stage to pass through. He'd fired into the woods at the most dangerous figure of the despicable pair. He'd fired at Letty. He'd been distraught when people from town had found him.

There was a reason Jonah had been unable to put the pieces together. Mike wasn't merciless. Letty was.

Scenes came to him—too fast to keep track of. Jonah couldn't type fast enough into his phone. But he didn't want to lose the story thread. He didn't want to lose anything.

There's no stink on me.

CHAPTER NINETEEN

EXTERIOR. A WAGON TRAIN DISAP-
PEARING IN THE DISTANCE. Mike
and Letty headed the other way in a
wagon. Mike is wearing thick glasses.

MIKE: You shouldn't have taken Mrs.
Granville's music box.

LETTY: Or Miss Hilliard's hair comb.

MIKE (softening): Or Miss Jenkin's silver spoon.

Their expressions lighten and they begin
to laugh.

EXTERIOR. SECOND CHANCE MAIN
STREET. Mike and Letty driving the
wagon through town as a snowstorm
blows in. They stare at the Mercantile
and Trading Post with interest.

MIKE: They sell gentlemen's clothes in there.

LETTY (smiling coyly at the black-smith): Your eyesight's growing weak, Mike. How much longer do you think you can support us selling suits? And who in the frontier will buy them? We need a stake and another wagon train if we want to get to San Francisco.

INTERIOR. THE SMITHY DURING A SNOWSTORM. Letty flirting with Jeb, who is busy making her a new frying pan.

JEB: I know I don't have much, Letty, but—

LETTY: I don't need nice things. (She laughs.) Except maybe a bigger frying pan now that I'm cooking for you and my brother. I'm afraid he's going blind.

JEB: I can take care of you, Letty. Both of you.

LETTY: I'm not the kind of woman who makes a good wife.

EXTERIOR. THE STAGE ROAD NORTH OF TOWN. A TREE HAS FALLEN ACROSS THE ROAD. Letty and Mike are both wearing fancy suits. At the sound of a stage approaching, they both pull flour sacks with eyeholes over their heads. Letty moves deeper into the trees and raises her shotgun.

LETTY: Stare at whoever's speaking. They won't know you can barely see.

Letty cocks her shotgun. Mike steps onto the road behind the tree, raises his arm and draws the hammer back on his six-shooter as the stage rounds the bend.

MIKE: This is a holdup. Throw down the cash box and everyone lives.

The guard begins to raise his rifle, but Letty shoots him first. He falls, dead before he hits the ground.

DRIVER: Who are you?

MIKE: The Merciless gang. Now throw down the cash box and no one else dies.

INTERIOR. THE DOCTOR'S OFFICE IN SECOND CHANCE. Mike's eyes are being examined.

DOCTOR: His vision is failing, miss. In a year, maybe two, he'll be completely blind.

Mike closes his eyes, visibly shaken. Letty presses her lips together, angry that with all their loot they can't buy back Mike's vision. She knows she can't pull off the robberies alone.
    The mayor enters, visibly shaken. Letty covers the stolen ring on her hand.

MAYOR: The Merciless gang struck again. Took the stage on the south road. I've sent for the sheriff. He'll be searching the home of every able-bodied man in the territory.

The mayor pats Mike's arm.

MAYOR: Not your home, Mike.

INTERIOR. THE SMITHY. Letty and Jeb are in the midst of an argument, whispering as Mike dozes on Jeb's cot in the corner.

LETTY: What do you want me to do? Our crop was ruined by that spring snowstorm. We're behind on payments. We're going to lose everything.

JEB: I said I'd marry you, Letty. I didn't say I'd steal for you. After all those robberies—the ones you say Mike did—they're going to hang him, blind or not. I'm going to turn him in the next time the sheriff comes to town.

LETTY: You do and I'll swear on a stack of Bibles you're one of the gang. No one will believe a blind man could pull off all those robberies.

JEB (looking speculatively at Mike): All those murders…

LETTY (milking Jeb's fondness for her): No more talk of blood and mayhem. Kiss me, Jeb. Kiss me like today's our wedding day.

EXTERIOR. THE STAGE ROAD NORTH

OF TOWN IN THE DEEPENING DUSK.
Jeb is riding his horse, scanning the dim
woods as he looks for Letty, hoping to
stop her from doing something stupid
with her brother's gang. Mike steps out
in front of him, wearing the flour sack
over his head and pointing a six-shooter
at Jeb.

MIKE: Throw down your coin, friend,
and I'll let you pass.

JEB (whispering): Mister…Merciless?

MIKE (chest puffed out with pride): One
and the same. Throw it down, friend.

Jeb looks into the trees as he reaches for
his newly purchased pistol.

LETTY (in a deep voice): Don't reach
for that gun, friend.

JEB (a determined set to his chin): You'll
be moving to another territory and leaving Miss Letty behind.

Mike seems taken aback. The "man" in
the woods stands. Jeb's attention is on

the shooter, the man he assumes is the real threat since he knows Mike is practically blind.

JEB: You'll be moving on...

Jeb draws his pistol and fires at the figure in the woods. A scream pierces the air.

MIKE (uncertain): Letty?

JEB (pale, leaps off his horse and runs to her side): Letty? Holy heavens! Letty?

Jeb reaches the fallen figure dressed in a man's suit. He pulls off the flour sack and cradles Letty in his arms as blood soaks her abdomen.

MIKE (kneeling next to them): Letty?

JEB (rocking Letty, crying): I'm sorry. I'm sorry.

The sound of an approaching wagon. Jeb raises his head, processing his options. He gently transfers Letty into her brother's arms, face strained with regret.

JEB: I'll tell them we struggled. I'll tell them I fought you. But you have to take her to safety.

MIKE (blinking eyes that can barely see): Where?

Jeb runs to his horse, brings her back to Mike.

JEB: There's a cave near Lookout Ridge. My horse knows the way. Take Letty there. I'll bring supplies later. Just keep her alive.

The sounds of the wagon grow louder, as does the sound of Letty's labored breathing.

JEB (stumbling to the road, staring at the blood on his hands): Go!

He waves down the wagon, prepared to feed them a story to save his darling Letty.

EXTERIOR. LOOKOUT RIDGE. Jeb digging a grave while Mike sits nearby, crying.

EXTERIOR. THE STAGE ROAD NORTH OF TOWN. Mike ties up Jeb's horse in the woods, pulls a flour sack over his head and steps out in front of the approaching stage to a chorus of shouts and screams. He shoots indiscriminately. The guard falls off as the driver pulls the stage to a halt.

MIKE: You remember to tell the sheriff that man's name. Wouldn't want it left off my wanted poster. Now throw down your cash box and move along.

The driver does as instructed, taking off almost before the cash box lands in the dirt. Mike waits until the stage is gone and then scrambles to the place he heard the box drop, shoots off the lock and grabs the sack of gold. The sound of a posse's thundering hooves fills the air. Mike stumbles into the woods and climbs on Jeb's horse. They race off, but instead of his mountain hideout, the horse runs back to the smithy, losing a shoe in the race.

INTERIOR. SMITHY. Jeb closes the doors to hide the fact that Mike is there.

MIKE: Stupid horse. Stupid lame horse. Jeb! You've got to hide me.

JEB: No. Your past is catching up to you.

Letty's music box is on a shelf. Jeb opens it up, filling the smithy with a bitter-sweet song—"You Are My Sunshine." The shouts of the posse reach them. Mike moves closer to Jeb and tosses the bag of gold to the blacksmith's feet.

MIKE: My sister would want you to save me. You know she'd want you to save me.

JEB (face contorted in grief and indecision): If you can make it to the cave, I'll bring you supplies tomorrow. But only if you leave town. Promise me.

MIKE (incredulous): I promise but the posse is here in town. They'll shoot me before I get across the road.

JEB: I'll slow them down. Go. Out the back.

Mike stumbles out to the old nag and climbs into the saddle. Jeb hides the bag of gold and picks up a hunting knife. He opens the door to the smithy that faces Main Street.

JEB: For you, my love. May this make up for all our wrongs.

He stabs himself in the side, being careful to miss anything vital.

JEB (stumbling forward): Help! Help!

The posse descends upon the smithy, guns drawn.

SHERIFF: Who was it? Who stabbed you?

JEB (sinking to the ground): Mike. Merciless Mike Moody.

EXTERIOR. MOUNTAINS. A rumbling rockslide kills Mike.

EXTERIOR. LOOKOUT RIDGE. Weeks have passed, Jeb places a headstone on Letty's grave.

Later still, Jeb and the schoolmarm climb atop the buckboard amid well-wishers congratulating them on their nuptials.

INTERIOR. MIKE'S HIDEOUT. Jeb painstakingly digs a hole in the rock wall inside the cave and hides the box of gold, keeping only one coin for himself. He sets off dynamite to cover the cave entrance with rock, sealing it from ever being found.

INTERIOR. THE BUCKING BULL RANCH'S FARMHOUSE. Jeb on his deathbed. His adult son is at his side. On a dresser, the music box plays.

JEB: That's why I buried your mother up there. It's where I want to be buried, too.

He presses a gold coin into his son's hand. His son stares at it in amazement.

JEB (drawing his last breath): In case you think I'm an old fool making up stories.

SON: Dad, is there more where this came from? Do you know where Mike Moody buried it? Dad?

CHAPTER TWENTY

"BEST FIRST DRAFT EVER." Jonah drank the last of his water and shouldered his backpack.

Yes, he'd taken some liberties with the timeline and Mike's blindness, but when a story worked, it worked.

With lighter steps than he'd had in days, Jonah headed back down the fire road, whistling as he took long strides. He rounded a bend and came face-to-face with a bull, the feral kind with long pointy horns and a distrust of people.

Especially Hollywood scriptwriters wearing red shirts.

The bull pawed the ground and snorted.

"Hey!" Jonah held up a hand. "Back away."

The bull snorted again.

Jonah side-stepped, heading for a tree with a thick trunk. Its branches were too high to climb, but it would provide some form of shelter. "Hey!" he shouted again when the bull took a step in his direction. "Get out of here!"

The bull seemed to reconsider his charge.

He turned around and trotted down the fire road in the direction Jonah wanted to go. No way was he following on the heels of that beast.

Franny had taken the Monroe men on a trail through the woods once. If he could find it, he could follow it down to the Bucking Bull's pastures.

EMILY PUT AWAY Razzy late in the afternoon.

The ranch was quiet without the boys or Franny around. They'd gone into Ketchum for dentist appointments. There was no Adam hopping about begging for sweets. No Jonah jabbering about Mike Moody.

Which was odd—Jonah not being around. If he wasn't writing, Jonah came to greet her at the barn when she returned. It'd been six hours since he talked about hiking up to Merciless Mike's hideout. He should've been back by now.

Emily knocked on the door to the bunkhouse, but there was no answer. A niggle of concern chilled the back of her neck.

She went inside the farmhouse and checked in with her grandmother.

Gertie was knitting in a chair by the front window where she could see all the ranch comings and goings, if there had been any.

She closed the music box when Emily came in. "I made cookies."

"Have you seen Jonah?" Was he napping or showering after his hike?

"Haven't seen him since he left after lunch."

The second niggle of apprehension ran down Emily's spine. She tried calling him on her cell phone. He answered, but all she heard was a garbled "I'm..." And then the line went dead. Two additional tries resulted in calls not going through.

The last person to go up the mountain and not return as planned had been Kyle. A sense of urgency had Emily racing for the door. "I think he's up on the mountain somewhere. I'm going out to find him."

"Take water and a med kit." Granny Gertie was nothing if not sensible. "And be safe."

Assuring her she would be careful, Emily returned to the barn, saddling Razzy and Deadly. "He's probably sitting up at the cemetery trying to intuit why Letty was a killer," she told Razzy. "This'll probably be a short ride."

"Hey." Bo entered the barn. "Have you seen Jonah? I need to tell him something."

"No. I think..." Em choked up. "I think

he's missing." She never should've let him go off alone.

"Did you check his room?" Gertie called from the front porch. "I could've missed him return while I was making cookies."

"He didn't answer before," Em said.

"He could've had his headphones on while he was writing." Bo led the way back to the bunkhouse.

If that had been the case, he'd have come out after the dropped call. Regardless, Emily knocked again, louder this time. When no one answered, they went inside.

Jonah kept the interior as neat as he kept his appearance. There was no pile of dirty clothes in a corner. No scattering of toiletries in the small bathroom. Everything was stowed in his travel bag. His laptop sat closed on the kitchen table, plugged into a power strip. He had one of those slim printers there, too. And beside it were two stacks of papers. His script, she assumed.

Emily glanced at the first page.

The City Slicker and the Rodeo Queen.

"What the…" She scanned the page, and then the next one. "He wrote about me. About us." Mostly about her. Emily had to put a hand on the counter to hold herself up. "This is…personal."

Bo picked up the other script.

Em was too upset to check what Jonah's cousin held. *The City Slicker and the Rodeo Queen* wasn't a script about Merciless Mike Moody and his sister Letty. It was a script about Emily and her quest to find a cowboy husband, aided by a clever matchmaker from Los Angeles.

"All this time…" All this time she'd thought he was writing a Western. And instead, he'd been writing about her. She flipped to the end, having the foolish notion that maybe he'd have written them together on the last page. But no. His pages ended with Emily putting on a dress and hot pink cowboy boots and bringing Bo lemonade. "Unbelievable." She dropped the manuscript on the table. "I feel so…exposed."

He held my hand. He kissed me.

It was one thing to hear Jonah talk about writing things that happened in his life and another to be the topic of his work.

Without my permission!

She'd thought he cherished her. If she didn't move… If she didn't do something, she was going to be sick.

"Do you know what this is?" Bo's voice was cold and hard. He held up the other script.

"No. And I don't care." She stomped out

of the bunkhouse, intending to put the horses back in their stalls and let the man rot on the mountain.

"It's a script," Bo said, still using that cold, hard voice as he followed her. "A story about Jonah, Aria and me. A flippin' romance. And he keeps insisting he doesn't want to write those anymore."

Technically, Bo's story had been a tragedy. Emily stopped, turned, wished this wasn't happening. "He wrote one about me and you, too."

Bo swore, pacing in a tight circle. "He always does this. He takes what happens around him and writes it into a script. Our childhood antics were immortalized in that sitcom he worked on. We were far enough removed from the events that it seemed amusing. But this…" His mouth set in a grim line.

"Was he in there?" Gertie called, sitting in a rocker on the front porch.

"No," Emily snapped. She wished he had been. She couldn't wait to lay into him.

The nerve! The gall! The shame of it all.

"You look like he was in there." Gertie stopped rocking. "You look like you found him in a compromising position with another woman."

"He's not here!" Emily shouted. "He's out

somewhere. If I'm lucky, he'll have been eaten by a bear or…" She'd been about to say trampled by a wild bull, but that was too cruel a wish, even to wish upon someone as shallow and uncaring as Jonah.

"I recognize that look on your face." Granny got to her feet, using her cane for leverage. "You're considering something foolish."

Emily stopped at the barn door, torn between rescuing Jonah, only so that she could give him what for, or letting him try to save himself.

"We Clarks always do the honorable thing," Gertie reminded her.

For once, mired as she was in anger and hurt, Emily didn't want to be a Clark. She wanted to be selfish and spiteful. She wanted to rail and belittle. That wasn't the Clark way. It wasn't the way of a rodeo queen, either. But that didn't change the fact that there was a growing pit of bitterness seething in her belly.

"I…" She couldn't tell Gertie she'd fallen in love with a manipulative con man. It was too painful to admit.

"He doesn't deserve a rescue," Bo said in a voice that matched Emily's. "But we're going to do it because we're better than he is."

Em nodded, heading to the tack room. "We're going to need another horse."

JONAH WAS LOST.

One tree was looking like another.

And it wasn't like he could open an Uber app and request a ride back to the ranch.

He'd just keep going downhill until he hit the highway and then he'd figure out where he was.

"Jonah!"

He'd finished his water an hour ago. He was parched and probably imagining things.

"Jonah!"

He stopped thrashing through the underbrush and listened.

"Jonah!" Emily was visible, riding Deadly on the slope above him. And behind her was Bo, riding Franny's horse, Danger.

"Over here!" Jonah waved his arms. He thrashed his way onto the narrow track she was using, stopping in a clearing wide enough for all three horses. "I ran into your future Buttercup and let him have the right of way on the fire road. I thought I knew the way back but—"

"You thought you were lost and about to die in the woods." There was no relief on Emily's expression or in her words, only pain and anger. "I can see it on your face."

"That would be the big yellow streak he tries to keep hidden." Bo was just as angry as Emily.

"I'm sorry you had to take time out of your day to find me. My cell is one big dropped call." Jonah was certain they'd been worried when he hadn't returned to the ranch on time. He stared up at Emily, at brown eyes ringed with red rather than worry, at the firm set of her mouth. And then he studied his cousin's face, the slash of lips, the bunching of biceps. He smiled, trying to defuse the tension. "I appreciate you coming to my rescue. Although I'd have made it to the highway. Eventually."

Neither one of them took his words and made a joke out of it.

Jonah's smile fell. "Has something happened? Is everyone okay at the ranch or...?" He glanced at Bo, looking for bad news about the Monroe family.

Bo stared at Jonah as if he could see right through him, as if there was nothing inside Jonah he wanted to see.

"Get on." Emily handed Razzy's reins to Jonah.

Everyone was all right, then. "Did I leave

the teakettle on?" Had he burned down the bunkhouse?

My laptop.

He refused to panic. He'd written the draft of the script on his phone and his other work wouldn't see the light of day. He waited to hear what had happened. And then waited a bit more. The birds in the trees had more to say than Bo and Emily.

"Where am I?" Jonah gave Razzy a friendly pat on the neck by way of greeting. "Besides in trouble with you two."

Neither one of them denied it. But neither one of them explained, either.

Jonah slid his arms through the backpack straps and then climbed into Razzy's saddle. Now that he was safe, the triumphant feeling he'd found on Lookout Ridge returned. "The good news—besides being found before nightfall—is that I've solved the plot of the Mike Moody story."

The three horses stood close in the clearing, but Bo had his force field fully charged and in place while Emily looked ready to launch a nuclear initiative at Jonah. He had to be patient and wait for them to unleash.

Bo spoke first. "You decided to stop torturing the living with your interpretation of their lives and focus on the dead? Why? Are those scripts back at the bunkhouse going to be shredded?"

Jonah's heart dropped down to his toes. They'd found his work.

"You wrote about me?" Emily pulled her hat brim low. "Me. Not Mike Moody. You made my dream of love into some huge joke. Why would you do that?"

"I didn't mean to." That was the truth. It hadn't been part of his career plan.

Emily trembled. "You wrote pages and pages. You wrote a beginning, a middle and almost an end." She jabbed her finger in the air between them. "Nobody writes that much without meaning to."

"Agreed," Bo said sharply.

"Let me explain." Jonah fought the rising panic, the rising sense of guilt, the rising sense that there would be no forgiveness for this. "I write. It's part of me. And the story of Mike Moody has been hard for me to crack. There were days when I wrote only one line." One line of Emily-inspired dialogue or a flat location descriptor. "I needed something to write to feel better inside, to rebuild my confidence. I didn't mean…"

Jonah stopped. The bottom of the proverbial hole he was digging collapsed. Dizzy,

Jonah gripped the saddle horn and sucked in air.

He couldn't lie, not to these two. He couldn't say, "I didn't mean to write scripts and sell them." Because even though he hadn't, when the opportunity arose, he'd put them out there, testing the market.

"You didn't mean to write about me?" Emily was seething with anger, sitting stiffly atop her brother's scary horse as if at any moment she'd cue him to rear up and frighten Jonah into racing away. "I don't believe you. There was a title page, Jonah. *A title page.* I'm such an idiot. I thought you cared for me and I..." Her jaw worked. "It's time to get you back home." She rode past him.

Jonah turned to Bo.

His cousin scowled at him. "Of all the stupid things you've done in the course of your life, writing these two scripts has got to be the dumbest, most insensitive ever."

"Yes." What else could Jonah say?

"What excuse do you have?" Bo leaned forward in the saddle and Jonah got the impression that if he was within striking distance, Bo would've punched him. "What could you possibly say that would make me understand? You printed them out, Jonah. You printed both scripts. I know what that means."

"Clearly, I need sensitivity training." Jonah tried to joke, knowing full well it was inappropriate to jest. "Maybe Shane can refer me to the place he attends when he's in Vegas."

"It's too soon for jokes." Bo's voice shook with emotion. "It may always be too soon for jokes."

"All right. Okay. I… That script started out innocently, too." Jonah hated that he'd hurt their feelings. "The irony of our situation last year wasn't lost on me. And I've always understood situations better if I put them on paper."

Bo nodded slowly. He knew that, too.

"But this Mike Moody script is going to be fantastic. And it's not based on anyone I know." The words burst out of him. It was such a relief. Shane would be ecstatic. The town festival would have their reenactment.

"I'm not interested in your stretch project." Bo's jaw worked. "I love Aria. I don't care that she's pregnant with another man's baby. I love her and I'm leaving tomorrow to make sure she knows it."

"Good," Jonah said woodenly. "You and I…" Jonah swallowed. "We've always been close. But there's also been this competitiveness, too. And then Aria came along and she… She looked at me. She looked at me the same way women have always looked at you." He was drifting into sappy territory. "And I thought, wow, *I* can be with *her*."

"You could have. You *were*." Bo's defensiveness turned to attack mode. He leaned forward in his saddle, eyes blazing.

"And when I realized I was with her for all the wrong reasons, I retreated," Jonah said emphatically. "I wanted her to know that you were the better man." Because he'd thought back then that she'd been perfect for Bo in a way no other woman had ever been.

"You used all your wily tricks learned from writing scripts with unexpected endings. You manipulated a woman you...loved."

"Yes." Jonah drew in a breath, hoping the oxygen would fuel his brain so that he'd choose the right words. He may have lost Emily, but there was still a chance for Bo, who remained by his side. "I'm sorry. That script won't go anywhere. I promise you."

"It's a little late for apologies," Bo said gruffly.

"But it's not too late for you and Aria," Jonah said softly.

Bo nodded stiffly and rode past him.

Jonah followed his cousin down the hill, letting Razzy choose his own pace, which was slower than that of the two big black horses. Jonah knew he still had many apologies and explanations to make. Emily would be waiting for him at the barn. She'd want to make sure Razzy was safely put away.

But it was a long ride back to the ranch.

"I DON'T WANT to talk about it." Emily was brushing Deadly when Jonah finally entered the barn leading Razzy.

Bo was nowhere to be found. He must have told Emily he was leaving. Jonah hoped he'd let her down gently.

"I'm sorry, Em. About so much."

"It was hurtful. You…" Emily turned, her eyes filled with tears. "You're hurtful. I should've seen it before, but I thought you were clever and cranky. I didn't imagine that you used people—real people—to steal their lives—their words—for profit."

"I didn't write that script to make money."

"But you haven't said you won't sell it now that it's done, have you?" Everything about her hardened—her expression, her words, her stance.

"That's not my plan." Why was every word he spoke coming out wrong? "What I mean is—"

"So you'd sell it." She blinked rapidly but didn't look away. "You'd sell *me* for the right price."

"No." He moved closer. "I'm honing my craft. Those scripts prove to people—important people—that I can write more than teenage stories."

"You showed them to people?" Her voice cracked as she backed away from him, her face pale. "You didn't even change our names!" She cast her gaze about, expression wavering from near tears to near disgust. "The only name you changed was yours... *Joe*. This is too much, Jonah. You have to know... My heart is broken."

"I know you're upset with me." Jonah came forward and tried to take her hands. "Neither script will see the light of day again. I promise."

"You promise?" Emily made a guttural sound, jerking her hands free. "What good is your word when you only speak in half-truths?" She took a step back. And then another. "My heart is broken. It's torn in two because I fell in love with a Monroe and then he betrayed me." Her eyes seemed luminous and her words...

Her words took a moment to sink in.

"You can't mean..." Jonah's breath caught in his throat. She loved him? "You couldn't have..."

"The last thing you have a right to do is to tell me what to feel or who to love." She darted past him. "Leave the horses. I hear

Franny's truck coming up the drive. I'll have Davey put them away."

Jonah stood in the barn, stunned.

Emily loves me.

On paper, they were worse for each other than he and Aria had been.

On paper, but not in his heart. The last act of Emily's script had always felt wrong, putting her with Bo. It'd felt forced. As if she shouldn't end up with her cowboy. And now he knew why.

I love Emily.

But since writing that awful script about falling into a creek and exposing everyone's weaknesses, he'd never let himself write his own happy ending.

But I love Emily.

And that love… It put a kink in his plans. He didn't belong here. He couldn't achieve his dreams in Second Chance.

I love Emily.

But the pieces of their lives didn't fit together. He couldn't weave them into a plot with a satisfying ending.

He may have solved the riddle of the Merciless Moody gang, but he was stumped by his love for Emily Clark, rodeo queen.

CHAPTER TWENTY-ONE

"I'M GOING TO head down to the Spring Rodeo for a few days." Sitting at the dining room table, Emily picked at her stew. Funny thing about tears. They stole your appetite.

She sniffed, doing her best not to think about the sharp stab of betrayal. The shocked look in Jonah's blue eyes when he realized she loved him.

Loved him. Past tense.

Listen up, eggs.

"You should be fine," Em continued, hardening her heart to thoughts of a smart redheaded man with a broken moral compass, "now that Zeke is back. Besides, Tina needs the moral support."

Franny stopped putting more peas on Adam's plate.

"We'll miss you, Aunty Em." Adam picked up peas with his fingers.

"Can I go?" Davey perked up. "I'm done with my schoolwork for the week."

Charlie grumbled. He was never done early with his schoolwork.

"It's kind of sudden. This trip." Gertie stared at Emily just as intently as Franny was. "Does this have anything to do—"

"I'm going to watch Tina compete. I'm loaning her Deadly." Emily set her fork down and met Franny's gaze. "If that's okay."

"He's more your horse now," Franny said carefully, drawing a deep breath.

"You're letting a girl ride Deadly in a rodeo?" Davey's jaw dropped. He stared at his mother. "You won't even let me ride him on the trail and he was Dad's horse."

"He's a lot of horse, Davey," Emily said as kindly as she could. "And I'm just loaning him to Tina. She rides him well. She'll win on him."

Davey stabbed a chunk of meat.

"I'll leave early in the morning." Before Jonah got out of bed. Emily gathered her dinner dishes, wanting to retreat to her room in case Jonah came around looking for her.

"Are you starting a fire outside tonight?" Granny Gertie hadn't stopped looking at Em since her announcement. "It's a beautiful, clear night."

"Not tonight." Emily busied herself with the dishes, helping as best she could to set the kitchen to rights. And then she realized there was a finality to what she was doing. Everything in its place. Everything clean and bright. Everything done so Franny wouldn't need to stress.

Franny wasn't going to stress. She had Shane to lean on.

Emily left the kitchen and hurried to her room before another round of tears fell.

She found a small duffel bag and started loading it with clothes.

A short while later, Franny knocked on her door, opening it without waiting for permission. One look at Emily's tear-stained face and she was at her side, wrapping her arms around her. "What is it? What's wrong? Is it Jonah or Bo?"

Emily told Franny about the dreadful script. "I'm not even sure it's dreadful. I was too shocked to know one way or the other once I saw my name on there and my words…" Lifted from real life.

"I'll have Shane sue him or something." Franny's words were as angry in tone as Emily's had been when she'd found Jonah aimlessly thrashing about the woods. Jonah was clueless about more than just another person's feelings. "We're not going to let him make a movie out of your life."

"I just…" Emily's breath hitched. "I just wish I hadn't trusted him." Or liked him. Or fallen in love with him. "I'm going to look for a job while I'm away." There'd be plenty of ranchers at the rodeo, plus the stock contractor.

"Don't rush into a decision you might regret later." Franny squeezed her tight.

"You mean like falling in love with a man over the course of a few weeks?" Emily blew her nose. "I never should have complained about a drought of eligible men in Second Chance."

"You're taking a little of my heart with you." Franny sighed. "But I understand. And Kyle would want you to be happy, whatever you decide to do."

"It's time, Franny. It's past time." Emily stood, folded a pair of jeans and tucked them into her duffel.

Franny got to her feet and wrapped her arms around her once more. "We'll be here for you. Always."

"I'll give you this." Shane threw Jonah's manuscripts on the fire at the lake camp. The pages shriveled and sent flames soaring before dying out to insubstantial ash. "You have a talent for writing a good romance."

"Thanks." Shane's praise for the script based on Emily was little consolation to Jonah. He was still stunned to recognize he'd fallen in love with her. And his talent with story wasn't going to undo the way he'd hurt her.

In fact, it was highly unlikely that Emily would ever talk to him again. Bo had left, apparently unwilling to hang around until tomorrow morning to talk. It might be another eight months before Jonah was able to heal the rift between them.

"You've got talent," Shane said. "That's why it's hard to understand your tendency for self-destructing romantic relationships." He stared up at the stars.

"It's not my fault." At Shane's pointed glance, Jonah admitted, "It's completely my fault." If he'd been more self-aware of his feelings instead of self-absorbed in his quest to change the course of his career… "Unlike Emily, I never dreamed of falling in love. I'm lousy at relationships. I made a mistake prioritizing my life." It should be Emily, Monroes, career. He knew that now. "You, of all people, Shane, can understand the pressure to earn a father's approval."

Shane nodded. "All the responsibility my father gave me was given with a challenge. I never knew if he'd be unhappy with me from one day to the next. Looking back now, I'm relieved to have found my own path, separate from Monroe Industries."

"That's exactly what I was trying to do." Jonah placed a log over the remains of his script and settled back onto his chair. "Make a name for myself separate from Monroe Studios."

Shane tsked. "The least you could have done was change the names to protect the innocent and avoid liability." He poked the fire with a tree branch. "Franny asked me if Emily could sue."

"That script is going nowhere." Jonah gestured to the fire.

"I reassured Franny the script wouldn't be sold. And as long as you don't sell it, Emily has no case against you."

"The scripts are dead to me." And to Maury, much to his agent's chagrin. "It's okay. I've worked out the hard parts of the Merciless Moody story line. I've even got an idea on how to condense it so you can put on a show at your festival." At least one part of his life was falling into place. But what did it matter without Emily in his life?

"Listen." Shane leaned forward. "Franny and Emily don't want anything more to do with you. You have to move out of the bunk-house."

The air left Jonah's lungs in a rush.

"I can't do that. I..." Jonah swallowed and let the words come out in a rush. "I love Emily. And I can't just walk away without trying to win her back."

Shane tsked. "Unfortunate word choice—win—given you and Bo were competitive over Aria and then Emily."

Shane was right. Jonah had backed himself into a corner where every ill-chosen word was a land mine.

"Emily's leaving for the rodeo tomorrow," Shane went on brusquely. "She'll be back in a few days."

"That's all I need," Jonah reassured him. "Just a few days to figure out how to apologize and convince her that I'll never hurt her like that again."

"My advice is to grovel, long and lovingly." Shane stood, digging in his jacket pocket for his keys. "It's what I did to convince Franny to marry me."

"Grovel. Right." Jonah might have put too much sarcasm into his words, because Shane frowned at him.

"If you love Emily the way I think you do,

you won't be so glib when your opportunity arrives."

Which was a grim observation given Jonah was cynical to his core. With good intentions, Jonah cleared his throat and tried again. "I'll grovel. Seriously." Because seriously, he loved Emily.

"Better." Shane walked away, leaving Jonah, the fire and an ash heap of regrets.

THERE WAS NOTHING like the bustle of a rodeo to distract a woman from her broken heart.

Emily relied on her decades-old rodeo queen training. She kept a smile on her face and had a kind word for all her old friends.

And if thoughts of Jonah snuck up on her and stole her breath midconversation, she faked a cough and channeled little Adam's angelic smile.

She watched Buttercup toss a championship cowboy into the dirt in under four seconds. Her bull's performance lifted her spirits, but only for a short time.

"He's a rodeo distributor's dream," Bradley Holliday told her. "Mean as spit and with the brawn to back it up."

"You aren't by any chance hiring?" Emily wished she had more confidence than smile in her question.

Bradley didn't seem to notice. "You know I already hired you two years ago, although it didn't stick. As ever, I'd be grateful to have you on our team. Call me Monday and we'll discuss the specifics."

Bradley wasn't the only one interested in hiring her. Tina's father had spread the word that Emily was looking. She had more interested parties than she'd ever imagined.

The rodeo queen competition was fierce. Thirty women from age sixteen to twenty-one. They were all beautiful, talented horsewomen.

During the introduction lap, Tina raced around on a sparkly, prancing black horse. Deadly was hardly recognizable with all that glitter. But Tina and her smile were. She was poised and sophisticated dressed all in black.

"That was Tina Reilly on Deadly, a very special horse owned by the Bucking Bull Ranch. That gelding lasted longer in the ring with Buttercup than most cowboys. Let's give those two a round of applause."

Emily clapped until her hands hurt.

And then came the pattern competition. Tina drew a lanky gray horse that rivaled Deadly in temperament. Tina guided the horse through its paces with an easygoing smile. The pair finished with two seconds to spare, eliciting applause from the crowd.

That night, the rodeo queen candidates lined up on a stage next to the rodeo ring. They wore their evening gowns. Tina had the requisite ringlets and dangly earrings but her dress was pinker than Em's favorite boots. Boy did she stand out. Emily sat with the Reillys and shrieked just as loud as Tina's mother when Tina made the final five. Emily even applauded for Madison when her name was called.

The finalists were ushered offstage and the interviews began. Each contestant was asked the same questions about political issues, animal husbandry, the state of rodeo today and what their dreams were.

Madison was adorable, but her answers were predictable. Madison prayed every night for world peace? She needed a dream that wasn't a cliché if she wanted to win.

Emily choked up thinking about dreams. Hers had been stomped on by Jonah.

Finally, it was Tina's turn. She showed her polish and her smarts with thoughtful answers and a smile as big as Idaho. And when it came to the dream question…

"I want to study animal biometrics," Tina said, her smile never dimming. "That may sound like a mouthful, but it's basically just using technology in new ways. So you all may see me managing my family ranch in the future, or you might just read about me developing an app that serves as an early warning system to detect sickness in cattle. But whatever dream I achieve, I will always remember my experience as a rodeo queen contestant. I cannot tell you how much confidence I've gained just by competing with these talented, wonderful ladies." She thanked the judges and practically floated in a hot pink cloud to rejoin the other four finalists.

Emily held her breath when it came time for the winner to be announced. And when she heard Tina's name, she leaped to her feet and hollered at the top of her lungs.

Not five minutes later, Tina came running down to greet her family.

"I won! I won! I won!" Tina hugged her parents. "I still can't believe it." And then she embraced Emily. "I couldn't have done it without you."

A petite blonde came up to them with a stunned smile on her face. "Congratulations, Tina."

The kind, benevolent, stock-in-trade smile appeared on Tina's face. "Thanks, Madison. I really enjoyed watching you ride today." Tina waited until Madison walked away to turn back to Emily with a soft *"Squee!"*

"You found something you respect about her." Emily hugged her again, but her gaze was beginning to roam, looking for a familiar redhead.

Which was silly. Jonah would never show up at a rodeo queen competition.

THE NEXT DAY, several little girls ran up to Tina, asking for her autograph and a picture. Then Tina and her court opened the rodeo with victory laps. Emily watched from the area outside the main gate. Tina and Deadly raced by her in a blur of black, the American flag flying above their heads.

The arena was slick in one corner from rain the night before. Emily held her breath until the girls closed out their last lap without any horse slipping and falling. Kyle's horse did everything Tina asked of him and with style. Her heart swelled with pride.

The rodeo hands opened the gates and the girls thundered through, pulling up a few feet away from Emily. She moved forward, prepared to take Deadly for a cooldown walk around the rodeo parking lot.

Tina smiled and laughed and congratulated

her court on a great performance. And then she hopped off Deadly and hugged him.

Emily's steps faltered. She let Tina have her moment.

The petite teen drew Deadly's head down and kissed his nose. And then she turned, wiping tears from her eyes and smiled at Emily. "He's the best, isn't he?"

Blinking back tears, Emily nodded.

She took Deadly and walked him through the horse trailer–filled parking lot to the Bucking Bull's trailer. She tethered the big gelding to the tailgate. "You're a winner, big fella. Kyle would be proud of you. He's going to be proud of me, too, whatever job I take."

She'd most likely wrangle bulls for Bradley Holliday, many of them from the Bucking Bull Ranch, but she was only allowed to have one horse on the circuit and it would have to be Razzy. Except...

Who would ride Deadly when she left? Who would love him for the smart, magnificent beast he was? Prickly though he might be...

For a moment, Emily's feelings toward Deadly became tangled with her feelings for Jonah. She wrapped her arms around Deadly's neck the way Tina had and hung on, not wanting to let go.

"You okay?" someone called to her.

"Yeah." Emily removed Deadly's tack and stored it in the trailer. And then with a halter on, she walked him to the Flying R's horse trailer.

"Here, I…" She leaned against Deadly's shoulder, knowing full well she'd have glitter on her back. There was already a layer of it on the front of her pink button-down. "I think a rodeo queen needs a mighty steed."

"Oh no, I can't." But there was longing in Tina's eyes.

Her father came for the lead rope. "Just for the rodeo season."

"Or longer," Emily murmured, because how could you deny a rodeo queen a love like that?

CHAPTER TWENTY-TWO

JONAH WAS PRINTING out *The Ballad of Letty Moody* the day Emily was expected to return from the rodeo when someone pounded on the bunkhouse door.

He'd stayed in the bunkhouse like an opposing general holding hard-won ground. He'd stayed, weathering Franny's scowls from across the ranch yard. He'd stayed and written faster than he'd ever put together a script before, even the one featuring Emily.

The knob turned and the door opened. "Hey, Jonah." Adam held onto the doorknob with one hand and gripped a half-eaten chocolate chip cookie with the other.

Bolt shouldered his way past Franny's youngest son and meandered over to greet Jonah. At least the dog still liked him.

"My mom wants to know why you haven't gone home." Adam took a bite of cookie.

"Well." Jonah scratched behind Bolt's ears, ignoring the way the dog raised his nose in the direction of Jonah's lunch plate and the remains of a tofu burger. Maybe the dog didn't like him as much as his food. "You can tell her I plan to make a move tomorrow." A move on Emily.

"Okay." Adam stuffed the rest of the cookie in his mouth and wiped his fingers on his T-shirt, which was black and didn't show chocolate smudges. He blinked up at Jonah, minus his usual smile. "Is it true?"

"Is what true?" Did the kid know about him breaking Emily's heart?

"Are you making Mike Moody's story into a movie?" Blink-blink-blink went his eyes.

Jonah laid a hand on the pages, still warm from the printer. "I'm setting things in motion. Maybe in a year or two the movie will be in theaters." If Jonah was lucky.

He'd sent a revised treatment to Maury, who'd crowed about the lack of stink, mollified after withdrawing Jonah's scripts from consideration.

Jonah hadn't sent a word to his father. Let the old man judge his efforts on the big screen.

Adam shrugged. "Adults take a long time to do stuff." He called for Bolt and slammed the door behind them.

Jonah set about cleaning the kitchenette

and packing his things. It didn't take long. He hadn't brought much to Second Chance.

Someone banged on his door.

Expecting Franny with an ultimatum to vacate the premises, Jonah opened the door with what he hoped was a placating smile on his face.

"Darn long walk from home to here." Gertie pushed inside past him, leaning on her cane as she headed for one of the chairs by the table where Jonah had worked the last few weeks. She sat down and plunked her bag of knitting on the floor.

Jonah closed the door and trailed after her, much like Bolt trailed after the Clarks.

"You've made a mess of things." She dug in her knitting bag.

"That I have." Jonah sat across from her, leaning his arms on the table. "You could've made it a little easier on me."

"Ha." She set her music box on the table between them.

It was exquisitely made. The wood worn in places where hands had grasped the sides of the lid. The top had a delicate inlay, a bird in flight.

Jonah opened the box to the notes of "You Are My Sunshine." "Is this Letty's music box?"

Gertie shrugged. "Who can say for sure?

All I know is Emily mentioned the things Letty stole and this has been in the Clark family for generations."

"So you didn't know if it was connected to the Moodys?" Jonah closed the lid, drumming his fingers on top.

"No." Gertie drew a deep breath and gestured toward Aria's watercolor portrait on the refrigerator. "That's a good likeness of you. It catches all your sharp edges and your sensitive soul."

Jonah stared at his face, trying to see the sensitive parts the old woman spoke of.

"That picture says there's more to you than meets the eye." She nodded toward him. "What are your intentions toward my sweet Em?"

"Good ones." Jonah remained close-lipped.

Gertie frowned. "Beyond good. What are you going to do to make her happy?" She reclaimed possession of the music box, tucking it between skeins of blue yarn in her bag. "I've been politicking for you at the house. Franny wanted to toss you out days ago."

"I appreciate your support." And given Adam's visit, he imagined Franny's indulgence of Gertie's whims were at an end.

She latched onto his forearm and squeezed, none too gently. "How do I know you won't ask Em to marry you and then break it off like you did before?"

"Because I love her. Absolutely. Whole-heartedly." Jonah covered Gertie's warm hand with his own. "Because when I think about a life without her my insides ache and my chest feels like it's filled with lead. Because everyone asks for things from Monroes, but she asks for nothing but love. Because…" He gently removed her hand and sat back. "All the reasons I love Emily… She's got to hear them first."

"I knew you'd come around." She pushed herself to her feet and winked at him. "I knew you'd make a good husband and father before you knew it yourself."

"I suppose you did." Jonah stared at Aria's painting of his face one last time before tearing it up and throwing it away.

WHEN EMILY GOT home from the rodeo, it was late. Everyone was asleep. All she wanted to do was collapse in her own bed, wake up early, pack what she'd need for the next few months and then leave in the morning. On to her new, Jonah-free life.

Jonah had other plans.

Her bed wasn't empty. A script rested on her pillow.

The Ballad of Letty Moody by Jonah Monroe and...

No.

She dropped the entire manuscript into her bedroom trash can and fell back on the bed, closing her eyes. The creep. He'd put her name on the title page underneath his.

Franny had texted that he hadn't left the ranch. Em knew he'd try to make up for what he'd done. She knew she had to harden her heart if he did. She'd rehearsed how she'd accept his apology. Graciously. Firmly. With just the right amount of distance to let him know there were no hard feelings. In fact, there were no soft feelings, either.

And then this.

Her name on the script. It felt like something important.

She rubbed the heels of her hands around her eyes.

What did her name on the title page mean? She wasn't a writer. She was a cowgirl.

The house was quiet. No creaking wood. No groan as it stood up to the wind. No one up to talk to about this peace offering of Jonah's.

Outside, the ranch was quiet, too. No cattle calling gently into the night. No owl announcing it was awake and on the hunt. No calls of one cowboy to another as there had been at the rodeo.

She should fall asleep easily. A few bedtime rituals and when her head hit the pillow, she'd close her eyes and it would be easy to forget Jonah. To forget his smile and snark, to forget how he held her tenderly and kissed her like he couldn't live without her.

But there was a script in her trash can about Letty Moody.

Letty, not Mike. And her name was on the first page.

She couldn't forget that Jonah was offering her a new dream to reach for. If she was brave enough to stand beside him.

Emily heaved herself out of bed. She did everything a non-brokenhearted woman would do before going to sleep. She changed into pajamas. She brushed her teeth. She filled a glass of water and put it on the nightstand. She slid beneath the covers and turned out the light.

She could try to forget Jonah or she could try to reach for something, like Kyle had wanted her to. Her insides were bottled up with fear.

There's always fear, Kyle had told her once after they'd dodged an ornery bull that got loose in the arena and tried to trample them.

There's always fear, but you just have to take a deep breath and work past it.

There was still a script about Letty Moody in the trash can.

Letty, not Mike. And her name was printed on top for everyone to see.

Emily took a deep breath, sat up and saved Jonah's work from the garbage.

CHAPTER TWENTY-THREE

"I MISSED YOU, AUNTY EM." Adam clung to Emily's leg while she buttered his toast the next morning.

"I missed you, too, bug." The words were hard to say. Not because she'd stayed up too late reading Jonah's script, but because she was going to miss Adam the moment she drove out the ranch gates in a few days to join Halliday's crew.

"Did Deadly win?" Davey smooshed his scrambled eggs between two slices of bread.

"Yeah, did he?" Charlie paused between bites of a similar breakfast.

"*Tina* won while riding Deadly." Emily had almost forgotten the news in the midst of her homecoming gift.

"Sweet." Davey spoke around his egg sandwich, holding it together with one hand. "I'll bring Deadly some carrots to celebrate."

"About that..." Emily got Adam situated at the kitchen table. "Deadly is on tour with Tina."

"What does *tour* mean?" Adam asked.

"She's going to travel around, ride in some parades and compete with him at the state level."

"But he's coming back," Charlie said past a mouthful of food.

"He's not," Davey said miserably, taking in Emily with a dark look.

"Boys, you have two minutes to finish eating before I drive you into town." Franny was in four-star-general mode, issuing commands. "Let's have some faith in Emily's choices and be proud of Deadly going on tour."

Davey brought his plate to the sink. He stared at Emily a moment and then hugged her. "I miss him."

Emily brushed a hand over Davey's thick brown hair, knowing he wasn't talking about Deadly. "I miss your dad, too, honey."

"In thirty seconds, I'm heading out the door," Franny announced, grabbing her cell phone.

"Go on." Emily held onto Davey's shoulders. "You can warm up the truck if you get there before your mom."

He backed away and then raced upstairs.

"First Kyle. Then Deadly. Now you." Franny stood with her arms crossed, frowning but not fooling Emily. There were tears waiting to flow behind that frown.

"It's just for the rodeo season," Emily said stiffly, turning to rinse off plates, staring at the spot in the backsplash where the grout was worn away. Wondering if Shane was going to get it fixed.

"Of course it's just for the season." Franny didn't believe Em. Her words were gruff and she sniffed.

"Out in the world, you're going to meet the cowboy you deserve," Gertie reassured Emily. "And start your own spread. Doesn't have to be like this one."

But how Emily wanted it to be. She loved the familiar rhythms of the Bucking Bull and the Idaho mountains.

"There's a cowboy outside." Adam ran to the front window and pressed his nose to the glass.

"Did you bring a cowboy home instead of Deadly?" Charlie hurried to join his brother.

Franny looked at Emily, a question in her eyes.

Emily raised her hands. "I came home alone."

"You boys don't know what you're talking about." Davey came thundering down the stairs. "That's Jonah."

Emily's heart began a thundering beat faster than Davey's feet had been.

The rest of the Clarks joined the boys at the front window.

Jonah stood in the ranch yard wearing cowboy boots, boot-cut jeans, a blue checked button-down and a white hat.

"What's he doin', Aunty Em?" Adam asked.

"He's waiting for a certain cowgirl." Gertie nudged Emily. "Go on."

"He's asking too much," Emily murmured, chest bound in fear.

"Emily Clark!" Jonah shouted, tipping the brim of his hat back. He wore a half smile and a worried look around the eyes. "Get on out here."

"He sounds just like the sheriff calling the bad guys out of the saloon." Davey glanced up at Emily. "What did you do?"

"Something bad, I bet," Charlie said, leaning on the windowsill.

"He's not the sheriff, but..." Adam stared up at Emily. "Did you do something wrong?"

"No." If anyone had done something wrong, it'd been Jonah. Emily went to her room, snatched up Jonah's script and marched outside. "Is this what you want?" She held it out to him, extending her arm as far as it could go.

Jonah raised his hands slowly, as if she held a gun. "Nope."

It sounded like chaos inside the ranch house. Emily bet the boys were running about, gathering their backpacks, pulling on boots, shouting at each other to hurry. They wouldn't want to miss the show.

Emily didn't want to be the show. "Go on." She shook the script. "Take it. And you can take my name off it, too."

"No." Jonah took a step back. "Didn't you read it? Didn't you see your words in there as dialogue?"

Emily wanted to say no. She wanted to say no, more than anything. "Yes," she admitted instead. "It's good, Jonah. Is that what you wanted to hear?"

A hint of a grin ghosted his lips. "One of the things."

"I don't deserve to have my name on this." The gravel still held the morning dew. If she dropped his work, the pages at the end would be ruined. She hesitated, held back by fear. And then dropped it. "I don't want to be associated with you or this."

His grin disappeared. "You deserve to have a film credit. I couldn't have unraveled Letty's story without you." He left the pages on the ground. "If it wasn't for you, I'd have

written a script about Merciless Mike Moody.
And as you once told me, any hack could
write a script about a male bandit."

She willed her feet to move back, but she
was caught in his gaze and in the words—her
words—that he'd handed back to her.

"I love you, Aunty Em." Only Jonah would
make a declaration with the nickname used
by her favorite people in the world. "I love the
way you don't take my guff at face value. I
love the way I can be me, unfiltered, and you
can be you, unfiltered, when we're together."

Emily's throat felt tight. She felt that way,
too. But she didn't move. She barely breathed.

"I love that you're part of a big family. An
integral part." He gestured toward her nephews coming out the front door. "I'm part of
a big family, too. Families can be messy and
feelings can sometimes get hurt, but I know
it's important to make amends, to keep family together."

His words dredged up the longing she had
for love, for family, for him.

Jonah stepped closer. He looked put together on the outside, but inside he was just
as scarred and scared as Deadly in the heavy
brush of the woods. "I know it's important to
say I messed up."

"Amen," Franny said from the porch.

Gertie shushed her.

Jonah stepped closer still. "I know it's important to say I'm going to try never to hurt you like that again."

Emily wanted to wrap her arms around Jonah and know he loved her as much as she loved him. But there was something that kept her rooted in place. It wasn't that his apology hadn't been epic. It wasn't that she didn't believe he could love her.

Her gaze drifted to the ground. To the pages of Letty Moody's story.

Jonah followed her gaze. "You see it, don't you? We're good together." One more step and he was in her space, in her life, in her world. "We're like sweet and sour, honey." His arms came around her. "Oil and vinegar." He drew her in close. "Those opposites are important because they complement each other. What would life be like without them?"

Franny was mumbling and Gertie was shushing her.

And Emily didn't care. Her arms came around Jonah's waist. She breathed in air through lungs that were heavy with grief and happiness, hurt and joy. She was going to forgive him. If she was honest with herself, she'd forgiven him when she read that script last night.

"I want you to be my wife." Jonah pressed a kiss to her forehead, so tender it brought tears to Em's eyes. His arms loosened and he got down on one knee on the gravel. "I want to have a houseful of kids that create a houseful of chaos."

Emily's eggs cheered.

Emily sniffed as a tear ran down her cheek. "Yes." She tried to tug him to his feet.

But Jonah wasn't done. "And I want you to be my writing partner."

Emily held her breath.

Jonah wasn't promising to buy her a ranch, but this was something important. Something that was just hers. And his. Something that scared her more than putting on fancy clothes and trying to look like she belonged at the side of a Hollywood Monroe. She opened her mouth to hedge, but Jonah was quick to stand and take her chin in one hand.

"Don't be afraid. You can do this, Em. We'll live in Hollywood during the cold winter months and we'll come back up here to ranch during the spring and summer. But we'll sit and banter and write some really incredible stories."

"But…" It was too much, too hard. Even if it was important.

"And someday, you can tell our children

about the legend of Letty Moody and all the other stories you brought to life on the page." He brushed his palm over her cheek. "And you can tell them how I'd be nothing without you. Because it's true."

And then he kissed her. He kissed her and the eggs were cheering and her family was cheering and Emily was consumed with the feeling of being loved.

And in that moment, as she nestled into Jonah's arms for what she hoped was forever, she knew one thing.

Thirty wasn't old.

It was just the beginning.

* * * * *

Don't miss more of The Mountain Monroes and their romances, available today from www.Harlequin.com!